A Country Affair

By Rebecca Shaw

A COUNTRY AFFAIR

A Barleybridge Novel

Rebecca Shaw

College of the Ouachitas

 THREE RIVERS PRESS · NEW YORK

Copyright © 2001 by Rebecca Shaw

This is a work of fiction. Names, characters, places, and incidents either
are the product of the author's imagination or are used fictitiously. Any
resemblance to actual persons, living or dead, events, or locales is entirely
coincidental.

All rights reserved.
Published in the United States by Three Rivers Press, an imprint of the
Crown Publishing Group, a division of Random House, Inc., New York.
www.crownpublishing.com

Three Rivers Press and the Tugboat design are registered trademarks of
Random House, Inc.

Originally published in Great Britain by Orion, London, in 2001.

Library of Congress Cataloging-in-Publication Data
Shaw, Rebecca, 1931–
    A country affair / Rebecca Shaw.— 1st American ed.
        p.   cm — (A Barleybridge novel)
    1. Veterinarians—Fiction.   2. Yorkshire (England)—Fiction.
    I. Title.
    PR6069.H388C68   2006
    823'.914—dc22   2005025251

ISBN-13: 978-1-4000-9820-0
ISBN-10: 1-4000-9820-3

Printed in the United States of America

Design by Barbara Sturman

10 9 8 7 6 5 4 3 2

First American Edition

PR
6069
.H388
C68
2006

List of Characters in the
Barleybridge Practice

Mungo Price .... *Orthopedic Surgeon and Senior Partner*
Colin Walker .... *Partner—large and small animal*
Zoe Savage .... *Partner—large animal*
Graham Murgatroyd .... *Small-animal vet*
Valentine Dedic .... *Small-animal vet*
Rhodri Hughes .... *Small-animal vet*
Errol "Scott" Spencer .... *Large-animal vet*

NURSING STAFF
Sarah Cockroft *(Sarah One)*
Sarah MacMillan *(Sarah Two)*
Bunty Page

RECEPTIONISTS
Joy Bastable *(Practice Manager)*
Lynne Seymour
Stephie Budge
Kate Howard

Miriam Price .... *Mungo's wife*
Duncan Bastable .... *Joy's husband*
Gerry Howard .... *Kate's father*
Mia Howard .... *Kate's stepmother*
Adam Pentecost .... *Kate's boyfriend*

The Barleybridge Practice

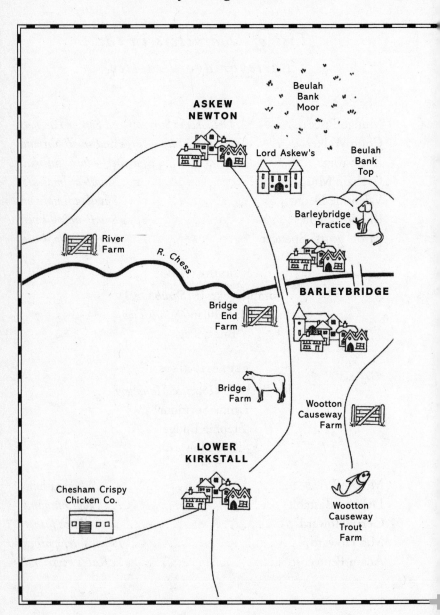

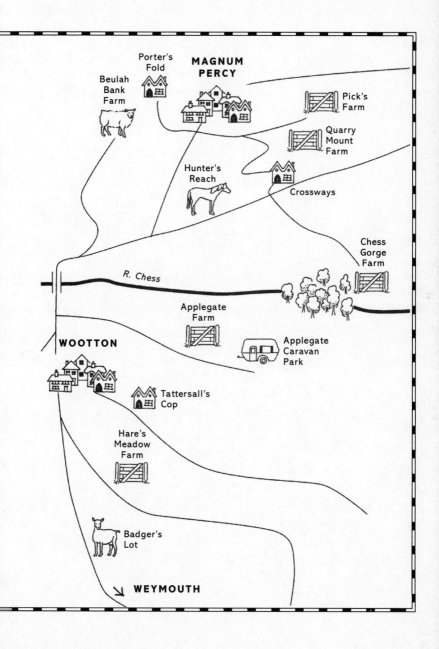

Chapter

· 1 ·

In the circumstances it would have been ridiculous to have arrived wearing a suit. So Kate had plumped for her smart—well, smarter—pair of black trousers, knee-length black cardigan and the pink shirt Mia had given her, which just managed to stay fastened without too much gaping between the buttons. That was one thing Kate envied about Mia—her ability to stay slim. She squeezed herself out of the car and looked around. It was certainly a beautiful setting. The hills rose almost immediately from the edge of the car park and if she shielded her eyes, she could just make out Beulah Bank Top, one of the highest of the surrounding hills. Dotted all over the slopes were sheep grazing in twos and threes. They looked to her to be Dorset Horns, lovely woolly sheep, grazing on land they'd grazed for hundreds of years, making, Kate thought, an idyllic scene. Turning around, she could see the town, which had now crept up the foothills, making the hospital the last bit of civilization before the hills.

Two Land Rovers, their wheels thick with dried mud, were parked in two of the spaces marked STAFF, along with several other cars, some large and opulent, others small and scruffy.

Her hand trembled as she locked the car door and shook as she walked around to the front entrance. This was worse than starting at a new school. At least in school she'd been one of many new girls; here she was the only new girl and very green at that.

Kate remembered the weight of the imposing double doors from her interview and knew that nothing less than a huge heave would open one. Then the inner glass door and she was in. Oh, God! That smell! She breathed it in, savoring the gloriously satisfying odor of disinfectant, of anesthetic, of . . . well, of everything she had ever dreamed of. At five minutes to eight the clients hadn't yet arrived, so she was alone. In front of her was the reception desk, strikingly new, very twenty-first century, white and clinical. To her right stretched the waiting room, well supplied with spanking-new, springy, bendy chrome chairs; a huge cheese plant reaching the ceiling; every windowsill filled with jaunty pots all bursting with plants still with the full flush of the garden center upon them. Four doors went off from the waiting area, each with the words CONSULTING ROOM in bold, bright-blue, up-to-the-minute lettering.

The first sign of life was the sound of two people arguing somewhere at the back behind the reception desk. She could hear the anger but not the words. Female voices, one belligerent, one patient. They must have moved closer to her, for now she could hear: "I know you've taken her on to replace me; I'm not stupid."

"I've told you twenty times she is not replacing you. Kate is here to work on reception as and when, but mainly to do the accounts."

"So . . . what have I been doing these last three months? The accounts!"

"Only because there was no one else and you volunteered. You're small-animal reception, Stephie, as well you know. You hate the accounts anyway, so I don't know what you're grumbling about. You should be relieved."

"Well, I'm not."

"I've too much on this morning to be bothered with your sulks, so you'll have to get on with it; and make jolly sure you hand everything over in a systematic manner and with good grace, or you'll hear further from me."

Kate heard a derisive snort and then: "You might be in charge here, Joy, but there's no need to take that tone with me."

An answer snapped back at her almost before she'd finished speaking. "Oh, I am in charge. There's no doubt about that and don't you forget it. Now get out on the desk and check today's appointments, there's a good girl."

A young woman about her own age came through from the back. She was a dowdy-looking girl with sallow skin; brown, lifeless hair tied back in a ponytail; dark, sulky eyes and a long, hollow-cheeked face. She managed a tight-lipped question: "Yes?"

Kate, determining to be cheerful in adversity, said, "I'm Kate Howard, the new receptionist." She held out her hand to this Stephie, hoping flesh on flesh might make for peace between them.

Grudgingly Stephie shook hands. "I'm Stephie Budge. You'd better report to Joy; she's in the back." The phone rang and Stephie quickly picked it up, answering it brightly with none of her bad temper evident in her voice: "Good morning! Barleybridge Veterinary Hospital. Stephie speaking. How may I help?" As she listened, she kicked out behind her with her foot and pushed open the door, nodding her head in the direction of the back office.

Kate walked around the reception desk and into the blessed warmth and comfort of Joy's office. Warm and comfortable not because Joy had the heating on, for it was still warm, although the start of September, but because of Joy herself. She must have been fifty, which when you're only nineteen seems ancient, but Joy's fifty was different from other people's fifty. Her smooth, unlined face glowed with an inner light, which enveloped you and made you smile despite yourself. She must have looked like this at twenty and would still at eighty. Her blond hair waved and curled about her face; her blue eyes twinkled at you with scarcely concealed mirth. Her office echoed her personality— soft-yellow walls, flowers, brightly colored files lined neatly on a shelf behind her head, on top of the royal-blue filing cabinet a fish tank with fish flashing around it among lush waving plants; even her state-of-the-art computer echoed the blue of her eyes.

Joy took to her new receptionist immediately. She'd liked her at the interview and had decided straightaway to employ her if she'd come. She liked the forthrightness of her eyes and the open expression on her face. Kate was apparently far too intelligent for the job, but if this was what she wanted, then so be it. Joy had liked the modest confidence behind the pleasant manner. She saw now that Kate was almost pretty; no, that wasn't right—more classically good looking perhaps, with a hint of good breeding. Most especially, Joy had loved her happy outlook on life and what was more, Kate reminded her of someone from the past whom she'd liked but couldn't quite put a name to. Joy stood up to greet her.

"Kate! How lovely! You are about to save my life. A nurse and a receptionist have called in ill this morning, and with Open Afternoon on Saturday that's all we need, so you're about to have a baptism of fire. But we'll cope; we always do! So you're on reception today; the accounts will have to wait. Welcome to Barleybridge!"

Kate drew confidence from her firm grasp and felt empowered. "Thank you, I don't mind turning my hand to anything at all . . ."

"Can't find time to sort out a uniform for you at the moment, but you look very efficient and that's the impression we always try to give: efficiency larded with compassion. Twenty minutes to liftoff. I'll give you a quick tour."

Joy came out from behind her desk and shot out of the door at the speed of light. Kate dashed after her, trying desperately to take in the operating rooms, the pharmacy, the cages in the recovery room, the animals' waiting room with its row of steel hooks for hitching dog leashes to, the staff room, Mr. Price's office, the washing machine, the dryer, the shower room, the staff wash rooms—endless space all so new, so ready for action.

"The consulting rooms are down that side with doors into the clients' waiting room and into the back here, of course. Golden rule: no clients beyond the consulting rooms. We've no secrets to hide but nevertheless . . . This is where you'll be doing accounts when you get a chance. The farm-animal vets are devils where keeping records is concerned and these new laptops they take with them are a real challenge for them. Keeps them on their toes, you see, and they're happier doing the job than keeping records; but as I tell them, if they don't make notes about all they do, we can't invoice the farmers and then there'll be no money to pay their salaries, so it's up to them." Joy grinned at her. "Lovely people, though. Here's one of them now." Joy was looking beyond Kate and giving one of her dazzling smiles.

Kate turned around and saw a lean, well-muscled man of at least six feet propped against the door frame. He wore one of those stiff-brimmed hats one imagines all Australian men wear when going walkabout, a pair of sharply creased khaki shorts, a bush shirt and a grin that almost split his face.

"G'day! You must be this new Kate they're all talking about. I'm Errol Spencer."

"How do you do."

Joy interrupted with: "He's Errol really, but we all call him Scott."

"Have you got Scottish parents, then?"

He burst out laughing. "Guess not. They're always getting Aussies passing through this practice, and the first one was called Scott and it's stuck. Saves a lot of trouble remembering names."

"How do you do, Scott, then." He was still holding her hand and she couldn't release it without making it obvious.

Joy raised an eyebrow. "Put her down, Scott; give her a chance to get in through the door." Kate blushed and Scott winked as Joy said, "Your morning visits await you at reception. Get cracking; you've a lot to get through."

"Slave driver, she is, beneath that charming exterior. Watch out for her; she keeps a whip in her top drawer and isn't afraid to use it." He bunched his fingers, kissed them and departed.

Kate was laughing; she really couldn't help herself. He was such *fun;* if all the vets were like him, she was in for a good time. Until now she'd thought of the veterinary world as a serious business, where saving lives and relieving pain were paramount; but apparently you could have an uproarious time, too, and that was just what she needed.

Joy looked up at her. "Take him with a pinch of salt, my dear; he's broken more hearts than I can count and he's only been here three months. Farmers' wives, farmers' daughters, farmers' mothers even, you name 'em; there're girls carrying torches all over the county for that young man. Still, he does add spice to life, doesn't he?"

When Kate got back to reception, she couldn't believe the change that had taken place in the ten minutes she'd been on her conducted tour. Stephie was at the desk, apparently answering three phones at once, as well as tapping furiously on the computer. The waiting room was filling up and that early morning clinical aroma was being submerged by animal smells. Animals of all shapes and sizes had arrived—big ones, little ones, furry ones, feathered ones, brown and black, white and gray, some cowering, some bold and barking, some cats peering suspiciously from their carrying cages, other cats spitting at the dog taking too much interest in them and a massive Rottweiler sitting propped against his owner's legs, aloof and slavering.

As soon as Joy saw him she said quietly to Kate, "I'd forgotten it was the first Monday of the month. Go and get the old fire bucket from the laundry room, fill it full of cold water and bring it here."

It seemed the oddest thing to be doing, but she filled it, carried it through—surprised at how heavy an old iron bucket filled to the brim with water proved to be—and asked Stephie where she should put it. Stephie pointed to the floor under the desk. "Down there. Thanks. Can you answer that? It's the farm vets' phone."

"Good morning. Barleybridge Veterinary Hospital. How may I help?"

The lilting Welsh voice, with its strong musical undertones, threw Kate for a moment, but when she had adjusted her mind to the accent, she realized the woman wanted to speak to Rhodri Hughes. "Hold the line a moment, please." Placing her hand over the mouthpiece, she asked Stephie what she should do. "Tell her he's out on a call, take her number and we'll get him to ring her back."

During a brief lull Stephie brought Kate up to speed on the telephone system. "It's all so clever now you wouldn't believe it. Talk about state of the art. All the farm vets have mobiles in their cars, so if they're out on a call and a request for a visit comes in, we ring the vet nearest to the farm wanting the visit and it saves them miles of driving. There're usually at least three vets out on call. Small-animal vets hardly go out on visits at all; most of the animals can come in, you see. This map on the wall here behind us, see, it's got a flag pinned on for every farm client we have, so you look on there, check today's lists and you know where they all are. Let's have a look at that number for Rhodri; see if I can recognize it." She studied Kate's writing for a moment, then said in a fierce whisper, "Welsh, was she?"

Kate nodded. "Very definitely."

"Look, I know her. That's Megan Jones. She fancies him something rotten, keeps ringing him up. He's not interested and he's desperate to avoid her. Next time say day off, or on holiday, or at a conference, or off ill or something—anything to put her off. If he speaks to her by mistake, he'll blow his top and that's not a pretty sight."

"How long has this been going on?"

"Weeks and weeks, every single day. She must be mad."

"Is he a good catch, then?"

Stephie looked skeptically at her. "If you fancy a short, thickset Welshman with a penchant for singing tenor in a male choir and a liking for ferrets and total independence for the principality of Wales, then yes. I don't really understand what she sees in him; he's not my type at all."

"What is your type, then?"

The phone rang again so Kate never got her answer. Then she spoke to an old lady who was so small she could only just see over the top of the reception desk about her nine o'clock appointment and whether that nice Mr. Murgatroyd was running late or had she time to go to the toilet, or should she delay going until after her appointment because she didn't want to be in the toilet when her name was called because her cat was so very ill she really mustn't delay her appointment and was she new she hadn't seen her before and what was her name she was such a pretty girl. Kate was about to advise her to go to the toilet first, though she hadn't a clue if it was the right answer or not, when a terrible snarling sound began that became louder and louder and louder. The fearsome noise turned out to be an Airedale terrier, which hurtled through from the back and, just missing knocking down the old lady, went like an arrow for the Rottweiler. But he was ready. At the moment they'd all heard the first snarling sound, the Rottweiler went on red alert, his fur bristling, his fangs showing, his feet ready for the inevitable skirmish. But it wasn't a skirmish, it was a full-scale fight. The owner was screaming, "Adolf! Oh, God! Adolf! Get that bloody dog off him; get him off!" All the clients clutched their pets to themselves and watched, frozen with horror. The two dogs took no notice whatsoever of Adolf's owner, swirling around, around and around, lunging and snarling openmouthed, each trying as hard as the other to sink its fangs into its opponent's neck or indeed anywhere it could get a hold.

Stephie, as was to be expected at moments of crisis, was answering the phone. She clapped her hand over the receiver and shouted, "The water! Throw it on them!"

Kate, too stunned to react for a moment, suddenly galvanized herself, grabbed the bucket and emptied the entire contents over the two dogs. The Airedale leaped back, shook itself free of the water, looked up at Kate and . . . well, he laughed at her. There was no other way to describe his expression: His tongue was lolling out of his open mouth, his eyes were bright with pleasure, his tail wagged furiously. She'd never seen a dog grin before, and it gave her the distinct impression he found the whole incident very amusing indeed.

Outraged, she said in a loud voice, "Who owns this dog? Because you're not keeping it under control. Please do so immediately." She glared around the waiting room, in her panic and anger not noticing the deathly hush that had descended.

The old man with two cats volunteered, "It's not none of ours. It's Perkins, Mr. Price's dog. Adolf and 'im are mates." This brought a chuckle from the regulars.

"Mr. Price?"

"Your Mr. Price."

Kate blushed. Stephie got off the phone, took Perkins by the collar and led him down through the back, muttering threats as she went. Joy emerged with a bucket and mop. "Mop up, there's a dear; we don't want anyone slipping on that water. Sorry about that, everybody. You all right, Mr. Featherstone-hough?"

Adolf's owner exploded. "How many times have I asked you to keep that blasted dog under control? You know I bring Adolf every first Monday for his injection and this happens every single time. You even have the water ready, so you do know what day it is. I shall be complaining to the Royal College of Veterinary Surgeons about this and don't think I won't because I shall. I've threatened before but this time I mean it. I know my rights. I shall sue your Mr. Price for every damned penny he's got if my Adolf gets hurt. This is just once too often, this is."

"Mr. Featherstonehough, I can't understand how Perkins knows you're here. He was upstairs in Mr. Price's apartment, safely shut away, and then somehow he realized you were here. And you know it does take two to make a fight, and Adolf does his share . . ."

A consulting room door opened and a gruff Northern voice called out, "Mr. Featherstonehough, please? Good morning, Adolf. Been knocking hell out of Perkins again, have you? Do come through."

Kate mopped up the water and went into th... empty the mop bucket down the sink. Joy came throug... tray of mugs in her hands. "Thanks for that. Coffee time— the weight off your feet. Here you are."

The coffee tasted wonderful, but as she drank it, Kate's conscience surfaced. "What about Stephie? Shall I go and relieve her?"

"We'll both go; you can't be by yourself, not yet. Take your mug, but if Mr. Price comes through, hide it. He doesn't like us drinking on duty—looks unbusinesslike."

Mr. Price, senior partner and lord of all he surveyed, did come through reception on the way to taking his orthopedic clinic, and he did see her drinking and reprimanded her for it, and made her feel knee high to a teaspoon and wishing the floor would open up. But of course it didn't, and Stephie heard the tail end of the conversation and sniggered. "Tut! Tut! How sad! On your first day too."

Kate ignored her uncharitable comment. "That's the great Mungo Price, is it? I'll never learn to put all the names to faces."

"You will, given time. But he's the one to watch. Old Hawkeye, I call him. Isn't he gorgeous, though? So suave, so sophisticated. He can ask eighty pounds for an orthopedic consultation. And that's just the consultation, never mind the operation, or the drugs, or X-rays, or the repeat visits. I can't even earn that in a day. Some people!"

"I expect he's worked hard for years to get where he is."

Stephie shrugged her shoulders. "Even so . . . Talking of working hard, I saw your CV. With A levels like yours, what you doing working here?"

"Ah!" Kate thought quickly. "Always wanted to work with animals. Bit mushy, I know, but there you are."

to one side and, looking quizzically at
y thing to me."

here? You must like animals just like

her shoulders. "'Suppose I must. It's the
and as for being a nurse? All that blood!
kely."

"But th... y is the sharp end, where it all happens."

"You sound a bit wistful to me. Why don't you be a nurse? The pay's not brilliant so they're always crying out for them." Stephie began shuffling her papers about, in preparation for leaving. "Anyway, I'm off for lunch, back at four. I hate split shifts. Too far to go home, really, too long to spend wandering around the shops; it only makes me buy things. Still, it's better than where the practice was before: at the back of nowhere. At least you feel at the hub of things here. Not a bad town once you get to know it. I'll be glad when the new shopping mall's finished; they say all the big stores will be there. Your mum and dad coming Saturday?"

"For the opening? Possibly."

"They'll like to see where you're working, won't they?"

"Have a nice afternoon."

"Thanks. We'll go through the accounts tomorrow. Can't afford to let them slip; otherwise it's hell. See yer!"

Kate watched her disappear through the big double doors. Funny girl. Nice one minute, nasty the next. Unpleasantness was one thing she hated and the conversation she'd inadvertently overheard when she'd first arrived had been unpleasant to the nth degree. She hadn't asked Dad and Mia yet, and rather guessed they wouldn't want to come. Not after the fuss Dad had made when she'd taken the job. She'd ask when she got home, the moment she got in the door.

. . .

DAD's car was in the drive; he was home early. Kate glanced at her watch—half past four; that was definitely early for him. She pushed down the door handle, which was slack and didn't always work at the first go, and wished for the umpteenth time that her dad would get around to mending it.

"It's me!" Kate flung her bag down on the hall chair and went into the kitchen. With her eyes shut she could have done a painting of that kitchen scene because it was so familiar. The kitchen table under the window with its blue-and-white checked cloth and its bowl of flowers. Dad lounging in his rocker by the side of the range, the stub of a cigarette in his mouth, his jacket lying on a kitchen chair. Lost in thought, his pale, fleshy slab of a face turned upward as though seeking heavenly inspiration, light-blue eyes focused on nothing at all, his stockinged feet thrust against the bottom of the range snatching at the warmth it generated and, without looking up, his muttered "You're back, then."

Even more predictable was Mia: thin, almost to the point of emaciation, seated on the special wooden kitchen chair she used when she was working. Mia raised her eyes, glazed with concentration, to look at her. "Kate! Sit down. I want to hear all." Putting down the tiny brush she was using, she sat back to study her work. It was a miniature painted from a photograph of a pretty girl, a present for the girl's twenty-first. Kate, always genuinely full of admiration for Mia's delicate skills, said, "Why, Mia! That's wonderful! She'll be delighted. So lively!"

"Kiss! Kiss! Please." Mia hooked her arm around Kate's neck to make sure her kiss reached its target. "Glad you like it; I think it's one of my best. There's such a glow about her, isn't there? Do you think I've captured it? I do. Such a zest for life, and I've caught the color of her hair just right. Tea's still hot. Pour me a cup too, and we'll listen to your news, won't we, Gerry? How did it go?"

"Absolutely brilliantly! I don't think I have had a more fantastic day in all my life. So interesting!"

"The staff, what are they like? Nice girls?"

"There're two Sarahs—they're nurses—and a round, plump one called Bunty. Two receptionists: Stephie Budge and Lynne Seymour, besides me. The senior receptionist—well, practice manager, I suppose—is called Joy. She was the one who interviewed me and she's lovely, but she does have a steely backbone when necessary, I think. I've met Mr. Price and got told off . . ."

"Trust you." This from Gerry.

"Gerry! What a thing to say. Kate's not like that. Go on, love, take no notice."

Accustomed to her father's diminishing remarks to her, Kate ignored him. "He is so superior. He can charge eighty pounds a consultation. Just think!"

"That could be you."

"Don't talk daft, Dad. He's Dr. Price, really, and he trained for years and years."

"You could have. With your ability."

"Give it a rest, Gerry." Mia reached across, patted Kate's leg and gave her a wink.

"I met this Australian called Scott, but his real name is Errol."

Gerry grunted. "Right wimp, he sounds."

"You should see him, Mia. Talk about drop-dead gorgeous!"

Mia giggled.

"He's a vet."

"Just what you should have been."

Both Kate and Mia disregarded Gerry's comments.

"I met Graham Murgatroyd, Rhodri Hughes and Zoe Savage. They're vets but there're others I haven't seen today. It's all so exciting, I can't believe how much I've enjoyed myself."

"You'd have enjoyed yourself a lot more if you'd done like I said."

"Look, Dad . . ."

"Gerry! Will you give it a rest. It's Kate's life not yours."

Gerry sat up, threw his cigarette stub on the range and said, "Did I or did I not *beg* her to take that A level again and reapply? She's wanted to be a vet all her life and one stumble, just one little stumble"—he measured the stumble between his thumb and forefinger—"and she throws in the towel." Gerry launched himself out of his chair. "If I had my way . . ."

"Dad! I did warn you that the school wasn't geared for teaching to a standard that would get anyone three A's even though it's easier now. I did say. So it's no good going on about it. If I'd stayed there ten years, I still wouldn't have got them."

Gerry wagged a finger at her. "Ah! But you'll soon have that money your Granny Howard left you. You could go private and pay for tuition."

In the past, Kate's immediate reaction to her father's ideas for furthering her career was flatly to deny them any merit, so she opened her mouth to do exactly as she had always done and then shut it again.

"See! I knew it! You have to admit it's quite an idea."

"No, it isn't. It's no better than all the rest of your ideas. I can't help but remember when I was working all hours studying you saying to me that nothing on earth was worth all that devotion. You've certainly changed your tune. Not only have I a full-time job but now you're expecting me to study too. Well, believe you me, I've had it up to here with studying and I'm not going to do any more, so that's that."

"You're a fool! One bit more extra push and you're there. A lifetime's ambition fulfilled! I'd be so proud of you. To say nothing of your satisfaction."

Mia stood up. "Think about it, Kate. No good finding when you're thirty that your dad was right all along and it's all too late."

"Oh, my word! My dear wife's agreeing with me! That's a first." Gerry disappeared upstairs, calling, "I need something to eat if anyone can spare the time."

Mia began to clear away her painting.

Kate studied the miniature Mia was about to put safely away to dry. "It's lovely, Mia, really lovely."

Mia smiled at her and reached out to place the palm of her hand softly on Kate's cheek, saying, "Thank you, Kate. You're my very dear girl. I love you very much and I'm glad you enjoyed yourself today."

Kate got up to get out the knives and forks from the kitchen table drawer. It wasn't possible, was it, that her dad could be giving good advice for once? "You think he could be right, don't you?"

Mia nodded. "Think about it. It means another year of waiting but think of the rewards if you . . ." She hesitated a moment to choose her words, not wishing to cause hurt. "If you win through, it's worth a try. You've already been accepted; it is only a question of improving your grades. Then you'd be wearing the white coat."

"I see what you mean. I will think about it, but only because you think it's a good idea. Perhaps I have given up too easily, too quickly. Do we need spoons?"

"Yes." Mia busied herself with the casserole that had been slowly cooking for most of the afternoon. She gave it a stir, added some cream and put it back in the oven. "Adam rang, by the way."

Kate's heart sank.

"He rang at lunchtime and again about an hour ago. He says he's coming around to hear how you got on. I told him to wait until we'd eaten. I thought you might need your meal in peace."

Gerry, reaching the bottom of the stairs as Mia told her about Adam, said, "Nice boy, that. Solid; good, steady job; you could do worse."

Kate snapped back at him, "Make up your mind, Dad; I can't marry Adam and go to vet college, can I?"

"True, true, but . . ."

"No buts, I can't." Kate contemplated marriage to Adam as she got the plates out of the warming oven and saw the years unfolding before her. The regulation two children, one boy one girl; the nice house on the nice road; the routine, the mind-numbing routine of Adam's life. The discussion of how close to the main entrance his current parking space was, of his desk and the quality of the chair he'd been allocated. Next year, perhaps, when they refurbished the office, he'd get a bigger, better one, then he'd know he was finally going somewhere. The ritual of the Sunday pub lunch; it's Tuesday so it's his tenpins bowling night; no, he couldn't go swimming because his sinuses were acting up—the terrible shattering monotony of a future like that.

Almost instantly a picture of Scott bunching his fingers and kissing them as he'd left her and Joy that morning came into her mind's eye. Catch Adam doing it. He'd dismiss a gesture like that as flamboyant Continental nonsense. How had she ever come to be involved with him? Well, she knew, really; she didn't need to ask. Because he'd been convenient, because he had money and she had only the money she earned on Saturdays working in the office at Apex Costings PLC and in the café in Weymouth in the summer holidays. Because she hadn't time for emotions when she was working so hard at school.

Because he was comfortable, like an old glove, and didn't demand anything of her. Because he was there and he was loyal in a kind of dumb-animal sort of way. Kate sat at the table.

"Is that enough potato for you, Kate?"

"Oh yes, thanks."

She told them the story of Perkins and Adolf, of the old lady worrying about the toilet and how very ill her cat was and how she didn't know what she would do if she died. And if Adam came, she wasn't in.

"Not in!" Gerry choked on a carrot. "Not in!"

"I can't stand him tonight. Tell him I've gone to bed with a migraine."

"You never get migraines."

"Well, a bad head, then. I'm too tired to bother with him."

Mia said gently, "Don't be unkind to him, Kate. He is genuinely concerned; he's rung twice, after all."

"All right, then. I'll see him but I'm going to bed early."

"Well, he'll understand that."

"So he should; he's always having to get a good night's sleep because he has a 'big day' tomorrow."

Her father chased the last of his peas around the plate and, having secured it, said, "I don't understand why you have such a down on him. He's a grand chap and I like him. He's got some worthy principles that I greatly admire. You'll always be safe with him."

Kate placed her knife and fork together on her empty plate. "Oh, very safe, but absolutely bored to tears. Is there a dessert?"

"Your favorite, my love, apple sponge."

"With cinnamon?"

Mia nodded. Kate rubbed her hands together. "Just what a woman needs when she's been at the coal mines all day." They all three heard the front door open and a voice call out, "It's me, Adam, the man of the moment."

Kate raised her eyebrows at Mia and they both giggled. Mia answered, "I know what you're doing, Adam Pentecost, and I have said before there's no need to take your shoes off when you come here."

His voice, muffled by his exertions, could just be heard: "Mum would kill me if she ever found out I hadn't taken them off."

Mia and Kate giggled again.

Gerry frowned at them and shouted, "Come on in, son. You're just in time for some dessert."

Adam stood in the doorway, glowing with self-satisfaction. Kate liked tall men and he was certainly that, but he was so thin he gave the impression of having outgrown his strength like a runner bean or something. Suitably, given his name, his Adam's apple was bigger and bonier than most, and bobbed up and down when he spoke; his shoulders were narrow, his bottom nonexistent no matter which trousers he wore. Even with all of that, there was something very appealing about him, a kind of vulnerability that made women feel he needed mothering. Kate could tell he was bursting for someone to ask him his news. "You've got something exciting to tell us, haven't you?"

He tried to dismiss his news as trivial but then couldn't resist telling them. "No, no, no, it's nothing, really. Well, it is. I've been short-listed for that promotion."

Mia congratulated him. "Oh, I am pleased. Your mum will be delighted."

Adam looked for a response from Kate. "That's lovely," she said.

"There's four of us, but I'm the most likely one to get it. Longest service and all that. Second interview on Friday."

"You'll have to get that best suit out." Kate put his dessert in front of him and gave him her spoon. "What will it mean if you get it?"

"I shall be second assistant to the deputy. It means another three thousand a year and a move to a vastly superior office. There'll just be the two assistants sharing instead of ten of us in that terrible temporary building. Another step up the ladder." Adam spooned apple sponge into his mouth, his self-satisfaction reaching new heights now that he had an admiring audience.

"This calls for a celebration, son! That red wine you bought, Mia, get a bottle out."

When they'd all finished their dessert, they moved from the kitchen into the sitting room; and Mia fussed about sorting out their best, long-unused wineglasses from the 1930s glass-fronted cabinet, giving them a surreptitious wipe first on a corner of her cardigan.

Gerry opened up the wine and took time sniffing its bouquet and studying the clarity of it by holding up the bottle to the window. "Try that, Adam, son, first rate I think you'll find. Mia's a gem at hunting down good wine." He flashed her one of his loving smiles, which Mia didn't notice.

They'd been sipping their wine and admiring it, and listening to Adam outlining the changes in his working practices if he got the promotion, when he suddenly interrupted himself and said, "Kate! I'm sorry I'm so taken up with my promotion. I've forgotten to ask you about your day."

"I've had an excellent day, the best day of my life to date."

Adam patted her hand. "That's good, I'm really pleased. Nice people to work with?"

"Absolutely!" For sheer devilment she overemphasized the merits of the male vets. "Scott's Australian and he's such fun, Adam, you've no idea. As for Rhodri Hughes, well! He's Welsh, which is obvious from his name, and he's handsome and he sings! And the clients all adore him. Terribly good vet. And you should see Valentine Dedic! Eastern European and sort of like Omar Sharif, olive skinned, and his smile! It's Open Afternoon on Saturday. I shall be busy but would you like to come? You'll come, won't you, Mia?" Mia nodded. "Are you coming, Dad? Last chance to see the operating rooms and the like, and a free feed."

Gerry grunted but it was difficult to know whether it was a yes or a no. Kate turned to Adam and waited for his answer.

"I think I should like that; I think that might be very interesting. Yes, I'll come. We could celebrate afterward, couldn't we? Me getting the promotion and you getting a good job."

Gerry interrupted Adam's fantasy with an emphatic "No. Not good enough, Adam, for Kate. She can do better than that. I want her to try again for veterinary college. Don't we, Mia?"

"It's Kate's decision. What do you think, Adam?"

"Frankly, I think she'd be happier doing what she's doing. Five years' hard work is a long time out of a life, and what's the point when she'll get married, settle down, have a family? She doesn't need to do it. No, not at all. She's better off where she is. Definitely."

"Who says I'll get married?"

Adam shuffled his feet in embarrassment. "Well . . ." Rather lamely he ended with, "There's someone not so very far away from you this very minute who would be delighted if you said yes to him."

"You mean *you?*"

Mia nodded to Gerry and they both slipped out quietly, leaving Kate laughing fit to die.

"I don't think it's that funny. I've been courting you for two years now. It's not altogether unexpected, is it?"

"Courting me? Courting me? So that's what you call it, is it?"

"Isn't that what I've been doing? I thought I was."

She stopped laughing because she realized she was being

cruel, and that wasn't fair. "I'm sorry, sorry for laughing, but I don't think a girl could have had a more peculiar proposal ever. Marriage is the last thing on my mind. Heavens above, I'm nineteen, that's all, and I've things to do with my life before I start thinking about babies and mortgages. Because I'm a woman it doesn't mean I take a job just to fill in time before I get married. I'm after a career. You're like something out of the ark, you really are."

Adam's dark-brown eyes looked searchingly into hers. She reached out sympathetically to touch his hair and found he'd put too much gel on it. "You're all sticky."

"Sorry."

"Anyway, if you want to settle down, as you put it, right now, then find someone else because honestly, Adam, I am not ready for marriage just yet."

"Even if you want to wait for us to get married, there's still no need to try for college again, is there? I mean, is there?"

"No. Only if I want to."

"I love you, you see. There's no one else for me, and with this promotion it makes it possible for—"

"Adam! You're tempting fate saying that. Stop it! Let's change the subject. Shall we go out for a drink?"

"Do you think we should? I'm wanting some early nights, you know, second interview Friday . . ."

Kate sprang up off the sofa. "Right then, you go get your early night. Be seeing you." She left the sitting room, leaving him to follow as and when. It might be an idea to try for college, she thought, just to spite him, him with his boring old-fashioned views. At twenty-five his attitude toward life was older than her dad's. Kate heard the quiet closing of the front door from the kitchen, where she was getting herself a drink of water. Mia looked at her. "Well?"

"There was no need to leave unless you were just too over-come with merriment to stay. Don't worry, I'm not marrying him now or ever. I'm going to bed. He is such a *bore*." Kate went upstairs, after giving Mia a goodnight kiss.

Gerry waited until the door was firmly shut and then asked Mia, "Did she say *bore*, or did she say *boor*?"

"The former for sure. Which he is; she's too lively for him. He'd snuff all her spirit out of her inside a year. Please, Gerry, don't encourage him."

"But he is a nice, reliable chap. He'd look after her, not half, and he and I get on really well."

"And that just about sums him up."

"Eh!"

In bed, Kate let her mind wander to Scott. She honestly could not imagine *him* wanting an early night because he had an interview on Friday. He'd be far more likely to be living it up somewhere—preferably, she speculated, with Kate Howard in tow. Then, blotting out that enthralling idea, came the memory of the warning that she'd had from Joy about taking him with a pinch of salt.

Chapter

· 2 ·

Saturday morning dawned cloudy but dry, for which Joy heaved a sigh of relief. It was still only six o'clock, so she lay down to snatch ten more minutes of peace before she got up. Her list of things to check was by the telephone downstairs and she resisted the idea of dashing down to take yet another look at it. Open Afternoons were no joke for the staff, at least not for her. The younger ones seemed to take them in their stride, but for her the smooth running of them entailed meticulous planning and, frankly, she had enough on her plate with the practice opening in a new building without the clients galloping about all over the place, though she knew she would enjoy it when it all started to happen. She turned over to find herself the only oxccupant of the bed. That particular discovery did not augur well for the rest of the day.

Joy sat up, drew up her knees, wrapped her arms around them and thought. Where could he have gone? So early too. Please, Duncan, please. Not today. But he would if he wanted. Nothing could stop him, not pleas, or cajoling, or shouting, or complaining—and certainly not begging. She smiled grimly when she thought what she did every day of her life, namely stand by her man. Would it be better if he didn't go to the Open Afternoon at all? No one would miss him, for Duncan was no conversationalist. No, she'd not remind him. Just go off as if it were an ordinary day and she was going to work. Which in part she was, as emergencies had to be dealt with by someone; one couldn't leave an animal in pain simply because they all wanted to have fun. Mungo and she would be on duty.

The very mention of his name could still melt her bones. They'd known each other for more than twenty years; she'd been his first receptionist when he set up for himself, and she'd stayed with him through all the ups and downs of his life. The worst had been when his darling Janie had been killed in that ferry disaster. After that, for almost two years he'd lived on automatic pilot, unapproachable, silent, detached; but she'd put up with all that and just when she thought her moment had come, he'd arrived out of the blue one afternoon with his new bride in tow: Miriam. Joy's pain and shock had been so great that she felt as though Miriam herself had taken dozens of knives and forced them straight through her heart. But she'd kept answering the phone, counting money, making out receipts, helping clients and making appointments as though having one's heart torn asunder was an everyday occurrence and not to be permitted to hinder one's devotion to duty.

The devil of it was that this Miriam was the nicest, kindest, loveliest, gentlest being any man could hope to have as a wife, or any woman hope to have as a friend; and that was exactly what Miriam had determined on, that she and Joy should be friends. Strange thing was, considering Joy's devastating disappointment, it wasn't difficult to be Mungo's wife's friend. After fifteen years Miriam still considered Joy her great friend, not suspecting for a moment how Joy felt about Mungo. Joy knew that even now Miriam would be up and about, getting the desserts and the savories she'd made for the lunch buffet out of the freezer, checking her lists of things to do and all for Joy's sake, not for the sake of the practice.

Thinking about Miriam didn't solve the problem of Duncan. Where the blazes was he? It was always the same when he was in the midst of one of his computer problems: He became totally absorbed by his work, with time for nothing and no one until he'd got it resolved; then gradually he came alive again and was reasonable to live with, and was more like the Duncan he used to be. Joy got out of bed and went to stand at the window. She could see way down the valley, could watch the road winding away down into the town, the gulls swirling and swooping in the brilliant sky, the cows returning to the fields from the milking parlor—all this but no sign of Duncan wandering about. Maybe he had been in the house all the time.

Joy showered, dressed, dried her hair and went downstairs. She found Duncan fast asleep in the armchair in his office. Dead to the world. His hands felt cold, so she fetched a rug from the linen chest on the landing and covered him. Why could he never find peace?

Duncan woke just as she was brewing the tea for her breakfast. "Bring me a cup!"

"You lazy monkey! Come and get your own, and eat with me."

Duncan ambled in and sat opposite her at the table.

"You know how much I hate unwashed people at breakfast."

He yawned. "Sorry! I'll go and wash."

"No, that's all right; I'll let you off. Here, toast?"

"Please."

"You don't eat enough."

"Tea?"

"Please. Working?"

"Yes." Joy felt deceitful and toyed with the idea of telling him about the lunch and the Open Afternoon, but she couldn't judge his mood. His heavy-lidded eyes in their deep sockets hid much from everyone including her; his high, domed forehead gave the impression of an excellent intellect and she could vouch for that, but spiritually she knew he craved peace of mind and it showed in the perpetual frown and the twitch by his right eye when things got too much for him.

"How are you today?" she asked.

Duncan was doing his Indian head massage to relieve his tension. When he'd finished, he combed through his hair with his fingers to straighten it and said, "Not bad, actually."

"Fancy an afternoon out? Well, lunch really."

"With you, you mean?"

"Me and about twenty others. It's the Open Afternoon. Lunch for staff and spouses et cetera at twelve, then open house till five."

Duncan nodded. "Yes, I'd like that. Yes, definitely."

"That's a date, then."

"I'll find my own way there."

"Are you sure? I could always come back for you."

"Not at all, you'll have enough to do."

"Thanks, I will. I'll get ready and be off; we've clients till eleven." Joy kissed him, glad he was feeling well enough to go.

THE next time she saw him he was in conversation with Kate in the accounts office. The computer was on and he was explaining something to her. She was nodding, obviously deep in thought, and he was more animated than she had seen him for a while. "OK, you two?"

They both looked up, said at the same time, "Yes, thanks," and went back to what they were saying.

"You're needed for lunch in the apartment. Right now, or you'll be too late. Sorry."

Duncan apologized. "We're coming. We'll talk about that later, Kate. It's so easy."

"For you maybe."

"No, for you too."

Kate laughed. "I doubt it. My hold on computer technology is slight to say the least."

"You do yourself an injustice. You've grasped the concept; having done that, you've nothing to fear." Duncan stood back to allow Kate through the door first and they sauntered amicably up to the apartment, followed by Joy. The cheerful noise of people enjoying themselves came down the stairs to greet them. Joy quaked with anxiety, wondering how Duncan would cope, but she'd forgotten how Miriam could always put him at his ease.

With arms wide stretched Miriam called out, "Duncan! You've come."

She embraced him with such open, genuine love that he succumbed to her warmth and found he could face the crowd with comparative enthusiasm.

"Joy! Hurry up or it will all be gone. Mungo! Drinks for Duncan and Joy, and for Kate—it must be Kate?" She kissed her too, briefly, on the cheek and Kate caught a drift of a flowery, old-fashioned perfume. "What will you have, my dear?"

Kate asked for mineral water.

"*Mineral water* on such an auspicious day?"

"I'll have something stronger when the clients have gone. I don't want to make a fool of myself."

"Wise girl. Come along and get some food; just pile up your plate. I don't want anything left over of this labor of love for Mungo and me to finish off." She grinned at Kate, who immediately felt drawn into her enchanted circle. She, Miriam, wasn't a beautiful person as such but somehow her joie de vivre made her so, and the large brown eyes and the well-rounded cheeks became beautiful without the aid of makeup. "Mungo! Where's Kate's mineral water?" Mungo didn't respond, so Miriam raised her voice. "Dearest! Mineral water for Kate. You're deserting your post."

Mungo came over with Kate's drink. "Here we are, Kate." He raised his own glass to her and said, "Hope you're getting well settled in."

"Thank you. I am. I have to say it's a pleasure to work here; everyone is so helpful and so kind to me."

"I wouldn't have it otherwise. There's no point in working with animals if you don't like both them and people, and I'm not talking about some slushy kind of sentimental love; I'm talking about *liking* them. There's no place for selfish sentimentality in veterinary work, you know."

"Indeed not." Kate felt something brush against her leg. "Oh! It's you. Hello, Perkins. You've forgiven me for throwing water over you, then?" Kate bent down to stroke him and he looked at her with a happy grin on his face, only his small front teeth showing between his parted lips. As she patted him, Kate looked up and gave Mungo a wide smile. "Isn't he great? He's the only dog I know who looks as though he's laughing . . ." Seeing the expression on Mungo's face, Kate stopped speaking. His color had drained away and his normally pleasant features had become pinched and anguished. His glass was rattling against his wedding ring, and to Kate's eyes he appeared to have experienced a tremendous shock. She was too inexperienced socially to know how to cope with the situation and all she could think to say was, "I'm so sorry if I've offended you."

Mungo visibly pulled himself together. He took a quick sip of his gin and said in a curiously uptight voice, "About the accounts. Do you feel confident about them?"

"I will shortly. There's a lot to get my mind around but I'll get there."

College of the Ouachitas

"Where did you learn?"

"I've worked Saturdays at Apex Costings for what seems like a decade and for some reason with what I'd learned at school I picked it up really quickly."

"Logical mind, that's what's needed. Must circulate." Mungo gave her an unhappy smile and wandered off to Miriam, who appeared to sense his desolation and, slipping an arm through his, offered him a plate of food. "Can't have you going out on a call the worse for drink, dearest." She handed him a fork and napkin, briefly kissed his cheek and dashed into the kitchen on some pretext or other.

Joy had witnessed the whole incident and, at the same time as Mungo had received his shock, she had seen what he had seen in Kate's laughing face and knew Kate would be dumbfounded by his reaction to her. So that was why Kate had so appealed to her at the interview. "Kate, you're not getting anything to eat. Come along now. We can't have you falling by the wayside halfway through the afternoon. Have your mum and dad not come?"

"They felt too shy to come for lunch so they're coming later in the afternoon. Have I said something I shouldn't? Like, been too familiar? Mr. Price looked really angry with me."

Joy said, "He's not angry with you, trust me. Probably indigestion—lives on his nerves, you know. Now, what will you have? Miriam has certainly done us proud, hasn't she?"

AT two o'clock the cars began to arrive by the score. Graham Murgatroyd had his work cut out organizing the car park, and Scott, who had been given the job of welcoming everyone at the main entrance, as only he could, and giving each visitor a map of the building, was in need of support. Joy, who'd been rushing around since eight that morning and was feeling distinctly jaded, rather than help Scott herself sent Kate to give him a hand and to get her out of Mungo's way. Joy went to supervise the girls in the reception area serving cups of tea and slices of Miriam's cakes to the clients on their way around the hospital. Duncan was comfortably seated in the reception area with a cup of tea, watching the world go by. At least he'd stayed; that was something. "OK?"

"Fine, thanks. They've done a wonderful job, haven't they, building this place? The capital involved! It's so well done, so pleasant; it's worth every penny."

"Glad you like it. It's taken a lot of planning."

"I've been listening to the clients' comments. They're well impressed. The client list is bound to increase."

"Do you think so?"

"I certainly do. When you think of those cramped premises the opposition has in the High Street, I reckon that practice will be out of business in six months. I mean there's nowhere to park, for a start."

"Out of business! Oh, I hope not. I wouldn't want that to happen."

Duncan looked at her and said, "Take a pew for five minutes. You deserve it."

Joy flopped down on the chair next to him

"Cup of tea?"

Joy nodded. Duncan walked across to the long table where Bunty and Sarah One were pouring the tea. She couldn't remember the last time he'd done anything for her in the way of looking after her. He was so totally absorbed by himself and his work that sometimes she could kick his computer to the bottom of the garden or better still into the sea at high tide. For a moment she enjoyed the idea of his being free of the damned thing, free as air, the frown gone, the twitch cast into oblivion. Oh, happy day!

As Duncan walked back toward her, Mr. Featherstonehough

came in. "Well, I've come. I said I wouldn't, but I have. If you're going to murder my Adolf on these premises, I might as well see for myself what they're like."

Joy jumped up. "How lovely of you to come. I am pleased to see you!"

"You are? I'm amazed."

She ignored his sarcastic tone and asked if he'd like tea and cakes first or to have a look around. No sooner were the words out of her mouth than Perkins hurtled into the reception area, braking the moment he realized that Adolf wasn't with his master. His tail began to wag and he greeted Mr. Featherstone-hough like an old friend. The old man couldn't resist his welcome and bent down to stroke him. "Oh, I see. I'm OK when Adolf isn't with me." Perkins wagged his tail even harder and trotted away through the back.

"I've written to the Royal Veterinary College, you know, telling them what goes on. It's not right."

"Adolf does quite enjoy sparring with Perkins, you know, and he's well able to defend himself. If he were too small to fight back, Perkins wouldn't bother with him."

Mr. Featherstonehough looked long and hard at Joy as though weighing how much of what she said was genuine and how much was a defense of Perkins. "You could be right. Yes, you could be right, but it's bloody annoying. Anyway, I've written."

"That's your prerogative. Now which is it to be, cake and tea or tour?"

"Tour."

"Tour it is. I'll get one of the girls to show you around."

"I just hope it's that pretty one."

"We're all pretty here."

He laughed. "You're right. But it's that nurse who held

Adolf for his injection last Monday, the one who's a bit too big for her uniform."

"You mean Sarah Two. I shall tell her what you've said. Wait there and I'll find her for you."

Joy got back to her cup of tea only when it was going cold, so Duncan kindly got her another one.

Long used to his silences, she was surprised when he took the initiative and said, "The new girl, she's got a good head on her shoulders. You'll have no trouble with the accounts once she gets cracking."

"Think so?"

"I do. She understands the principles, you see."

"Of bookkeeping? I should hope so; that's supposed to be the main object of her employment."

"Of computers, I mean. Logical brain."

"Very bright. Too bright for what she's doing."

Duncan had lost interest and was staring into his empty cup. "Going?"

He nodded, got up and walked out.

Joy sighed. People must think him really peculiar. Just for once she would have enjoyed him being around, talking, helping, just being *there*.

KATE asked Scott would he mind if she left him to do the meet and greet on his own while she took her parents around.

"Moment they come you leave me to it. There's not so many arriving now anyway. What you doing tonight?"

"Going out with my boyfriend."

Scott pulled a face. "Boyfriend? What does he do for a living?"

"Manager of the dispatch department at that big computer warehouse out on the bypass."

With a wry twitch of an eyebrow, Scott asked, "Important job, is it?"

Kate giggled. "He imagines it is, but it's mainly moving paper about, especially in triplicate. Order this, order that, see it gets to this company and that company—quite boring really. He should be here, but he's late. I tried to ring him last night. He had a second interview for promotion yesterday and I thought he would ring, but he didn't. Talk of the devil, there he is."

Adam parked his little Toyota, locked it and began to walk between the cars toward the entrance.

Scott muttered out of the side of his mouth, "I don't see any horns." They both laughed.

Seeing the two of them standing there in the sun, Adam thought they looked like a gilded couple in an exclusive club to which he knew he would never belong. He felt bitterly excluded, but to save face he determined not to let it show. He raised his arm in greeting. "Hello, there!" To indicate to who-ever this Adonis was standing beside her that Kate was his, Adam put his arms around her and kissed her lips as though he hadn't seen her for a month.

Kate pushed him aside as discreetly as she could but saw the amusement on Scott's face and knew her action hadn't escaped his notice.

"I rang last night, but you weren't in. What happened?"

He chucked her under her chin. "Ah! Ah! Surely you know the answer to that?"

"You got the job!"

"You said it!"

"I'm very glad, very glad indeed. So pleased. Aren't you clever? So where were you last night when I rang?"

Adam smirked. "Out with the boys, actually."

To Kate this seemed the oddest thing for him to do and for

a moment she didn't believe him, but then she remembered he never lied, so it must be true.

Scott said, "Congratulations," and held out his hand. Adam pretended to have just noticed him. Scott added, "I'm Scott from Aussie land."

"How do you do. I'm Adam Pentecost. Pleased to meet you."

"You haven't seen Mia and Dad on your way, have you?"

"No. Should I have?"

"They said they were coming." Kate scanned the car park as though by doing so the two of them would materialize, and they did. Gerry's Beetle trundled steadily into the car park. Kate waved and darted between the cars to where Gerry was carefully parking his treasure.

"That's Kate's ma and pa, is it?"

Adam nodded. "Her dad and his second wife. She's a bit odd. Not quite my cup of tea. Paints."

"Oh, well then. Wonderful car."

"He's besotted with it. Can't think why; it costs him a fortune in upkeep."

"Here, have these; I'll go take a look."

Adam watched Scott amble away and resented being left holding the maps for handing out to the clients. What cheek! Leaving him to hold the fort while he pranced about like an idiot, admiring Gerry's car. He could see from her body language that Mia had taken an immediate liking to Scott and recalled the sneer in his voice when he'd said, "Oh, well then." Adam found he had taken an instant dislike to Scott. This should have been his day and it wasn't; it was being snatched from him by a fly-by-night, here-today-gone-tomorrow type of chap, with more dash and go than he would ever muster. Life simply wasn't fair. He sank further into the depths of gloom.

At the deepest moment of his despair, Joy came out to tell

Scott and Kate they might as well come in now, seeing as it was half past four and they couldn't expect any more clients.

"Good afternoon, I see you've been left in charge."

Adam thrust the maps into her hands. "Yes. I'm Kate's boyfriend."

"How nice to meet you. Scott's commandeered her, I see. Is that Kate's mum and dad?"

Adam didn't proffer the full explanation. "Yes."

"I'm Joy, by the way. You're . . ."

"Adam."

"We're just about to clear away the tea things. I'll go and put a halt to it." Joy went back indoors, leaving Adam alone.

He joined Gerry and Mia, accompanied by Kate, who energetically explained everything as she took them around the various departments and introduced them to all the staff, poured cups of tea for them and handed them cake; but he couldn't raise any enthusiasm. Stephie Budge made a fuss of him, which pleased him, but other than that all he could see was that the whole place, in which Kate appeared to be so comfortable, presented a threat to his plans for his life. In no circumstances must Kate be permitted to go to college because if she did, he would lose her for evermore and that wasn't to be allowed.

Mia helped Kate and Joy with the clearing away, so Adam and Gerry hung around in reception.

"I'll take Mia home if you like; there's no need for you to stay."

Gerry shook his head. "We're going to a friend's straight from here, thanks all the same. Thought you and Kate might like a bit of privacy tonight." Gerry nudged his elbow.

Adam blushed.

"What do you think, then, about this place? It's certainly cost a packet."

Adam nodded.

"Oh yes! But I've said this several times and I shall say it again. My Kate should try again for veterinary college. You can feel the . . . well, is it aura or is it privilege or is it authority or self-confidence or what that all these vets have? But whatever it is, you can feel it and I want it for our Kate."

A rage grew up in Adam's narrow chest; it grew so huge he thought his chest must have swollen to twice its size. Anger flushed his face, swelled the blood vessels at his temples and finally exploded into words. "Not if I can help it. I love her and I want her to marry *me* and settle down with *me*. All this"—he made a vigorous dismissive gesture with his hand—"is nonsense."

Gerry looked at him, amazed. It was the first time since he'd known him that Adam had displayed such powerful opinions . . . no, they weren't opinions, they were emotions. "Why, Adam, you're not jealous of her, are you? There's nothing for you to be jealous of. You're climbing that ladder you've talked so much about too—you know, with this promotion."

Adam's reply was a snort. He stood up and said, "I'll see her back at your house."

Gerry called after him, "You'll need the key; you can't get in . . ." but he was too late. Adam had gone.

So he was outside the house waiting in his car when Kate got home well over an hour later. Before she left, Kate and Joy and Stephie and the two Sarahs, with Bunty and several of the vets, had all gone up to Mungo and Miriam's apartment to eat some of the food left over from the lunch buffet.

"Otherwise Mungo and I will still be eating it this time next week, so you must. I insist."

Joy said Miriam had provided far too much and Miriam's reply, spoken with her face alight with laughter, was that her generous nature was to blame.

Mungo, who'd been out on a call during the afternoon, was

back, tucking into the food. Whatever it was Kate had done to upset him seemed to have been forgotten, and he appeared relaxed and amused them all by relating the funny side of the call he had just made. Before she left, they'd all decided that after they'd indulged themselves with Miriam's food they didn't need to eat, so they'd all go out for a drink together. Only Kate had declined, saying she had arranged to go out with Adam.

"Bring him with you," said Stephie. "We'd like to get to know him and it's a good chance for you to meet everyone too. Go on, give him a ring on his mobile."

"He hasn't got one."

Stephie thought about this and said, "If he's at your house waiting for you, go home and tell him we're going to the Fox and Grapes. He'll jump at the chance, believe me."

So she did just as Stephie said. She tapped on the car window. "Hi!"

Adam wound it down and snapped, "Where have you been? I've been waiting ages."

"I'm sorry. Miriam asked us all up to the apartment to finish off the food. It would have been discourteous not to have accepted her invitation. If you hadn't gone off in a huff, you could have gone upstairs too. Anyway, I'm here now. Come in while I get changed and have a wash because we're all meeting up for a drink and you're invited."

"I've not eaten yet."

"You can eat at the pub. They do lovely food there."

"I thought we were celebrating tonight, just the two of us."

"Look, I'm the new girl and I want to belong and I don't yet, so going out with them all will help. It'll be such fun. So please, for my sake."

Adam didn't reply, but stared straight ahead, ignoring her.

"Please, you'll like them all. I know you will; they're such a friendly lot. Go on, please. Come in and wait. I shan't be long."

"I think you'd best go on your own. I'll be here tomorrow at twelve as usual."

Incensed by his refusal to indulge her, Kate said, "Don't bother, Adam, thank you."

"Not go out for lunch? But it's Sunday!"

"I know what day of the week it is. If I didn't know better, I'd think you were jealous."

"Of what?"

"Heaven alone knows. Go on, then, spend Saturday night with your mother. I'm sure she'll enjoy your company, which is more than I would with you in this mood."

Kate slammed into the house, absolutely furious with him. She went to the Fox and Grapes, fully intending to have a good night. Which she did and later, in bed, she decided that she'd enjoyed herself an awful lot more than she would have if she'd gone out with Adam. Then she felt guilty, then decided she didn't care if he didn't come around ever again, changed her mind and wished she had gone out with him, and changed her mind again when she finally came to the conclusion that Scott and Graham and Rhodri were much more fun, to say nothing of the two Sarahs, who were such an incredibly funny double act they'd had her in stitches. She was in so much turmoil that it was two o'clock before she got to sleep.

AROUND that time Duncan came home. Joy had gone back straight from the practice, expecting to find him waiting for his meal, but he hadn't been there. She made it for him anyway and kept it under a plate, ready for the microwave when he did finally decide to return. But two o'clock in the morning was excessively late even for Duncan.

Joy leaped out of bed when she heard his key in the door and went downstairs dreading what she would find. If it was possible, he appeared wearier than ever, his dark stubble emphasizing the exhaustion in his face. He was soaked to the skin.

"Duncan! Duncan! Where on earth have you been? Here, let me help." Between them they stripped off his wet clothes. Joy got a huge well-warmed towel from the airing cupboard and wrapped him in it. "What you need is a hot shower. Have you eaten?"

Duncan shook his head.

"Come on, then, upstairs you go for a shower and I'll get your food ready. Clean pajamas in your top drawer."

When he'd finished eating and been warmed by the heat of the stove and the food in his stomach, Joy said, "We can't go on like this."

Duncan huddled still farther into his dressing gown until it seemed as though all there were in the armchair were a dressing gown and a head. He stared at the logs burning away. "It would be so easy to seek peace in drink."

"I know. I know."

"While ever I've got you . . ."

"I know." She knelt beside his chair, laid her head on his chest and hugged him.

Duncan stroked her hair. "I don't deserve you."

"No, you don't. You do nothing to deserve me."

Duncan chuckled. "You're supposed to say 'What nonsense.'"

"It was the truth."

"Ah! The truth. Don't give me any more truth, thank you, I may not want to hear it."

"Best not. Eh?"

Duncan nodded his agreement. "Great day today. I envy all of you, your purpose in life."

Joy sat back on her heels. "It did go well, didn't it?"

"Excellent. Such a turnout of clients. I doubt there was anyone left in the shops in town; I think they all came to see the new place." Duncan rubbed a hand on her back. "All thanks to you."

"Where have you been?"

"Mostly sitting up on Beulah Bank Top. Great place for thinking."

"What about?"

"Me."

"Ah! Very self-indulgent."

"More harrowing, really."

"Did you come to any conclusions?"

"That I'm trapped, in a cage, and they've thrown away the key."

"Duncan!"

"I'm going to bed."

And he went.

Joy cleared up, closed the doors of the stove and followed him up the stairs. He was already asleep, curled in a fetal position as always and on her side of the bed. She pulled the duvet around his shoulders and climbed in herself, and thought about her day.

If she rated it on a score of one to ten, then taking everything into consideration it rated ten—well, perhaps nine and a half, as she remembered Mungo's face when Kate had stroked Perkins and looked up at him with a smile. Joy sighed. One day she'd explain to Kate. Dear Kate, she was going to be such an asset to the practice. Joy cuddled up to Duncan's back and, letting the warmth of his body seep into her, fell asleep, enriched by the satisfying pleasures of a successful day doing what she loved most.

Chapter

· 3 ·

Monday morning dawned wet and cold, a typical English autumn day. Heavy traffic in the town center had delayed Kate so that it was already just after eight o'clock by the time she parked her car. The wind blew down from Beulah Bank Top, making the car park the very last place on earth that she wanted to linger. Nothing irritated her more than being held up in traffic with the wipers going hell for leather all the time and being scarcely able to see where she was going. As she leaped out of the car, the wind blowing down from the hills hit her full in the face. Not stopping to lock it and with the hood of her anorak pulled over her head, she made a run for the main entrance.

Stephie had already laid a long length of matting from the glass door to reception to save the floor and was on the computer checking through the appointments for the day, and as Kate wiped her feet on the mat, the farm practice phone began ringing as well as one of the others.

"Take that, will you, Kate."

Answering the phones before the fourth ring was practice policy, so Kate, without removing even her anorak, drew a deep breath and picked up the receiver. "Good morning, Barley-bridge Farm Practice. How may I help? Rhodri Hughes? Hold the line a moment, please." She went into the farm practice office to see if Rhodri had come in yet and found him sitting with his feet propped up on the desk opening his mail. "Phone call for you."

"This early?" He picked up the receiver, saying, "Rhodri Hughes speaking."

Kate went back to reception and replaced the receiver. "Client?"

"Don't know. I'll be back—just going to get myself organized. My shoes are soaking wet."

Using the mirror in the women's staff cloakroom, Kate combed through her hair and wished for the thousandth time she had naturally curly hair that would bounce back to life immediately after she'd removed her headgear. But she hadn't, so she combed through it, pushed it about with her fingers a bit, found she'd buttoned her uniform up wrongly and thought to herself that that fact alone augured a bad day.

The moment she opened the cloakroom door, she could hear Rhodri shouting. Stephie was shouting back at him: "I didn't answer the phone. It was Kate."

Joy came out from her office saying, "This noise is quite unacceptable. Kindly refrain, the pair of you. I will not have my staff spoken to like this, Rhodri. Whatever is the matter?"

"That bloody Megan Jones. They put her through to me. They know—I've told them—I don't want to speak to her. How many times have I to say it?"

Joy grinned. "We're not here to field your personal calls, you know. You should tell her the truth, that you're not interested."

"I don't want to hurt her feelings."

"Oh, poor dear boy. If you're so kind, why not take her out?"

Rhodri shuddered. "Not likely. She's not my type."

Kate apologized. "I'm so sorry; it didn't click that it was her. I'd just rushed in and . . ."

"That's no excuse. Her accent is recognizable, for God's sake, surely. Don't ever do it again." His dark eyes were almost boiling with temper and he quite intimidated Kate.

"I am so very sorry. I promise, cross my heart, that I won't let it happen again; it was just that . . ."

Rhodri wagged his finger at her. "Best not, because I can't answer for the consequences."

Joy bristled at his threat. "Mr. Hughes! You will not threaten my staff, if you please. It is entirely your fault that this situation has arisen. Apologize immediately."

Though startled by the level of anger in Joy's voice, Rhodri had to recognize the rightness of what she said: He'd caused sweet-tempered, gentle Joy to become distinctly ungentle all in a moment.

"I beg your pardon, Joy and Kate, for losing my temper . . ."

Stephie pouted at him. "And what about an apology for me? You shouted at me too."

"Yes, and you too, apologies all around."

Joy stood with her hands on her hips, head to one side. "So, are you going to sort it out or shall I?"

Rhodri pondered the way out she had offered him. "No, thank you. I'd be less than a man if I allowed you to do it. It's something I must do, hurt feelings or not." He grinned. "I've taken her out three times and I've known from the start she wasn't right for me. Let's face it, she was revolted by Harry and how can a man go out with a girl who doesn't like Harry?"

Kate, wondering who on earth Harry was, asked, "Harry? Who's Harry, for heaven's sake?"

"My ferret."

Kate began laughing and found she couldn't stop. Rhodri

looked at her and for a moment she thought he was going to be angry again, but he wasn't. He caught the infection of her laughter and he too began to laugh, the rich, musical sound echoing around reception to the delight of the clients who were just beginning to arrive.

When finally he stopped and had wiped his streaming eyes, he said between gasps, "I'll have to be cruel and do the dirty deed. Tell her straight from the shoulder that it's no go. I'll ring her tonight. Curse the woman."

Joy suggested a stiff whiskey prior to dialing her number.

"Maybe you should give up Harry," said Kate.

Rhodri looked appalled. "Give up Harry? Certainly not. Love me, love my ferret." He turned on his heel and went back to opening his mail.

Stephie put down the receiver, altered an appointment on her computer and turned to Kate. "Can you imagine that? 'Love me, love my ferret.' I ask you. It's a rotten, smelly thing; I've seen it. I can't believe anyone could fancy him, never mind him *and* a ferret."

Kate's eyes twinkled. "Oh, I don't know, all that Celtic emotion. He's quite attractive once he gets worked up."

"He might be laughing now but he won't forget what you've done. He's like that—bears a grudge, you know, for ages."

"In that case I shall deflect his annoyance by showing an interest in his ferret."

Stephie raised an eyebrow. "Well, if you're that hard up . . . Adam OK?" She looked slyly at Kate during the lull in ringing phones and then asked again, "Adam OK?"

"He's fine, thanks. Yes, fine."

"Did you go somewhere exciting yesterday?"

Kate, who was printing out the visiting lists for the farm vets, shook her head and asked casually, "Did you?"

"Well, Sarah One and I went to this new leisure complex that's opened. Expensive but brilliant. You and Adam should try it. I expect he's a good swimmer with his build."

But the morning had begun in earnest and the two of them got no further opportunity to discuss the weekend, for which Kate was grateful. She hadn't, in fact, seen Adam apart from when he had sat outside her house from twelve until one, waiting for her to come out to go for their regular Sunday pub lunch. Her dad and Mia had gone to a factory outlet place first thing, so they hadn't seen him, and Kate had refused to go out to speak to him. She'd already told him she wasn't going and, being in a temper because of his refusal to join her and the others for a drink the previous night, had decided he could sit there till the cows came home if he wanted to; after all, it was a free country. He had a right to park his car where he chose as long as he wasn't on a double yellow line. She'd peeped through the net curtain several times and nearly gone to the door twice to speak to him but defiantly changed her mind.

In fact, trying for vet college again had become more of a distinct possibility each time she'd looked out. Adam's horizons were so limited, and how could anyone be such a fool as to sit outside all that time and not knock on the door. But then he had never knocked on the door on Sundays; he'd always simply parked and waited for her to come out—something about not disturbing Mia and her dad on a Sunday. Other days he knocked and walked in. A creature of habit was Adam. How he'd cope with the new job she couldn't imagine. But she was glad he'd got it, even if his behavior had become so odd. Going out with the boys for the evening! That was a joke, surely?

"Kate! Hello-o-o!"

Jerked back into the present, Kate looked up from her lists. "Sorry, Scott, just printed out your list. Here you are."

"How's my favorite girl this morning?"

"First, I am not your favorite girl; and second, here's your list; and third, it's a long one; and fourth, this call here I've just added on sounds critical."

Scott groaned. "Oh God! Not Applegate Farm. I swear there's a curse on me. Cross it off my list and give it to Zoe, please, I beg you." Scott got down on one knee and put his hands together as though in prayer. "Please. For your favorite Aussie?"

"You know that Zoe, being pregnant, can't go because it's an abortion, so you'll have to go."

"Stephie! Tell her I can't go. Please."

But Scott's mistake had been calling Kate his favorite girl. "Kate is in charge and she's right," Stephie said. "Zoe can't go."

"Very well, but if something goes wrong, I shan't be responsible for my actions. That farm is the filthiest . . ."

Kate stopped him speaking by placing her finger on his mouth, which he swiftly took the opportunity to kiss as she said softly, "Not in front of the clients, please."

Looking suitably chastened, Scott ambled out. He closed the glass door behind him and turned to press his face, contorted into an alarming grimace, against the glass. Kate waved her hand at him and then ignored him. He came back in to make another remark but thought better of it and left when he saw Joy taking over the reception desk.

"Accounts, Kate. You'd better get on."

"Right, I will. Scott didn't want to go to Applegate Farm."

"He never does, but he must."

"Why doesn't he like it?"

"Because," Stephie said, "he always makes mistakes there."

"Mistakes?"

Joy denied this. "For some reason, things always go wrong for him there and he's got a thing about it now. But he can't pick and choose."

So the clients couldn't hear, Stephie whispered, "Nasty man is Mr. Parsons. Very rude. You should hear him on the phone. Disgusting!"

"Only because Mr. Parsons thinks Mungo is the one vet capable of attending to his animals."

Stephie muttered, "Some animals! Well, we'll see what he has to say when he gets back."

"That won't be for ages. I've given him a list long enough to keep him busy all day."

"So you should, Kate; he has to earn his money. He gets paid enough, believe me. Off you go and you too, Stephie, and take a break. Please."

SCOTT flung himself into the Land Rover, opened the windows wide, turned on the radio, checked he had his laptop with him, swung into gear and charged out of the car park in despair. Sure, he'd played the fool in his attempt to avoid this call, but underneath it all he seriously—oh, so seriously—didn't want to go. Most especially on a wet day. If only there'd been a nurse free to go with him, that might have helped, but with Bunty still away . . . He had a suspicion that her absence would be put down to him. How could she expect a young, virile man to resist her charms? She was round and cuddly and blond and tanned, and had what his ma would have called come-hither eyes. It had all happened so quickly—she eager, he hungry—and those sexy legs and the swing of her slender hips as she walked across the farmyard to the Land Rover for his drug box . . . well, what with the dark and everything, what else could she expect, having spent the evening egging him on?

But he hadn't meant for this to happen . . . just the once, as Pa would say if he were here, it only needs once, just once and she's up the spout. He brushed aside the thought that a little Spencer had most assuredly had his life snuffed out this week, signaled left onto the Applegate Farm track and thought about the thick mud that always covered the yard, be it drought or flood, and planned his precautionary strategy. Scott took off his precious Timberland boots and changed into his Wellingtons before he got out. As his feet touched the ground, a voice shouted, "Taken long enough. Come on, then. Be sharp. It's Zinnia."

"Morning, Phil. Wet day."

Phil Parsons was a short, stocky man with a rotund waist-line and massive red, swollen hands and an overlarge head. He was never without, summer or winter, a black balaclava, which entirely covered his face and head except for a slit where his mouth and nose were, and two holes through which his eyes could barely be seen, as the holes didn't quite match where his eyes came. Consequently, one never quite saw both eyes at once, which was disconcerting and affected one's relationship with him. Added to which, if one got too close, he smelled strongly of the all-pervading odor of someone whose program of personal hygiene had been severely neglected.

From the back of the Land Rover, Scott pulled out some equipment he thought he would need, and slid and slithered his way to the cow barn. It was windowless, so the only light came from the open door and two hurricane lamps hanging from the cobwebby ceiling. In addition, today there was Blossom Parsons, Phil's young wife, holding a torch.

"Morning, Mr. Spencer. Poor morning. You been on call all night?"

"For a change, no, I haven't, Mrs. Parsons."

Scott, from the first moment he had met her, had retained a certain formality when speaking to Blossom Parsons, for he was intensely aware that she fancied him and she made it abundantly clear even in front of her husband. Scott's technique was to ignore her remarks as though concentration on the animal he'd come to see was taking up all of his mind. He went to have a word with the cow. He stroked her head and spoke softly to her, looked at her eyes to judge her temper, checked her gums to see if she was in shock.

"Hold the torch for me, Phil, right here, please. Let's see what's come away."

"No, no, I can do it." Mrs. Parsons laid a hand on his back as she leaned forward to get the beam shining where he wanted it. Her fingers began very subtly massaging his spine.

"She's not got rid of it all and she's not well either. Got a temperature, I would think. What is she, about fifteen weeks?"

Phil scratched his head through his balaclava. "Couldn't say for certain, but about that."

"Look in your records."

"Do me a favor. Natural farming I go in for. If they're in calf, they're in calf and if they're not, they're not. Writing it down doesn't put them in the club and what's more it takes up my time." Phil peered at the bloody mess surrounding the tiny, immature dead calf laid on the barn floor. "My bull knows his business better than me. Don't need no pen an' paper, he don't."

"I see." By this time, Scott had his hand in the cow's uterus and Mrs. Parsons had stopped massaging him.

"I'll go put the kettle on, shall I?"

There were some farms where Scott could enjoy a mug of tea sitting at the kitchen table talking farming, and there were some where he couldn't. Applegate Farm came into the latter category. When he'd been offered tea the first time after a long, cold wait for a calf to arrive, he'd accepted and eagerly gone inside to get warm, but after the shock of seeing their filthy kitchen and the indescribable chaos that reigned in there, he had vowed he'd die of hypothermia before entering that kitchen again.

"No, thanks, Mrs. Parsons. I've more calls this morning

than I can cope with. I'll just take a couple of blood samples and give Zinnia an antibiotic, and then I'll be away."

"I'm real disappointed you won't have a cuppa. I made cherry cake yesterday and there's a slice left. Let me put it in a bag and you can take it home to finish your lunch with. Won't be a minute."

"She should be all right now, Phil. Any ideas why this happened?"

Phil shook his head. "None. Just one of them things."

"I've said this before and I've got to say it again: This place needs cleaning up. Milk produced here! God help us! No wonder Milkmarque says you don't reach its hygiene standards and refuses to collect."

"There's plenty of people'll buy my milk. Don't need no puffed-up officials, I don't."

Scott held up his hand to silence him. "Say no more; I don't want to know. Right. But it's a disgrace. A complete disgrace. If I mention it in the right quarter, you'll be in deep trouble, so make sure when I come back the day after tomorrow to see Zinnia that you've made a start. No, more than a start, actually done it. The cow barn, the yard, everywhere. Right?"

"I heard." Phil sniffed his disgust and turned on his heel back into the barn.

Hoping to escape before Mrs. Parsons came out of the farmhouse with his cherry cake, Scott headed straight through the yard, out of the gate and across the farm track to where he'd left his vehicle. He had stored his equipment and stripped off his protective clothing when she bellowed from the farmhouse doorway, "Scott! Your cake! Here!" Mrs. Parsons held up a brown paper bag, making no attempt to walk across to him. There was nothing for it: Politeness and good client relations demanded that he walk over to get it. Taking a moment to replace his Wellingtons, Scott crossed the farm track and slurped his way over to the house. The route from the barn to the track he knew, but he'd never walked from the track to the farmhouse door before and he unwittingly dropped up to his chest into the slurry pit which, through years of practice, Phil and Mrs. Parsons and Zinnia and the rest of the herd would have known to avoid. The farm always smelled, but by disturbing the slurry, as Scott did with the speed of his fall, he spread an extra layer of stench not only over himself but also the whole yard.

They pulled him out between them without a word being exchanged. Phil got a bucket, filled it from the tap in the yard and threw it over him, then another and another.

"No, no, come into the house. You can stand in the bath and strip off in there. I'll lend you something of Phil's."

Three buckets of water had made little impression on the stinking mess that was Scott. His spanking-clean chinos were now thick with cow dung; his checked shirt, bought in Sydney the day he left, was weighed down with the thick sludge; his boots were filled with it; his bare arms and hands oozed the stuff. He took a moment to be grateful that he hadn't had time to change into his Timberland boots before she'd called him. Bitter desperation filled him. Strip off in front of Mrs. Parsons? Not likely! An outfit belonging to Phil? Even less likely!

"Thanks all the same. Do you have some newspaper for the car, Phil? I'll get back to the practice and shower there. I keep a spare set of clothing there just in case." He didn't, but in circumstances like these a lie was neither here nor there.

He lumbered across to the Land Rover with filth squelching in his boots at every step. Before he got in, he smoothed his hands all over himself and squeezed away as much of the loose stuff as he could. The newspapers he spread all over the seat and the back of it, and gingerly climbed in. Scott opened every window, reversed and was about to stamp on the accelerator when Mrs. Parsons appeared beside him.

"Your cake! Don't go without it." She held the bag up to the window, and Scott reached out a stinking, filth-streaked hand and thanked her politely for it. The ludicrousness of the situation struck him and he began to laugh and was still laughing, but by then somewhat hysterically, when he arrived back at the practice.

Finding the back door locked and no amount of hammering bringing a response, he clumped around to the main door and went in.

When the smell that was Scott reached Joy, she looked up from the desk and saw him standing dripping on the doormat with pieces of the newspaper from the seat still stuck to his back. The astonishment on her face struck Scott as highly comical. But there was nothing funny about her reaction. "Get out, you absolute nincompoop! Out! Go on! Out!"

The clients patiently waiting their turns protested loudly at the smell. Covering their noses with handkerchiefs, they shouted, "Get out, Scott! What a smell."

Slowly the sodden cow dung on his socks began sinking into the doormat. Scott looked down at the mess he was creating and muttered plaintively, "I can't help it. No one answered the bloody door when I knocked."

"Oh. Language!" someone said.

Joy endeavored to retrieve the situation by telling him to go around the back and she'd send someone out to help. Which Scott did. A client got up and opened the windows to let out the smell while Joy went to ask Kate to give a hand outside.

She stood him on a grate by the back door and hosed him down till he was shuddering with cold. "I've got to take my clothes off."

"I'll go in and start the shower; leave your clothes out here and I'll sort them out, and please dry yourself off a bit with this dog towel before you come in."

"Dog towel! Oh, thanks! Good on you, mate!"

"Otherwise, we'll have filthy water everywhere. Go on, do as I say."

Showered and warmed and dressed in Mungo's gardening trousers and shirt, Scott sat in the accounts office drinking the scorching-hot coffee Kate had made for him, muttering threats about Applegate Farm. "I shall report him. I said I wouldn't, but I shall."

"For what?"

"For selling milk on the quiet when Milkmarque won't collect from his farm. For keeping animals in disgraceful conditions, though I have to admit they do seem happy and are not actually in any danger. He knows every one of them by name."

"How did you come to be like this?"

Scott's eyes gleamed with amusement over the rim of his mug. "I fell into the slurry pit."

"You didn't! How could anyone do that? Weren't you looking where you were going?"

"Parsons's pit isn't fenced."

"But what about the cows, don't they fall in it?"

"Oh no! They know where it is and walk around it. Trouble is the yard is so thick with mud and mess you don't see where the mud finishes and the pit starts. Thank God they were there to pull me out."

Kate knew she shouldn't laugh because Scott was so dejected, but she couldn't help it and it began to bubble up inside her. He caught her eye and they both laughed.

Kate pulled herself together and said, "Look, there's the rest of the calls still to do. You've got to go."

He stood up. "You're getting as bad as Joy, you are, and you've only been here a week. To cheer a miserable Aussie up, will you come out with him tonight?" Seeing the doubt in her face he added, "For a drink?"

Gravely Kate studied him and answered, "All right. I will. Just for a drink."

"But of course, sweet one, as you say, just for a drink. Fox and Grapes about eight?"

MIA, Gerry and Kate were finishing their evening meal when the front door opened and they heard Adam's "It's only me."

There he was in the kitchen in his tenpins bowling outfit.

Gerry covered Kate's and Mia's surprised silence by saying, "Come in, Adam. There's still some tea in the pot. Like some?"

Mia got up to get the extra cup and Kate looked up at him. "Yes?"

Adam didn't quite look her in the eye but answered, "Thought I'd just pop around."

"I didn't think you would be coming for me tonight, after Sunday."

"Here, son." Gerry pulled out the chair next to Kate. "Sit here."

Mia passed him his cup of tea and pushed the sugar bowl across to him.

Gerry made pleasant remarks about the weather, trying to lighten the atmosphere, and wondered why things didn't seem right.

Adam ignored him and said to Kate, "I waited outside on Sunday but you didn't come out."

"I know I didn't."

Gerry and Mia tried to disguise their surprise. Gerry asked feebly, "Why didn't you?" but got no reply.

"Well?"

"I told you not to come. I said I wouldn't go out to lunch."

"But we always do."

Seeing that Adam was disinclined to look at her, Kate twisted around in her chair and glared at him. "You are a chump, Adam. Who in their right mind would sit outside a house for a whole hour and then drive away?"

"But I never knock on Sundays."

"Exactly. But just once perhaps you could break the habit of a lifetime and knock. Where are you expecting to go tonight?"

Adam looked down at his beige sweatshirt and trousers, which in the catalogue had been described—stylishly, he thought—as taupe, and his immaculate white socks and bowling shoes. He plucked at his sweatshirt and said, "Isn't it obvious?"

"Perfectly. Unfortunately, I've made other arrangements for tonight."

He couldn't have looked more surprised if she'd said she was going skinny-dipping. "Other arrangements? What do you mean? It's Tuesday."

Mia gently interrupted this painful dialogue. "Adam, just for once Kate wants a change. Don't you sometimes want to do things differently?"

"Well, no, I don't. I'll miss it if we don't go."

"I shan't. You're not very good at it and I'm tired of making a fool of myself for your sake. I try not to win and I do, every time."

Mia couldn't believe how hurtful Kate was being to Adam and neither could Gerry, who felt a conciliatory word was required. "I think you should cancel this outing you've planned and go with Adam, Kate. It's only fair."

Kate got up from her chair. "I don't want to hurt your feelings . . ."

Adam looked angry now and his anger disturbed Kate more than she liked to admit. Usually he flushed when he was upset but this time he was white to the gills. Through gritted teeth he said, "It's too late; you already have."

"To be honest, I've arranged to have a drink with . . . someone from work."

Adam got to his feet. "Well, there's no point going on my own." Pushing his chair under the table, he asked her outright, "Is it that Aussie?"

"Well, yes, it is. He's had a really bad day today and he needed cheering up, and I thought after Sunday you wouldn't be coming."

"I knew you should never have gone to work there. I just knew it. How can you contemplate having an evening out with someone else when you're *my girl*? You always spend Tuesday night with me. Ring him up and cancel it like your father said." Kate didn't make a move, so Adam pounded his right fist into his left palm and added with an unwholesome attempt at authority in his voice to which all three took exception, "Do as I say!"

Mia, with unaccustomed forcefulness in her tone, said, "Don't speak to my Kate like that; I won't tolerate it. She's a free agent; she can go out with whom she pleases and wherever she is going is all right by me because I know I can rely on her. You don't own her, Adam, and you'll do well to remember that."

Gerry was about to add his own comment to Mia's statement and opened his mouth to do so, but Adam glared at each one in turn and left the kitchen without another word.

When the front door slammed, Gerry sat back appalled. "What the blazes is up with him?"

Mia, very troubled by Adam's reaction, said, "He's turning into a bully, that's what. Speaking like that to Kate! Don't let it spoil your evening; that Scott is a nice boy."

"Perhaps I should go after him . . ."

Gerry, who'd championed Adam through thick and thin for the last two years, said, "No, best let the dust settle. The prospect of that promotion has gone to his head, speaking like that to you in my house. I won't have it." He took out his wallet and, picking out a ten-pound note, handed it to Kate. "I know you're short till you get your first month's salary, so here, take this. I want you to be able to stand your corner. Doesn't do to be beholden to anyone, not even that Scott, nice though he is."

"There's no need, Dad, but thanks."

WHEN Kate went into the Fox and Grapes, she found Scott already there. He was sitting at a corner table with an enormous plate of food in front of him. She saw him pick up his knife and fork and begin to eat, and judging by the enthusiasm with which he dived into his food, she guessed he hadn't eaten all day, so she decided to spend a couple of minutes in the ladies' room to give him a little time to take the edge off his hunger.

Her reflection in the mirror in there quite pleased her. She'd taken the trouble to put on makeup, which she didn't do every day, and she admired her new eye shadow, then looked a little closer at her forehead, thinking she could see lines appearing already and no wonder. What on earth had gotten into Adam? He had never been an emotional person, but now, since his promise of promotion, he'd gone distinctly highly charged in the most unpleasant way. Perhaps she was to blame, for she hadn't been quite fair, but there wasn't any need to go quite as ballistic as he had done tonight. Even Mia had taken exception, and her dad. Anyway, she and Adam weren't engaged or anything, so if she decided not to see him again, she wouldn't. An evening with Scott was a very interesting alternative to trying to lose at bowling. She winked at herself in the mirror and charged out to find Scott.

When he saw her crossing the bar, he put down his knife and fork and stood up. "Kate! You've come!" He kissed her cheek.

She kissed him back. "I have."

They both beamed idiotically, enjoying the sight of each other.

"Here, look, sit down; I'll move my coat. Will you excuse me if I finish my meal?"

"Of course. Can I get you a drink? What would you like?"

"A coffee first, please. Here, let me . . ." He dug his hand into his pocket and brought out loose change.

Kate said, "This is on me."

The cappuccinos looked tempting, and Kate spooned some of the froth and the chocolaty bits into her mouth. Looking up, she found Scott watching her and caught a look in his eyes she'd never seen in Adam's. Kate blushed and, to pass off her embarrassment, picked up a sugar sachet, opened it and let the sugar cascade into her coffee. Then another.

"Hey!"

"I like my cappuccino sweet. It's one of my things."

"You're quite sweet enough."

"That's a corny remark if ever there was one."

"I meant it, though. Thanks for coming out this evening; I've had a rotten day."

"I know. That's why I came."

Scott finished his meal and eyed the menu. "One of my things is ice-cream sundaes."

"And mine."

He ordered two strawberry sundaes and waited at the counter while the girl made them up. She was laughing so much at his comments that it was a wonder they got their order at all. Kate couldn't quite put her finger on why it was he had this effect on women, but he did. And on her. He was so light-hearted and such fun that one really couldn't take him seriously.

They chatted and laughed their way through their desserts, enjoying the thick, cloying strawberry sauce, the nutty bits sprinkled on the rich cream piled right to the very top of the glasses and the fresh strawberries they kept finding even right down at the bottom of the glass.

"I've never had such a delicious sundae in all my life."

Scott winked. "She knows me, you see; she knows what I like."

"You come here a lot, then?"

"When I've worked a ten-hour day and I've a night on call to face, believe me, I'm in no mood for cooking when I get home; and a fella needs food if he's to function well."

"I wonder how the farmers take you seriously."

"What do you mean?"

"You don't seem like a responsible person."

"Where my work is concerned, I am. I know I play the fool and such, but I do know my job."

"You enjoy being a vet, then?"

"I wouldn't want to be anything else. Nothing else in the whole wide world."

She sensed passion and conviction in his voice, loved the light in his eyes and asked him which parts he liked the best.

"A cold winter's morning with a brilliant, rosy-red dawn just breaking, a warm cowshed, a fight to get a calf born alive, the sight of it slithering out and the joy of it breathing, and the mother, all toil forgotten, bending to lick it." Scott looked embarrassed. "Sorry for going all poetic, but that's what I like. Then you wash under the tap in the yard, or if you're lucky, someone brings a bucket of hot water into the cowshed and when you're clean, you go into the warm kitchen and have a coffee laced with rum and a comfortable chat about things that really matter; then you go home." He looked somewhere beyond her shoulder, lost in thought. "More often than not, though, it's pouring with rain, pitch black and you're chilled to the marrow; and the wife's away, so there's no coffee, but still I love it. And lambing—now, there's a job and a half. You put your hand in and find two lambs tangled together and the ewe can push neither of them out; and you straighten them up, move a leg here and a head there, and hey presto, two beauties and the mother as proud as punch. Brilliant!"

Wistfully, Kate said, "It must be great." And before she could stop herself, out poured all her terrible disappointment about missing vet college, something she'd promised herself she would never do.

Scott listened hard to every word she said. When she'd finished, he took hold of her hand, saying, "Look here, if you feel as strongly as that, isn't it worth having another try? Why stand on the touchline of life? Get in there and on with the game, a bold strike straight for the goal. This isn't a practice game, you know; you only get the one chance. For someone with your passion for the job, that's the only thing to do; otherwise, there'll be a terrible vacuum in your life all your days. What's holding you back?"

"I don't know, really."

He encouraged her to explore her problem. "You must know."

"Well, it's the thought of all that studying. I tried so hard to succeed and it all came to nothing. I don't know if I can face such a defeat all over again. And that's only the start of it; five solid years of slog ahead."

"But you've only the one grade to improve, not three."

Kate nodded. "I know."

"Your ma and pa, what do they want?"

"They're like you, they want me to try again."

"Well then, there you are."

"Adam doesn't want me to; in fact, he doesn't want me to work at the practice even."

"You need to ditch that medieval horror."

Kate withdrew her hand from his and said indignantly, "Ditch him?"

"He's smothering you."

"He isn't."

"He is. He's a nutter."

"He isn't."

"Believe me. He is."

Kate stood up. "I wish I'd never told you how I felt. I promised myself I wouldn't tell anyone and I've told you, and now look what's happened; you're organizing my life for me."

"So why have you lost your temper? Is it because you know I'm right?"

His mobile phone began to ring. "Damn." He listened, answered and switched off. "Got to go. Sorry. Should have known not to invite you out when I'm on call. We'll do this again one night when I'm not."

"We will?"

Scott took her hand in his and squeezed it. "Don't be cross, not with me. Just think about what I've said. I'm right about trying again and very right about that damned Adam. Good night, sweet one."

He hurtled out of the bar, blowing a quick kiss to the barmaid who'd made the sundaes for them and calling "Good night" to everyone as he went.

Kate bought herself a vodka and tonic, and sat thinking about Scott. There was nothing more poisonous than living one's life with regret . . . thinking "if only" all the time. She liked his analogy of the game of life. She'd give it serious thought, but she'd have to be quick or the opening would be gone. It would mean good-bye to Adam, for he wouldn't tolerate her going to college for five years; in fact, she knew he would actively persuade her not to try. The expression "wouldn't tolerate" hung about in her mind and she thought, *What am I saying here? "Wouldn't tolerate." Is that love?* No, it most certainly wasn't. If he loved her, Adam would be encouraging her, surely?

Someone opened the door into the other bar and briefly she caught a reflection in the mirror behind the bar of someone standing there and she thought it was Adam. God! Now he was haunting her. Swiftly Kate finished her vodka and left.

Next morning, as though to confirm to her that Scott's advice was sound, the letter came from the solicitor with the check for ten and a half thousand pounds promised her in Granny Howard's will.

Chapter

· 4 ·

"Have you a first-class stamp, Mia? I want to get this letter in the mail on the way to work. Before I change my mind."

Mia passed her the fresh pot of tea. "You've definitely decided, then?"

"Yes, I have. The shock of not getting three A's totally threw me and I realize now I was far too hasty in giving up all hope of being a vet and applying for this job."

"I thought you liked the job. Don't you?"

Kate pondered Mia's question for a moment. "I like this job so very much. I like the people, I like the place, I like the animals, I like keeping the accounts in good order; *but* at the same time, I know I need more fulfillment. I'm not using my brain as I should and I know I would regret all my life not giving it another go."

Mia patted her hand across the breakfast table. "I've been dying for you to do this, but I knew it had to be wholly your decision. Your dad will be thrilled. It's what he wants for you too."

"I know. I'm ringing Miss Beaumont tonight to see if she'll tutor me."

"I thought that thin little man—I forget his name—taught you chemistry."

"He did and I never got on with him because he was lazy. That's why I didn't get an A. He was useless. Miss Beaumont is brill; we got on really well."

Mia brushed a strand of loose hair away from Kate's face. "I'm so proud of you."

"Thanks, Mia. I'm not telling anyone what I've done. Not till I've got a grade A, then if I don't, they won't be any the wiser."

"I think Adam should know."

Kate put down her slice of toast and studied Mia's loving face. "He'll do his best to stop me."

"He can't, though, can he, actually stop you? You're a free agent."

"He'll finish with me."

"Haven't you already finished with him?" The questioning look on Mia's face made Kate stare at her.

"Do you know, I think I already have, as you say. He's so peculiar at the moment. I don't even like him."

"I certainly didn't like him the other night."

"Truth to tell, you never really have liked him, have you?"

Mia fiddled with the sugar basin, put two spoonfuls into her cup and then, without thinking what she was doing, added another. "It's that obsession of needing to do the same things at the same time every week. It demonstrates a strange kind of insecurity. Or is he a power freak? He lacks spontaneity. It's odd in such a young man. I never noticed it at first, or has it gotten worse?"

"Worse."

"You see, it's only fair to tell him because if you do get in, it means he must wait another five years and he should know, or if he wants to find someone else, he should know where he is . . . with you."

Kate stood up to go, having seen the clock. "Sometimes one has moments of blinding insight when one sees so clearly it's almost frightening." Mia nodded. "You asking me if I hadn't already finished with him made me realize that yes, I have. Trouble is, will he finish with me?" Kate shuddered slightly.

"Well, you must be honest; tell him outright, but very kindly. You know."

"I know. Thank you, Mia, I don't know where I'd be without you."

Staring into the distance, Mia answered, "Whatever you do, you mustn't drift into marriage just because someone is there and there isn't anyone else on the horizon, and he's comfortable and suitable. You mustn't fool yourself. You've got to marry for love."

"Did you marry for love?"

Mia looked up at her, smiling. "Oh yes! I married for love." She reached out, and taking Kate's hand in hers, pressed it to her cheek.

Kate's face lit up with amazement. "Not of me?"

Mia nodded.

"I didn't know. Thank you." She was silent for a moment, taking in the full implication of Mia's words and of how she'd taken Mia's love all these years without giving it a thought, then brought things back to normality with, "See you tonight. I'm split shift today, so I'll go shopping this afternoon and be home about seven-thirty, with any luck. If you and Dad are going out, don't worry about me. OK?" Kate bent to kiss Mia's cheek. "Bye! Let *me* tell Dad."

· · ·

BEARING in mind Gerry's warning not to fritter away her granny's money, Kate decided to spend some of it that very afternoon. She desperately needed new clothes and she also intended treating herself to a nice lunch in the Bite to Eat café in the shopping precinct to celebrate having taken the big decision.

Most of the dress shops in her spending bracket had autumn sales on, so after a splendid lunch, which she thoroughly enjoyed, she set off to spend, spend, spend.

It was a day for swift decisions, and she made them. A suit, a party dress, some lingerie and a jacket. She came out of Next, turning left to head for her car, intending to put all her bags in the trunk and to return for a pleasant reviving cup of tea in the Food Gallery surrounding the main shopping square. Kate set off at a pace and had gone quite a way when she realized she'd left the jacket she'd just bought in the shop. Without stopping to inspect her bags to make sure, she swung around to return to the shop and bumped headlong into Adam.

"Ooh! Sorry! Adam! What a surprise! What are you doing here?"

Adam appeared as surprised as she was and twice as flustered. Kate asked him if he was not working today. "Having a late lunch." He looked at her, long and deep, and put out a hand to take her bags. "If you're leaving, I'll help you with those to the car."

"I've just bought a jacket in Next and I've left it on the counter, so I'm going back to get it."

"I'll come with you, then."

Kate retrieved her jacket and went with Adam to the car park. On the way she debated whether or not to go straight back to the practice, thus avoiding a talk with Adam, but she decided there was no time like now and asked him if he had time for a cup of tea. He glanced at his watch and accepted. "I've put in a lot of hours this week. They can't complain."

His Adam's apple was bobbing up and down quite vigorously and she wondered about the stress he must be under with this promotion. "Are you settling in?"

"Settling in?"

"In your new job?"

"Oh yes! Day off, is it?"

She explained about the split shift.

"I see." He gazed over the balustrade, watching the shoppers walking about below. "Nice spot, this. Come here often?"

"No, just sometimes. I got Granny Howard's money this week, so since I needed new clothes, I came shopping."

"Come in handy, that will. Take care of it."

"Handy for what?"

"Our deposit on a house."

A terrible feeling of suffocation came over Kate and she had to breathe deeply to rescue herself. Things were much worse than she had thought; he must be losing his marbles.

"There're some nice starter homes being built the other side of town. I thought we might go and look at them."

"You might, but I'm not."

Adam picked up his cup and toasted her with it. "To us. We'll look somewhere else, then."

"We won't. I'm not ready to get married yet. Not for a long long while." Now was the time to tell him what she'd done this morning on her way to work, but something in his eyes held her back from spilling the beans.

He continued eagerly, as if she'd never spoken, "I've just had the most tremendous idea. Mother's house is not suitable for an up-and-coming man. How about if she sells and we use the money and your granny's to buy a bigger house, and we all live together? That way, if I work long hours, which one does if one is in a top executive position, you'd always have someone at home for company and to give you a hand with the children. What do you think, eh? Good idea, isn't it?"

The nightmarish turn his conversation had taken scared Kate to death. Live with his mother! That martinet! That nitpicking, overindulged, idle hypochondriac of a woman! He must be going mad, or else she was. Kate, overcome by her inability to deal with the situation, glanced at her watch. "Look at the time! I'm going to be late."

"You've half an hour yet. What's the rush?"

"Anyone would think you hadn't a job to go to. Well, I have and I can't be late."

"Think about it, will you, Kate?" He looked pleadingly at her.

"Adam, I've told you. I'm not ready to get married yet."

"But I love you."

His vulnerability, which she'd successfully ignored these last two or three weeks, struck her anew. She patted his clenched fist, saying, "I know you do and I appreciate how you feel, but I don't want marriage and babies right now."

"We'll go out for a drink tonight and we'll talk some more. I'll come around about eight. You've no other plans, have you?"

Kate sighed within herself. "All right, then."

She left him sitting at the table finishing his cup of tea. Looking back at him as she left the café, she paused for a moment, trying to see him as others did. With great clarity of mind she recognized him as a loser: head down, shoulders bowed, clenched fists laid on the table, he seemed . . . Suddenly he looked directly at her and a shiver of fear ran down her spine. It confirmed as nothing else had done that Adam was not for her.

THE clinic that afternoon was busy; it seemed to her that every single animal on their books, both large and small, had decided it was dying on its feet. Kate always found the four-till-seven clinic busy, but this was ridiculous.

At five past four, little Miss Chillingsworth came in with her cat. "I know I haven't an appointment, Kate dear, but she really is very poorly today."

"Vomiting again?"

Miss Chillingsworth nodded bleakly. "She can't keep a thing down. I've casseroled some chicken for her, but she can't even manage that."

Privately Kate thought Miss Chillingsworth would be all the better for eating the casserole herself, for today she seemed smaller and thinner than ever. "Take a seat, Miss Chillingsworth, and I'll see what I can do. I've no doubt Mr. Murgatroyd will find a space for you."

Miss Chillingsworth's face lit up. "Oh, he will when he knows it's me. He loves my Cherub." As if to emphasize the fact, Cherub Chillingsworth howled pathetically. "You see, she is in pain."

Kate broke off to answer the phone and squeezed in yet another client appointment for Valentine Dedic in room three. Catching Graham between clients, Kate asked him if he would fit in Cherub Chillingsworth.

Graham grimaced. "Not again. I swear there's nothing wrong with Cherub but old age and too much coddling. However, I will see her. Wheel her in after this next client. It's only a booster—shouldn't take long."

Graham weighed Cherub and found she had lost weight—not much but enough to make him think Miss Chillingsworth might be right. "Now see here, Miss Chillingsworth, we've done blood tests, found nothing; we've kept a close watch and found nothing, and now Cherub has lost weight again."

"I knew she had; I could tell." Miss Chillingworth's eyes flooded with tears.

"I'd like to x-ray her, her stomach and such, but . . ."

"Yes?"

Graham propped himself against the examination table. "But I hesitate to suggest it because it will cost money, you see, and you've already spent a lot. How do you feel about it? She's very old." He checked the computer screen. "Yes, as I thought, seventeen. That is old to go through an X-ray because she'll have to have an anesthetic, you see, which won't be good for her."

Her bottom lip was trembling, but Miss Chillingsworth did her best not to let her voice shake. Defiantly she said, "She may be old, but she's . . . lively and still has a good quality of life, you know, when she's well."

"I know. Yes, of course." Gently Graham suggested, "You could always go to the RSPCA. They can do it for nothing."

Miss Chillingsworth was shocked. "I am not in need of charity, Mr. Murgatroyd, no, certainly not, and whatever Cherub needs, she will get. I'll find the money."

"Very well, but even if she has an X-ray, that's no guarantee we can sort out what ails her. At her age . . ." Graham gravely shook his head.

"I know what you're trying to tell me, but Cherub and I will go down fighting."

"Bring her tomorrow. Eight A.M. Can you manage that?"

Miss Chillingsworth drew herself up to her full height. "Of course I can." Picking up Cherub, who looked up at her owner as though she'd understood every word, Miss Chillingsworth went out of the consulting room.

Kate saw her sadness immediately and managed to catch Miss Chillingsworth's eye. "How're things with Cherub?"

Miss Chillingsworth put Cherub gently on the reception counter and while Kate stroked the old cat comfortingly she got her answer. "Dear Mr. Murgatroyd, he's going to x-ray her tomorrow morning. Now, my dear, I want him to know he can do his very best for her without any anxiety about money. So can I put her in her carrying cage and leave her here while I go to the bank to get the money out? I shall feel happier if it's here waiting and then Mr. Murgatroyd can go ahead with whatever he needs to do."

"There's really no need. You can pay tomorrow when you come to collect her. It's quite in order to do that."

"No, my dear, I want the money here on the premises and I want you to tell Mr. Murgatroyd it is here waiting and that he won't have to hold back on anything he needs to do."

"But . . ."

"No, I insist. I don't like the idea that he might think I'm too poor to pay and will take short cuts because of it. I shall feel more comfortable if he knows the money's waiting."

"But I don't know how much it will be."

"I shall bring one hundred pounds and if it's not enough, I shall bring the balance. If it's too much, then I know you'll take good care of it for me and give me back what's left over."

"I don't know if I'm supposed to do this."

"Well then, it's just between you, me and Mr. Murgatroyd. Now here's Cherub. You keep her behind the desk; she doesn't like all the dogs, you see." She handed the cage over to Kate, who put it on the floor near her feet.

"Mind how you go, Miss Chillingsworth."

"I will."

Lynne Seymour was on duty with Kate that night, but somehow she had managed to disappear at the crucial moment when all hell was let loose. Two dogs had a serious go at getting a cat out of its basket, someone taking a sympathetic peep at their budgerigar let it out by mistake and to cap it all, someone's dog cocked a leg down the front of the reception desk.

"Lynne! Lynne! Can you come, please?" Kate shouted, and eventually, at a pace more suited to a summer's afternoon stroll, Lynne appeared.

"What's up?"

"What's up?" Kate was on the brink of giving her a piece of her mind, but just then Miss Chillingsworth came back clutching her bag. She waited until peace was restored and handed the money to Kate.

"I'll give you a receipt in just a moment."

"Don't worry, my dear. Please. I want to get home. Cherub must be tired."

"I'd much rather . . ."

"Not at all."

"Well, I'm on first thing tomorrow, so . . ."

"Good night, dear. And thank you. Tell Mr. Murgatroyd." Miss Chillingsworth trotted out with her cat, waving cheerily to Kate. "I'm full of hope for tomorrow."

Kate didn't have her confidence. She wrote "Miss Chillingsworth" on the envelope and put the money in a drawer under some papers until she had a moment to open the safe, which had to be done when two of them were free to do so.

The evening dragged its feet and by the time the last client had gone, Kate was exhausted. Home, a meal and bed was all she could think about and then she remembered Adam was collecting her. *Blast.* She heard Graham and Valentine talking about the meal Valentine's wife had planned for the two of them, and Lynne and the two Sarahs agreeing to go to the Fox and Grapes.

Seeing a way of avoiding a whole evening chewing over

Adam's plan of marrying her and dumping his mother on her, Kate asked, "Could I join you there? Would you mind?"

Sarah Two looked at her and smiled. "Why not? The more the merrier."

"The only thing is Adam will be with me; do you mind?"

"Not at all. Lynne's dragging her two brothers out with her, so we'll make a night of it. It'll be fun."

"Thanks."

IN fact, the evening that Kate had dreaded but had hoped to rescue by giving Adam no chance to talk about their future turned into a complete disaster. First, Adam hadn't wanted to join them all, but Kate had insisted. Lynne's brothers teased Adam mercilessly but in a very subtle way so that they were partway through the evening before Kate even realized what they were up to.

Finally, she made a move to leave while the night was still young.

"Don't go; the party's just getting going," Lynne protested.

"I don't intend to sit here to watch Adam on the receiving end of your brothers' sarcasm. He's been very patient so far, but that's it. I've had enough."

Eyebrows raised in surprise, Lynne pretended innocence. "I don't know what you mean."

"If you don't, they do." Kate turned to the two young men and said, "I think your behavior has been childish in the extreme. It's about time you grew up and learned good manners. Good night."

She stormed out, followed by Adam, who had not recognized what they were up to. Kate, now thoroughly upset because she could hear the two of them laughing as they left the bar, turned the wrong way in the car park and had to ask Adam where his car was.

"It's over there on the other side. I thought they were interested in what I did. They kept asking questions."

"Oh, they did; they were just leading you on. Didn't you see that? They are absolutely so arrogant. They think your job's the biggest joke ever."

"Joke? But it isn't; it's important. What do they do, then?"

"They both work in the City at something exotic, which means they earn thousands and thousands a year. They were both at Oxford and think themselves exceedingly superior. Which in my opinion they most certainly are not."

Adam unlocked his Toyota. "I see."

"Drive me home."

"But they kept asking me questions about what my job involved."

Kate sighed. "Honestly Adam, you are dim sometimes. They were mocking you. Couldn't you tell?"

"No." He crashed the gears, which made him wince. "I don't understand why they wanted to do it to me."

"Well, you wouldn't, would you." She shut her lips tight for fear she might tell him why. They'd set out to humiliate him because his job in their opinion—and she had to admit sometimes in hers too—was so ridiculously trivial as to be ludicrous and he hadn't realized it. She should have felt sorry for him, but instead she felt nothing but . . . *Well, go on, then, Kate Howard, what do you feel?* That Adam was a joke? That her own self-worth made her not want to be associated with someone so full of his own importance that he couldn't recognize blatant mockery? Sorry for him? A bit. But most of all she wanted to laugh. For a little while she smothered her true feelings and then they burst out of her in loud laughter. With her head thrown back, she simply roared.

The more she laughed, the more annoyed Adam became. His driving became erratic and finally he pulled into a turnout at the side of the road, switched off the engine and folded his arms.

Kate had to stop out of consideration for Adam. The first thing she did when finally she could speak was to apologize. "I'm so sorry, Adam. I don't know why I laughed. I shouldn't have done, but I did. Those two arrogant, pompous . . . Who do they think they are."

"I did say you shouldn't go to work at that place. I think you should give in your notice. In fact, I insist."

"You do?"

"Oh yes!"

"You're on thin ice telling me what to do." It was too dark for Adam to see her face. If he could have he would have noticed that her lips were pressed firmly together.

"But if we are to make a go of it, we ought to make decisions together."

"But you've just *told* me what to do and I won't be told."

"It's for the best if they're people like that."

"They don't work with me; they just happen to be Lynne's brothers. This is getting nowhere. Drive me home."

"See here . . ."

"See here nothing. Drive me home. Please."

"I think there's one thing that should be understood between us: I'm the man and . . ."

"You are?"

"You're in a very funny mood tonight."

Kate turned to look at him. "I think we'd better finish, you and I, don't you?" Kate caught sight of his face in the headlights of an approaching car and wished to God she hadn't said what she'd said. "You know, we're just not on the same wavelength anymore and I think if we cooled it . . . you know . . . for a while . . ."

Adam gripped her forearm hard and pushed his face so close to hers that she could see in minute detail the tiny hairs in his nostrils and the beads of sweat on his upper lip. Taken totally unawares, Kate hadn't a chance to escape. With his blazing eyes focused on her own she knew real fear for the first time in her life. "What are you doing? Adam! Let me go."

His grip on her arm tightened. "When I'm good and ready. If anyone is going to say we're finished, it'll be me. Not you. You're mine, my girl. Do you hear? Mine."

"Let go!" Kate tried to force his fingers from her arm but didn't succeed. "Please!"

"You were laughing at *me*, weren't you? Not at them. *Me!*"

"I don't know who I was laughing at. Honestly. Just let go." His breathing was getting faster and deeper, as though his anger was coming to boiling point. His racing heart was pressed against the arm he held and the pain in it was increasing as fast as the fear in her heart. His other hand grasped her knee and Kate realized her predicament was becoming extremely serious. One wrong move and he'd do something she'd have to live with for the rest of her life.

He squeezed her knee hard.

"Get off me, Adam! What do you think you're doing? You're hurting me. Stop it!"

Her anger was inciting him to intimidate her further and she knew she'd have to change her strategy.

"I shan't ask you to go out with them again. You're right, as always; we won't bother with them anymore." His grip relaxed slightly. "They're not worth it." He relaxed a little more. "They're cheap little nobodies, that's what, and not even amusing. I should have listened to you. You've more wisdom in your little finger than . . ." She reached up as though to stroke his hair. Catching him off guard, she took her chance. The chill night air hit her as she leaped in one swift movement out of the car and without stopping ran up the impossibly steep embankment onto the level bit at the top, then pelted hell for leather toward the chain of lights that she knew was Sainsbury's car park. For one blind, panicking moment she thought she heard Adam's footsteps behind her, but she was wrong. It was only his voice calling demandingly, "Kate! Kate! Kate! Come here!"

Mia always insisted she have a phone card on her and Kate thanked her lucky stars that she did. "Dad! Dad!"

"Kate?"

"Dad! I'm at Sainsbury's, you know, the twenty-four-hour one. Can you come to pick me up? I'll wait in the main entrance."

"What the blazes are you doing there at this time of night? Have you broken down?"

"No. Just come. I'll explain." Gerry caught the panic in her as she began to make a mewing sound, too frightened now to speak.

"All right. All right. Calm down. Stay in the entrance where there're lights and somebody about. Ten minutes. Right."

SHE fell into Mia's comforting arms and wept. "I'm being stupid, Mia, I know I am, but I'm so frightened. He's not himself at all."

"There, there, love, you're all right now. Mia's got you. Let's go, Gerry. You can tell me all about it when we get home."

"Been trying it on, has he?"

"Gerry!"

"Might as well be honest about it. Well, has he?"

"No."

"That's all right, then."

"Sometimes, Gerry Howard, you need to engage your brain

before you speak. There, love, calm down now. Here's another tissue, look."

"I don't know him anymore. He's gone mad."

The brandy her dad poured for her when they got home calmed her fear and Kate explained to them both why she'd had to ring. "He went completely berserk. I should never have laughed, but it struck me as so funny that anyone could sit there all that time and never realize those chaps were having him on. He's so full of his own importance, the stupid man."

"Let me see your arm." Mia turned to Gerry. "He's bruised her arm. Just look at that bruise!" Gerry caught Mia's eye and frowned. Not a word passed between them, but each knew what the other was thinking.

"Listen to me, my girl." Gerry learned forward and took Kate's hand in his. "If he rings and wants you to meet him somewhere, you agree so's not to anger him, but *don't go.* Come home and tell Mia or me, and we'll stay at home with you. You're not to go with him anywhere at all, and if he's waiting outside the practice when you finish work, go back in and get that nice Mrs. Bastable to help. First thing tomorrow when I'm on the road I'm getting you a mobile phone."

"Dad! There's no need. When it came to it, Adam wouldn't hurt me."

"Oh, really? Well, I say there is. If there's much more trouble with him, I shall go to the police."

"No. No. Don't do that! There truly is no need. It's just me being daft."

Gerry pushed back her jumper sleeve and pointed to the bruising. "Being daft? You say he loves you? Huh! You've heard what I've said and I mean it. Now, bed, with a couple of Mia's herbal thingamajigs to help you sleep."

Chapter

· 5 ·

In the cold light of day, Kate decided she'd panicked un-
necessarily and that she'd made a complete idiot of herself over Adam. Her dad gave her a kiss as he left that
morning and told her to be on red alert when he got back
because he'd have her new phone with him. "There's no need,
honestly, Dad."

"Can't a dad buy his daughter a present now and again?"

"OK, then, and I shall be glad of it."

Mia waved Gerry off to work and came back in to sit with
Kate while she ate her breakfast. She poured Kate a fresh cup
of tea and asked her if she wanted more toast.

"Yes, I will. Are you eating this morning?"

"Don't feel like it."

"Mia, you must. You're not worrying about me, are you? I'm
all right now. I've come to my senses this morning, got things
in proportion, you know. Come on, have this other slice of
mine; I only need one."

"All right, then. I will."

"I've got to hurry; I don't want to be late."

"You enjoy it, don't you?"

"Yes. Miss Chillingsworth's bringing Cherub in this morning. She's such a dear old thing and so worried about her cat. When you haven't got a pet of your own, you don't realize how much people care about them till you see them in tears."

Mia patted her arm. "Don't take it too much to heart, will you, or you'll spend all your veterinary career weeping."

"What career?" Kate had to laugh. "You're right, there's no room for tears, is there?"

"I bet that Scott gets upset over things."

"I believe he does."

"He's a nice chap."

Kate giggled. "He is; women eat out of his hand."

"Given half a chance, so would I." They both giggled with mouths full of toast.

"I'm off."

KATE parked her car in her usual place, picked up her bag, got out and as she locked the car, she glanced up at the hills and drew in a deep breath. This weekend she'd go walking—with weather like this, who could resist? There was a slight mist at the peak of Beulah Bank Top. Other than that, it was as clear as clear, looking out across the hills. The wind was slightly blustery but pleasant. Kate dropped her car key, bent down to retrieve it and as she straightened up, caught sight of the mawkish purple of Adam's car, all by itself at the top of the car park, where the staff never needed to park.

If she'd been electrocuted, she couldn't have felt greater physical fear. Her scalp prickled and her hair felt as if it stood on end. She staggered to the safety of reception as best she could. Halfway there it occurred to her that he might already be inside, for she was certain he wasn't sitting in the car. Or was he? Should she look? She glanced briefly over her shoulder. He didn't appear to be. Joy! Joy was on duty this morning. Joy.

She pushed open the glass door and called out to her, "Has anyone been asking for me?"

Joy looked up. "No. Should they be?"

"No, not really. There's no one been here, then?"

"No, definitely not. I'm the only one here. My dear, what's the matter?"

"To be honest, it's just me being ridiculous." Nevertheless, she went into the laundry room, which gave her a view of the car park, and Adam's car wasn't there. She was definitely going mad. How could she be so stupid? What on earth would he be doing at this side of town at this time in the morning when his office was seven miles out on the other side? Come to that, though, what was he doing in town yesterday, having what he called a late lunch? Being paranoid about time, he would never take the risk of driving so far and back and eating lunch all in an hour. She must have dreamed his car was there. It couldn't possibly have been.

As she put on her uniform and sorted out her mind for the day ahead, she remembered Miss Chillingsworth and Miss Chillingsworth's money. Heavens above, she'd never put it in the safe.

Kate went straight to the drawer where she'd put it for safekeeping, pushed her hand under the papers and couldn't feel the envelope. The phone rang twice for farm calls before she could get back to searching again. She took all the papers out of the drawer and put them back in one by one. No, the envelope hadn't slipped between anything at all. It was missing. She stood, looking at the drawer. Had she got the right one? Yes, she had. Had she and Lynne put it in the safe and she'd forgotten? The moment Lynne came out of the loo she'd ask her.

"I don't know anything about any money. We certainly didn't put it in the safe. I would have remembered. Sorry."

Joy, watering the plants on the windowsills, overheard and asked what money they were talking about.

Now very worried about the whole incident, Kate went across to Joy to explain what had happened.

"You shouldn't have accepted the money, you know, Kate."

"I know that; I was only trying to help. She was worried that Graham wouldn't do all he could for fear of embarrassing her about the money. Which I don't think she has, really. I think she's short but can't bear the thought of losing Cherub. She only wanted us to know the money was *there.*"

Joy emptied the watering can on the last plant, tested the soil with her fingers and said after a moment, "Well, now it isn't. We have a golden rule, you see. Any money taken during the day must be entered and accounted for *on that day.* Otherwise, with different people being on duty we'd get into no end of a mess. Lynne should have done the sheet last night before she left and that hundred pounds should have been on it."

"I know, but we were so busy we could have done with three of us on. She did do the sheet, but of course the hundred pounds wasn't on it."

"You did it with the best of intentions, I know, but I shall have to report it. You've thoroughly searched the drawers?"

"I've searched the one I put it in, yes."

"Had everything out?"

Kate nodded.

"Say nothing at all to Miss Chillingsworth. She's brought Cherub, has she?"

"No, which is surprising because she promised to be here at eight."

"That's odd. Leave it with me. I'll tell Mungo in my own time, but it'll have to be today."

Kate had to say the words she didn't want to have to say: "I haven't stolen it; I promise you that."

Joy looked her in the face, frankly and openly. "You don't need to say that to me, my dear. I know that. You're as honest as the day is long."

"Thank you. I'm so sorry about it and if it doesn't turn up, I'll find the money, because it was my responsibility."

"That's a very fair offer, but I can't accept it. You haven't worked here a month yet, so I know for a fact you haven't received a penny in salary."

"Yes, but my granny Howard left me some money in her will and I got it this week, so by coincidence it isn't a problem."

Joy patted her arm. "Leave it with me."

One by one the two Sarahs and Lynne were called into Joy's office for a discussion about the missing money. Hidden away in the accounts office, Kate was in anguish fretting and fussing over it, thinking of all the possibilities of where it could have gone. When she heard Mungo's footsteps coming down the stairs from the flat, her heart sank. It could mean her instant dismissal and she didn't want that.

Joy called out, "Mungo! Have you a minute?" Joy's office door was briskly snapped to and Kate knew her fate hung in the balance.

"Good morning, Joy. What's up? Can't be long, my first appointment's in ten minutes and I've still got the notes to read up."

"Sit down. Won't keep you two minutes."

Mungo folded his long body into a chair and waited. Loving him hopelessly, as she had for twenty years, Joy still experienced an instant explosion of happiness when she saw him. Was it his lean, intelligent face, his perfectly beautiful large brown eyes under their heavy brows, his handsome head of thick, well-cut black hair, or simply his lovableness that enraptured her?

"Yes?"

"Sorry. We have a problem. One hundred pounds has disappeared." He listened gravely while Joy told him the whole story.

"Kate was trying to help, you see."

"Help? Surely she knew our rules."

"Of course, but she thought about efficiency well larded with compassion and it was the compassion that won."

"She should have had more sense, a girl with her intelligence."

"We are shorthanded at the moment, Mungo, as you well know. She's new and was doing her best to cope."

"New or not she should have known better."

"And hurt Miss Chillingsworth?"

"The very least she could have done was to put it in the safe."

"Exactly. I know that. I've interviewed the others and they claim no knowledge of the incident. Lynne was there when Kate put it in the drawer, but it doesn't mean she saw her do it and it doesn't mean she didn't. As I say, they were very busy last night."

"So what does Kate propose to do about it?"

"She's offered to pay back the money."

"Hm."

"Well?"

"She'll have to be dismissed. Today."

An angry flush flooded Joy's cheeks and she exploded with temper. "Oh no, she won't. I won't have it. She's the best girl we've employed in years. Efficient, caring, quick to learn, enthusiastic, hardworking; I don't want to lose her. I know, positively know, she isn't the kind who would steal. In any case, I have her word on that and I believe her. We're short enough as it is. Bunty isn't back until next week and we're still one receptionist short. If you're prepared to do the accounts . . ."

"You'll cope."

"I won't."

"I can't spirit new staff out of the air."

"I don't expect you to; that's my job. I've only informed you because I must. You've always left the staffing to me. Anyway, I wasn't asking for your advice, simply telling you what had happened."

"So . . . I still say she should be dismissed."

Joy tried a different tactic. "I've worked for you for twenty years and striven always to do my best through thick and thin, but if you insist on Kate's dismissal, then you'll have to dismiss me too."

Mungo looked at her, eyebrows raised in amazement. "You too? What do you mean? We can't manage without you. You know everything there is to know about this practice."

"I'm not a permanent fixture here, you know, I am free to go if I wish."

"But you wouldn't leave me!"

"Wouldn't I just! Might be the best move I've made in years. Better for all concerned. Fresh start. Break the old ties. I'll go to the practice in the High Street. I understand they could do with some help since we've opened up here."

Mungo was lost for words.

"I know why you're taking this stance. I saw what you saw when Kate looked up and smiled at you when she was stroking Perkins. She brings back too many memories for you, doesn't she? Dismissing her would be a good way of ridding yourself of the problem."

"You're being bloody stupid, Joy, or more likely bloody-minded. Sometimes you lose your sense of proportion, you know, always have done at moments of crisis." He stood up and turned away from her to look out of the window, aware he'd been more rude to her than he had ever been and knowing she was right about Kate: That look she had given him at the lunch had rocked the boat and no mistake.

"Well, there's been plenty of moments of crisis working for you, believe me." As an afterthought and between clenched teeth she snapped, "And don't you dare swear at me."

Mungo recognized the fury in Joy's voice and knew he'd gone too far. He held up a placatory hand. "I'm sorry, love. Truly sorry. I shouldn't have lost my temper and I shouldn't have sworn. I won't tolerate theft, though. We have to be seen to take steps. React in whatever way you think fit. I'll leave it to you. Must go." He opened the door, then looked back at her and smiled as only Mungo could. "I'm sorry. You know? Friends?"

Her anger at his attitude melted away at his smile and she said, "Friends."

She could hear him greeting his clients and their dog, using all his charm to ease their anxiety and succeeding, for the clients were eating out of his hand before the had even reached the consulting room. Joy smiled a little grimly at the way all his clients worshipped the ground he walked on. No wonder, though, because he was immensely good at his job. However, he couldn't solve her present crisis, could he, for all his charm and talent?

At lunchtime Joy issued an ultimatum. If the missing money was back in the drawer by the time they closed the cash sheet for the night, then nothing more would be said. She knew she was avoiding the main issue entirely and that, in fact, it solved nothing, but at the moment it was all she could come up with.

During the afternoon Miss Chillingsworth was discovered by Kate sitting quietly in the reception area, having made no one aware of her arrival. "Why, Miss Chillingsworth, you've come. I'll tell Mr. Murgatroyd."

Her tear-stained face told Kate all. "Oh no! Oh, dear, I am sorry."

"In the night."

"What happened . . . do you know?"

"I am sorry. In the night I woke up and had this dreadful feeling inside. I went downstairs to the kitchen and there she was. She'd struggled out of her basket by the stove—she always sleeps there: it's warm all night, you see—and was lying on the floor, breathing all funny, and I picked her up and loved her, and she died as I held her." Tears rolled down her face.

Kate took a clean tissue from her pocket and offered it to Miss Chillingsworth, but she was too overcome to notice, so Kate gently wiped away her tears for her. "What a lovely way for her to go, though, in your arms. That must have been so comforting for her."

"She looked up at me as if she knew, just knew it was all over. Seventeen years we've been together, the two of us. I'm not going to be able to go back into the house and find her not there, but I had to let you know because you were expecting me."

"Well, that was kind of you, to come to tell us. A cup of tea. How does that sound?"

"Thank you, dear. Yes, that would be nice."

Kate told Graham and he came out of his consulting room to see her. "Miss Chillingsworth, let's go in the back and you can tell me all about it."

"Oh, Mr. Murgatroyd! What am I going to do?"

"You're going to be thankful that Cherub found a lovely way to go. She didn't have to be anesthetized for the X-ray and she didn't have to go through an operation. She just quietly slipped away as though she knew it was of no use whatever we did. Be glad for her."

"Oh! Mr. Murgatroyd, you expressed that quite beautifully.

I should be glad, shouldn't I, that she didn't have to suffer anything at all but simply went to her Maker as gently as she could?"

"Exactly. And what's more, she had you to comfort her, didn't she?"

"You're right, and I did."

He handed her the tea Kate had brought her and watched her drink it while he searched for the right words to say. "Sometimes I think animals are wiser than we humans realize. They seem to have an intuitive sense about when the end is in sight. It's almost as if they are resigned to what happens to them and it makes life easier for them finally. They don't fight what is happening to them, if you see what I mean." He paused for a moment and then asked, "So if I might mention it, where is she now?"

There was a short silence, then Miss Chillingsworth said, "I've buried her in my garden under a tree she liked to climb in her youth. I did the whole funeral service for her, every word. I just hope the good Lord didn't mind her being a cat."

Graham patted her shoulder and looked away.

"I'll take my money, that is if you don't mind. You won't need it now."

"Of course, Miss Chillingsworth."

She got to her feet. "You're a dear boy." They shook hands and she left to collect her one hundred pounds and he to catch up with his client list.

Kate needn't have gone to the bank on her lunch break to get out the money, for the envelope with "Miss Chillingsworth" written on the front of it in Kate's own hand was in the drawer ready and waiting. Kate watched Joy hand it over and she broke out in a sweat of relief—relief which couldn't be measured.

When Miss Chillingsworth had left, Joy winked at her. "You needn't have gone to the bank."

"But who . . . ?"

"No idea. But in future you make very sure all money is registered and banked. For whatever reason, do not promise to take care of money for clients. Ever. There's a powerful lesson to be learned from this."

"I know. What I can't understand is who and why?"

Joy had her suspicions but had vowed to keep them to herself and to keep a closer watch in future. She replied, "Can't answer that because I don't know."

Scott came in at about four, just as Kate was leaving. "Sweet one! Long time no see. Just finished? Great!"

"Why?"

"Why?" Scott clapped a hand to his forehead in mock despair. "She asks why. Because I've had a rotten day and need your company."

"I see."

"You haven't a prior engagement, have you?"

"Are you leaving right now?"

"Just got these samples to hand over to Joy for dispatch and then I'm all yours."

"I'll wait in my car."

Out of the corner of her eye Kate saw Lynne watching her with a slightly malevolent expression on her face and it occurred to Kate that it might be Lynne who'd removed the envelope from the drawer. But of course she wouldn't have, not Lynne. Now had it been Stephie . . .

Scott slid into the seat next to her and grinned. "So where shall we go?"

"Actually, I can't go anywhere tonight because . . ."

"You're not going out with that Adam fella, are you?"

"What if I am?"

"I've told you he's a nutter."

Memories of running along the embankment toward Sains-

bury's car park flooded back. She avoided the issue
I tell you where I'm going, you're not to breathe a w
la

"Cross my heart and hope to die."

"This is my first night going for tutoring for chem

Scott turned a delighted face to her. "You're no
decided, then."

Kate nodded.

"Well, I am pleased. Really pleased. You've made th
decision. Yes, definitely. My chemistry is rusty, but if yo
any help, shout for Scott."

"She's a great teacher and thrilled to be helping me."

"Good girl! This calls for a celebration."

"I need to eat before I go."

"Quite right. Won't Mia be expecting you?"

"She will. I'll go back in and give her a ring."

Scott scuffed about in the cavernous pockets of his Barbou
and proffered her his mobile. "Here, use this."

"I don't know how."

He squeezed closer to her and showed her how to make a
call.

Kate spoke to Mia and explained. "Now, how do I switch
it off?"

"I'm amazed you haven't got one of your own. Time you did."

"I shall have, tonight, if Dad does what he says."

"He thinks you should have one, does he?"

"He does. Your car or mine?"

"Mine, of course. The whole inside absolutely stinks, so I'll
put a cloth over the passenger seat. It still hasn't recovered from
my episode with the slurry pit."

Kate smiled. "I keep having a laugh about that; I thought it
was so funny."

"Thanks! Trust a Limey to find it amusing. Doesn't say
much for your sense of humor."

"Oh! Sorry. It's a sign of maturity, you know, to be able to laugh at oneself."

"Is it, now?" He spread a clean cover over the seat and she climbed in.

"Where are we going?"

When he looked at her, there was that same gleam in his eye that she'd seen before and she felt a blush creeping over her cheeks. His admiring gaze stayed on her face while he said, "People who show dogs use the expression 'It fills the eye,' meaning it's a first-rate dog with that special something that they're keen to find. That's just what you're doing tonight, filling my eye." He leaned toward her and placed a gentle kiss on her lips. Nothing more. "Not the Fox and Grapes, I think. No, this calls for the King's Arms."

"I'm not dressed for the King's Arms."

He assessed her suitability by examining her from head to foot. "Like I said, you fill my eye, so there's no need to worry. I've a clothes brush in the back for emergencies like these and I'll brush my trousers before I go in, and then we'll both be suitable. What the hell, they won't be feeding us for nothing, you know, so they'll put up with us, believe me."

"I expect you know them all."

"I do."

"Thought so."

And he did. He was greeted like an old friend by waiters and bar staff alike.

"Is there any place where food is served that you haven't tried?"

"Not many."

They all looked curiously at her and she guessed he'd been in there with other girls before her. She wouldn't ask. What she didn't know wouldn't hurt her, as Mia would say.

They both ordered steak with French fries and vegetables, and Scott asked for lager for himself and cider for Kate. While they waited they discussed work.

"What's this I hear about Mungo and Joy having a row about you? What have you been up to? Explain yourself."

She rounded off her explanation by saying that she could hear the raised voices but not the words and that they both sounded furious with each other but not angry about her at all.

"Ah! Well, didn't you realize that Joy carries a torch for Mungo? Has for years, apparently."

"But she's married."

"So? People marry for all kinds of reasons."

"But she wouldn't, not Joy."

"Wouldn't what?'

"Love someone else when she was married."

"Like I said, people marry for all kinds of reasons."

"So in your opinion why did she marry that nice man Duncan?"

"I haven't the faintest idea."

"You're no help at all. I'll ask Bunty when she comes back on Monday. She'll know. She knows everything about everybody."

"Does she?" Scott took a long drink of his lager and asked casually, "She's been away two weeks, is it?"

"She's left-handed, so she couldn't assist at operations with things all bandaged up, or whatever."

"All bandaged up?"

"Her finger."

"Explain."

"She dislocated the little finger on her left hand in an accident playing netball at school and since then it's kept dislocating itself on the slightest excuse, and it's so painful when it happens and puts her out of action for a few days each time, so they've operated on it and hopefully this will cure it for good."

Kate realized that Scott was paying very close attention to every word she spoke. "OK? Is there anything else you'd like to know? Like her blood group, for instance?"

"Is this true?"

"Why would I lie? Of course it's true."

Why Bunty's finger being operated on should silence Scott, Kate had no idea, but it did. He cheered up a little when they ordered their ice-cream sundaes and was forcing himself to be chirpy by the time their bill arrived at the table.

"Mustn't be long." He looked at his watch. "Nearly time to go. The sundae wasn't as good as the Fox and Grapes'."

"You're right. Thank you, though, I have enjoyed it. I'll be off. I shall need a lift back to the practice to pick up my car, if you wouldn't mind."

"Of course. Yes."

He waited until she'd started her car and returned her wave as she drove out of the car park.

So the question was, was Bunty pregnant and remaining so or had she fooled him completely by making him think she was away from work having an abortion when all the time she was having her damned finger operated on and she wasn't pregnant at all? Or was the dislocated finger a blind to cover a trip to an abortion clinic? If she was pregnant and she intended keeping the baby, should he do the right thing? Not likely. Marriage wasn't for him and most definitely not for him and Bunty. Women! Why did he bother? Well, he knew why he bothered, but why did he always bother with the wrong ones? Answer: because they were the most fun.

But Kate was the exception. She was delicious, in a quiet, innocent kind of way. Refreshing, untouched. That was what made her so fascinating. And a virgin, because that Adam wouldn't have the guts. Well, he'd better not have. That clumsy, blundering nutter would have as much subtlety when making love as a bull in a china shop. But if she got her chemistry A level, then that would be the key to getting her away from that blasted Adam. What was it about that nutter that made an insensitive, unperceptive Aussie feel such concern? The question hung about at the back of his mind all weekend.

Chapter

· **6** ·

On the Monday morning, having decided to tackle Bunty first thing before he went on his calls, he found her in the laundry room sorting the operating linen from Sunday. "You're better, then."

Bunty's bright-blue eyes met his. They stared at each other for a moment and Scott asked her again if she was better.

She turned back to the washing machine. "As well as can be expected in the circumstances."

"What are the circumstances?" He'd shed his normal casual approach to everything outside his work and was standing, hands out of his pockets, waiting to pounce like a panther. Bunty might not have been looking at him but she was fully aware this was a different Scott from the one she had known that hot, passionate night they'd shared.

"Well?"

She still didn't answer, so he covered the space between them in a moment and took hold of her arm. "Look me in the face and tell me straight out. Why have you been absent from work?"

"Worried?"

"No, I am not. Just asking on a need-to-know basis, that's all."

Bunty dropped the last of the bloodied linen into the machine and faced him. Holding up her left hand still encased in a plastic glove she said, "Operation on finger. OK?"

A huge sweat of relief came out on Scott's body, which just as quickly disappeared when he realized how she'd tried to trick him. "You lied to me. That's nasty, that is, Bunty, downright evil to lie about something as important as that."

"Disappointed there isn't going to be a little Scott Spencer for you to coo over?"

"I would have walked away quick smart, believe me, nothing surer. You could bet your life on it."

"That's nice, that is."

"It isn't, but it's the truth."

"Typical man."

"Believe me, I don't feel good about what's happened, but it did take two of us and I most certainly didn't force you."

Bunty peeled off the plastic gloves, flung them in the bin and stormed out. Scott shrugged his shoulders. He caught up with her as she began preparing the operating room for the day. Putting his head around the door he said, "By the way, you've not switched the machine on." He slammed the door shut before whatever it was she'd thrown at him reached its target.

As he retreated he bumped into Joy, who was looking for him. "Scott! There you are. Your list awaits you. What are you up to?"

Scott flung his arms around her and kissed her on both cheeks.

"You naughty boy! What brought that on?"

"My reprieve! I'm on my way. I reckon I'm the only one who does any work around here."

"You're not, believe me." Joy watched him disappear into reception and went to greet Bunty on her first day back.

"Hello, Bunty. Now, how are you, dear?"

"I'm fine, thanks, Joy. Quite glad to be back. Mum's been fussing over me all the time."

"So she should. You be thankful she did."

"Yes, I expect you're right."

"You're still looking peaky, though. Are you sure you should be back?"

Bunty was laying out instruments on the trolley cart and, without turning around, she said, "I'm fine, thanks. Fine."

"Finger working OK? Let me look."

Bunty waggled her finger in the air. "They've done a good job. I'll need a morning off in two weeks for a checkup."

"Tell me the date and I'll fix it on the roster."

Bunty nodded. "Thanks."

Joy, glad that the nursing side of her responsibilities was fully manned, closed the door behind her and went out to reception. On the counter were the appointment lists for the small-animal vets and the lists of calls for the farm practice side. She briefly checked them through. Rhodri and Scott were out on call this morning with Zoe, and Colin, now that he was back, would be starting work at one. Graham and Valentine would be consulting this morning. Mungo's list was crammed with appointments all morning and he had two operations in the afternoon. She studied the names of his clients. Some she knew, others . . . The phone rang. The Welsh accent gave the caller away.

"I'm sorry, but Rhodri is out on call all morning. I thought he'd asked you not to call him anymore at work. I can't employ staff to field his personal calls and I've told him so, and he promised it would stop. I'm sorry."

When she replaced the receiver, Joy pulled a face at Kate. "Honestly, that woman! You'd think she'd have more pride, wouldn't you?"

"You would."

Clients always checked in at reception when they came, and a steady stream of them and lots of phone calls kept Joy and Kate busy for the next half hour.

It was Kate who answered the next time Megan Jones rang. "I'm so sorry, but Rhodri is still out on call. He's attending a whelping and it could be all morning. After that he has a full list of appointments. Good morning."

Kate put the receiver back and said, "That's a new line. Now she's talking about a sheep needing looking at."

Joy raised her eyebrows and laughed. "Our Rhodri must have a lot more to him than we realize."

"I think he's really nice."

"He is. But he's a dyed-in-the-wool bachelor. Forty and set in his ways."

"Pity, that; he'd make a nice dad."

"You're right, I think he would. How's your Adam?"

Kate didn't answer straightaway, having a client who'd made a mistake about his appointment time and was over an hour late.

"Please take a seat. I'll tell Mr. Dedic you're here and he'll fit you in. Yes, you're right, it is difficult to read the time on your card. We'll have to make sure we write more clearly next time. I haven't seen Adam for over a week; we've had a fallout."

Joy looked speculatively at her. "You don't appear to be unduly worried."

"I'm not. He's started getting possessive and ordering me

about, and I won't have it. Also he's boring!" She looked at Joy and smiled a little bleakly.

"I see. It's none of my business, but I'm quite glad; I didn't think he was the one for you."

"You didn't? Neither does Mia."

"She seems nice; in fact, very nice."

"She is a love. She's been so good to me. We get on so well. Same sense of humor, you know."

"How long has she been your stepmother?"

"Since I was eighteen months old. I've no recollection of my own mother at all."

"Your mother died, did she?"

Kate found a client far more important than answering Joy's question and Joy took the hint. Obviously, it was delicate ground and she'd better keep off it. If Kate hadn't seen Adam for more than a week, why had Adam's nausesating purple car been parked down a side street on Friday, obviously waiting to catch Kate leaving work? A shudder went down Joy's spine and she wondered if she should say something. She'd ask Duncan what he thought.

At this moment Rhodri bounded in, back from his whelping. "Nine! And they're all beauties. All alive and kicking, born without a hitch. The first one was crossways on; that was the problem, but hey presto, after I'd straightened him up, they popped out like shelled peas." He was exhilarated and completely wound up with excitement. He clutched Joy around the waist and twirled her around, saying, "Nine! All beauties worth five hundred pounds apiece. Mrs. Kent is so grateful." He released Joy.

She pulled her uniform back in to place and wagged a finger at him. "I need a word with you." Taking his hand, she pulled him into her office.

"Aren't you glad for me? My reputation has rocketed sky high with Mrs. Kent. She's weeping with gratitude, having thought she was going to lose both the bitch and the puppies."

"Of course I am, but . . . this morning we've had two calls from that Megan Jones. I thought you'd stopped her ringing."

Rhodri groaned. "Not again. I told her, I did, I really did. She doesn't ring me at home anymore. Honest, Joy."

"I believe you. But one more and . . ."

"What?"

"I shall have a word with her. She's even mentioning sheep now, saying she has one in need of veterinary attention. I mean really! It's her in need of the veterinary attention, not a sheep."

Rhodri spread his arms wide. "What can I do? Eh? Advise me."

"Well, I think you should . . . What the blazes is going on?"

Even though Joy's office door was closed, both of them could hear the commotion outside in reception and Rhodri was convinced he could hear a sheep bleating.

"My God! That sounds like a sheep."

"Don't be ridiculous."

"It is. It's a sheep."

They both rushed out into the reception area to discover a woman standing there with a full-grown sheep on a lead. It wasn't enjoying its adventure and was tossing its head and stamping its feet, and bleating for all it was worth. The woman, well dressed in a Barbour jacket, brown cords and smart brown leather boots, appeared unconcerned by the commotion she was causing.

Kate was saying, "Please, we don't have sheep in here; this is for small animals only. Please take it out."

"I have been endeavoring to get a vet to come to my farm and attend to this sheep, but each time I get an answer, someone says that I can't speak to Rhodri Hughes as he's at a whelping. I don't want to speak to Rhodri Hughes, at a whelping or not. All I want is someone to look at my Myfanwy and tell me what's wrong with her."

"You're . . . ?" Kate asked.

"Megan Jones, Beulah Farm. We're new."

It was Kate who found her voice first. Joy and, in particular, Rhodri were too struck dumb with surprise and embarrassment to answer. "Ah! It's a case of mistaken identity. I'm so sorry. We've been having nuisance phone calls, you see, from someone called Megan Jones and we mistook your calls for hers. I am very sorry."

"There must be hundreds of Megan Joneses all over the world, so I can understand your mistake."

"Look, Mrs. Jones . . ."

"Miss."

"Sorry, Miss Jones, would you be so kind as to take Myfanwy outside and I'll get a vet to come to have a look at her. Or if you prefer, you could take her back home and someone will visit."

Miss Jones thought this over for a moment and decided she'd have someone look at her straightaway. "It is urgent, you see."

Rhodri, poleaxed by his first impressions of this new Megan Jones, found his voice and said, "Could I be of any assistance?"

Miss Jones studied him coolly.

He nodded vigorously to encourage her to agree to his examining Myfanwy.

She nodded. "Are you experienced with sheep?"

Joy knew he wasn't, not since his college days, and waited with bated breath to hear what appalling fib he was going to use to ingratiate himself.

"Oh yes! My favorite animal. Dorset Horn, isn't she?"

Inwardly Joy groaned.

Miss Jones nodded. "Yes. Come on, then, boyo." Myfanwy took some persuading to leave and it needed Rhodri, Miss Jones and Joy to get her out through the door. As she and Rhodri heaved and pushed from the rear, while Miss Jones pulled from the front, Joy muttered, "For God's sake, mind what you do. If in doubt, shout."

Finally Myfanwy was forced into departing. Joy returned to the desk and Kate asked quietly, "Does he know anything at all about sheep?"

"Not a damn thing, not since college, anyway. I've never known him to do a thing like this before; he must have gone mad."

"By the looks of Rhodri, he believes he's met his soul mate." Kate laughed.

If Joy hadn't been so anxious, she would have laughed too. "I'm going to wash my hands—I stink of sheep—then I'm taking a peep outside from the laundry window. You look after the shop."

One of the regular clients called out, "Kate! There's one thing about coming here: You do see life. It's the first Monday, so Adolf will be here soon. I just hope Graham's running late with his appointments or I shall miss the fun."

"Oh, drat! I'd forgotten."

Kate raced off into the laundry room for the fire bucket but got tempted into joining Joy at the window. Rhodri and Megan were holding an earnest discussion.

"Joy, are we witnessing the meeting of true minds here?"

"I reckon we just might be. This could be a moment in history to be savored."

"I wish these windows weren't double glazed and we could hear what they're saying."

"Kate, honestly!"

"I wonder if she likes ferrets."

"Had we better warn her before things get too advanced? Oh, look! There's Mr. Featherstonehough's old van."

"Adolf!"

Kate grabbed the fire bucket, Joy fled to shut the door to Mungo's flat, and Rhodri and Megan were left to discuss the nitty-gritty of Myfanwy's symptoms unobserved.

Both Joy and Kate were intrigued to know what had happened between the two of them, but Rhodri returned by the back door and went straight to his consulting room without entering reception. The first they heard of his return was his singing "Land of My Fathers" in his wonderful tenor voice with such enormous enthusiasm that one was made deeply aware of the passion therein, but whether or not the passion was for Wales or for Miss Megan Jones, they could only guess. Kate and Joy raised their eyebrows at each other and laughed, but not for long.

Miriam came down from the flat, carrying a cake for the staff in honor of Mungo's birthday, and before they knew it, Perkins was down the stairs and in reception, going like an arrow for Adolf.

Joy shouted, "I don't believe it!" But she was too late. He'd passed her, and Perkins and Adolf were in the throes of yet another major fight. She grabbed the bucket and emptied it over them, but they were too quick for her and she missed them both. "Oh no!"

Kate grabbed the bucket again and fled to fill it up, returned, aimed again and this time scored a hit. The two dogs broke apart and both shook off the water right in front of Joy, drenching her before she could leap back.

"You two naughty boys! What are we going to do with you? Look at me." The only sympathy she got from them was Perkins grinning at her. Adolf completely ignored her and went to sit, propped against Mr. Featherstonehough and wetting his trouser legs in the process.

"Dry-cleaning bills, that's what you'll be getting next."

Miriam apologized. "I'm so sorry, it was my fault, I left the door open to our flat. I just don't know how Perkins knows you're here."

"Neither do I. I could always move and go to that place in the High Street."

"Well, of course, the choice is yours, but we'd hate to lose you." Miriam smiled her most enchanting smile.

Mr. Featherstonehough, a womanizer in his time, couldn't resist her charms and melted before her eyes. He rubbed a wry hand over his bristly chin and said slyly, "Of course I could be persuaded to stay. Like I say, your staff are all so pretty, especially that one who spills out of her uniform."

Miriam pretended to be shocked. "Well, really, I must say, so that's why you're a client of ours. It's our attractive staff, not the expertise."

"And you too, Mrs. Price. I could do with you holding Adolf for his injection. Very nicely I could."

"You flirt, you!" Miriam patted his arm and left with Perkins amid muffled giggles from the other clients waiting their turns.

THAT night at Mungo's birthday dinner, Joy related the episode with Mr. Featherstonehough to Mungo and he found it hugely amusing. "The old reprobate. Threatening to leave me, is he? Well, he won't. We go back a long way, him and me. He wouldn't possibly leave *me*."

His words were an echo of the ones he'd used to Joy when she'd threatened to leave the practice and she raised an eyebrow at him, but he avoided her eyes. "Do you know, he was my first client, was old Mr. F. He had a huge Rottweiler then called Fang, a massive creature, totally unpredictable. He clamped his teeth on my arm more than once, the nasty devil." Mungo pushed back his shirt cuff and showed a scar. "See! I begged him to have him put down, but he wouldn't and then the dog bit his wife, and I mean bit, cracked a couple of bones in her wrist, he did, and she issued him an ultimatum: either the dog went or she did. It took him a week to make up his mind, which wasn't very flattering to his wife, but eventually he came in one day heartbroken and declared that he wanted him put down. He wept. Left the surgery with tears streaming down his face. I met him in the street weeks afterward and he told me that the damn thing had bitten him more than once and that I'd been quite right; he had been dangerous, and at bottom he was glad he'd had him put to sleep."

Miriam said, "After all that, he's gone and bought another one."

"Yes, but not until after Mrs. F. had died. Adolf's a big soft beggar; wouldn't hurt a fly."

Duncan said he found it difficult to understand why people needed animals to love.

Miriam was appalled. "Oh, Duncan, how can you say that? They're wonderful. Look at our Perkins. He's such a love." Perkins, banished from the dining room while they ate, was sitting outside the door, heard his name and whimpered loudly to remind them of their extreme cruelty to him.

"You've got Mungo to love. Why do you need a dog too?"

"Well, he's not my dog, is he? He's Mungo's."

"Why have you got him, Mungo?"

"He's my third Airedale and I wouldn't be without one."

"There must be a reason. Come on."

Joy kicked his foot lightly under the table. "Just because, darling."

"Joy's just kicked me to tell me to shut up, but I honestly want to know. Why do you need a pet to love?"

Mungo shuffled uneasily in his chair and then answered, "If you must know, my Janie bought me an Airedale puppy for a wedding present and I loved him from the first moment. Don't ask me why, because I can't tell you, but I did."

The silence this comment brought about was uncomfortable for all of them except Duncan, who remained unmoved. Joy because she knew the pain it caused Mungo even to say Janie's name, Miriam because she wondered if Mungo would ever love her as he had loved Janie, and Mungo because of the searing pain memories of Janie could still inflict.

"You see, you have no rational explanation, have you? How a highly intelligent, well-setup man of the world like you can find himself muttering about loving a *dog* I do not know. A dog! God!"

Mungo, on the verge of losing his temper, said tightly, "I do. Let it be the end of the matter. Right?"

"So you're irrational, then."

"If love is irrational, yes. Perkins is all I have left of Janie; his bloodlines are related to the first one she gave me and that's enough for me. Brandy, Duncan?"

"No, thanks. I think I'll be off." He stood up. "It's the same with children. Why do people bother? God! You can't go anywhere, do anything without them damn well trailing after you making a noise and embarrassing you with their supposedly innocent questions. Their continuous demands on your time, your money, your nerves! Who'd have children?"

Joy gasped in astonishment at his thoughtlessness.

"I would, Duncan, any day." Miriam looked up at him, her eyes full of tears.

Duncan, brought up short by the sadness in her voice, remembered too late. "I'm so very sorry, Miriam. Please forgive me. I'd forgotten."

"That's all right. I can't expect other people to keep our

tragedy in their hearts forever as I do. They'd have been four-teen and twelve now if they'd lived."

"Damn bad luck, that. Both of them. How careless of me and how inconsiderate. Forgive me. I've got the black dog on me tonight. I'd better leave. See you at home, Joy."

The three of them listened as Duncan clattered down the stairs to the ground floor. Joy spoke first. "There are times when I could cheerfully kill him. I'm so sorry, Miriam; he doesn't mean half he says, he just enjoys argument."

"Not your fault. It's a long way for him to walk."

"Do him good. I'll go too, but not before I've helped you with this lot." She waved an arm at the cluttered table.

"Certainly not. I don't expect my guests to work. I'll do it." Miriam pressed her hands on the table and heaved herself up. "Won't take long."

Mungo sprang up. "I'll help. Shall I see you to your car, Joy?"

"I do know the way! I'd rather you helped with all this, salve my conscience a bit. Bye-bye and many thanks. I'm sorry Duncan spoiled your birthday, Mungo. Don't invite him next year."

Mungo kissed her cheek. "Don't worry about it, not your fault, but he could do with keeping some of his opinions to himself."

Joy kissed Miriam and squeezed her arm. "Sorry! Night-night." Joy picked up her bag, slung her jacket over her shoulders and left.

Miriam sat, head down, staring at the table. "It never leaves us, does it? Always there, dogging the footsteps?"

Mungo placed a hand on each side of her head and lifted it so he could see her face. "Expand on that. What dogs your footsteps?"

Miriam chose to say, "The children." Best keep Janie well pushed away so she couldn't hurt. "Still, there we are." She sighed.

"You must let them rest. Let go. Just let them go."

"You've let them go, have you, then? The son the image of you. The daughter so unbelievably pretty?" A deep sob escaped before Miriam could stop it.

"Darling!" He hugged her close. "If I could turn back the clock . . ."

"They'd still be ill, wouldn't they? Still be incurable."

"Indeed. Good thing we found out in time before we had any more." He was silent for a minute and then said gently, "Lovely dinner, as always. You go to bed. I'll do this lot."

"Why do I like Duncan so much when he's so odd?"

"Perhaps because he *is* odd."

"He needs hugging, you know; that's what he needs, lots of hugging to convince him he's worthwhile."

"So do I."

Miriam laughed. "You! You've an ego the size of a watermelon. His is the size of a grape, if he has one at all."

"Well, don't you go hugging him or Joy might have something to say."

Miriam watched Mungo stacking plates and then answered, "I don't think Joy thinks about him like that; she really wouldn't mind if I did. They have the most peculiar relationship, haven't they? They've kind of stayed individuals and haven't melded."

"Haven't noticed."

"We've melded."

Mungo thought about what she'd said and nodded. "Yes, you're right, we have. I'll see to Perkins. Off you go. It's raining now. Can you hear it? Duncan will get soaked; it must be all of five miles. Serve him bloody well right. I take a certain amount of pleasure at the idea of him getting a soaking, the thoughtless sod."

• • •

BUT because of the rain, Duncan hadn't taken the path over the fields as he usually did; he'd kept to the road. Consequently, Joy had caught up with him and given him a lift. They drove home in stony silence. Duncan unlocked the front door; Joy put the car in the garage and stalked upstairs to bed. She was seething with tumultuous emotions, none of which she could come to terms with. When she came out of the bathroom, Duncan was already lying on the bed, wearing his pajamas. She looked down at him. "Pleased with yourself?"

"Not at all."

"I should think not. How could you be so crass? Have you forgotten all those agonizing years of theirs? How *you* couldn't even go and see the children because you were made so desperate by their plight? Remember?"

Duncan turned over and groaned. "Of course."

"So?"

"I got carried away with my argument and didn't think."

"Exactly." Joy sat on the edge of the bed and set the alarm for morning.

Duncan rolled over and disappeared into the bathroom. When he returned, he got under the duvet and lay on his back with his hands clasped beneath his head. "I get so involved with my work I forget human beings. Do you know that? I forget feelings and things, you know. I think everyone's automatic like me and they're not."

"Really!"

"Yes. First and foremost I should have thought of Miriam's feelings and they never occurred to me. Not once."

"I blame computers."

Duncan thought about this for a moment and nodded his head. "You could be right. They've no emotion, you know, none at all, no flexibility, no give and take. They're programmed that way. Did you realize that?"

"Of course."

"Maybe I've lived with computers for so long that I've grown like them."

"Could be."

"Become devoid of emotion—that's why I act so strangely. I think only of myself."

Joy pretended surprise. "No!"

"Tomorrow first thing, I shall go down to the florist's and organize a bouquet of flowers for Miriam with a card written in my own hand."

"What will the card say?"

"It will come to me by morning."

"Right."

"Maybe it's a new disease that will shortly be discovered by science. Maybe it's at the root of all our troubles, people turning into robots through continuous association with computers. I may have hit on something here."

"I shall be hitting you before long."

"Maybe all the violence in the world is caused by computers because they've made people no longer feel anything at all. Consequently, we're free to damage other human beings and things without any conscience whatsoever. You know, the damn things are dictating our behavior and we've never realized. So computers *are* taking over the world as we threatened they would and carelessly we all laughed at the idea." Duncan sat up. "Joy! I feel so dreadful about Miriam. To do that to such a lovely person. I'm ashamed of myself."

Joy took hold of his hand. "She understands."

Duncan sighed. "Joy?"

"Yes?"

He lay down again, still holding her hand. "You can't stop loving him, can you? I can see it in your eyes when you're with him. It's not fair to Miriam, you know."

Joy didn't answer but leaned on her elbow and kissed his cheek.

Duncan's deep-set eyes looked up at her. The lamp cast shadows in the hollows of his eyes and she couldn't read what they were saying. She knew what she wanted to say, but she didn't say it. Instead: "And there's you, saying you've lost all feeling to that computer of yours."

Duncan lay silent for a while, then rolled onto his side and drew up his legs till his knees were almost touching his chin. "I'm for sleep. Remind me in the morning. Flowers. Good night."

"Good night."

Before she knew it, he was breathing heavily, leaving her wide awake and in turmoil.

"How could anyone do such a dreadful thing? Abandoning them like that? It's so cruel. Look at the dear little things! Is that one asleep or . . ."

Kate and Stephie were peering into a cardboard box a client had found at the main entrance. Inside were four kittens—two tabbies, one black and one black with white markings. The black-and-white one was lying very still. Kate lifted its little head with her finger and it flopped. "I've a nasty feeling that one is beyond help."

"Beyond help? You don't mean it's dead?"

"I think so. In fact, I'm sure so. How old are they, do you think?"

"I don't know, but let's get that one out that's dead. Here, look, put it in this." Stephie rooted in the waste bin and brought out an empty tissue box she'd that moment thrown away. "You lift it out. I'm not very good with them when they're dead."

Kate carefully lifted out the dead one and laid it in the box. "It's so cold." They covered it with a clean tissue and then gave their attention to the ones that were alive. Three pairs of bright little blue eyes peered up at them out of the depths of the box. The kittens looked so appealing that both Stephie and Kate said, "Ah! Aren't they sweet?" Kate laid a gentle hand on each in turn and came to the conclusion they were all cold. "You'd think they could have put a blanket in for them, wouldn't you? We'd better get them some help. What a lot of noise you're making! I bet you're hungry, aren't you?" She rubbed her finger under their chins, each in turn, and wished she could take one home, but Mia's asthma forbade it. Responding to her touch, they began clawing at the sides of the box, trying to get out, their mouths opening into triangular shapes revealing tiny snow-white teeth as they mewed for help.

Stephie suggested they should get one of the vets to look at them.

The client who'd found them said, "They look big enough to me to lap up milk. You can't 'elp but love 'em, can you, Kate? They're so lovely. Wish I could lay my hands on the pigs who did this to 'em. What 'arm 'ave they ever done?"

"Well, perhaps their mother has died or the person who owns them couldn't afford to keep them. They do get quite expensive to feed once you start weaning them. At least they brought them where they could get help. Sometimes people leave them in a bin or in a hedgerow somewhere and that really is cruel. See if Rhodri's still here, will you, Stephie?"

"He'll want us to call the RSPCA."

"They'll be adopted quickly, won't they? There's no one going to come forward to claim this little lot. Fancy being homeless at this age."

"I'll get Rhodri."

Moved by Kate's sympathy for them, the client put a finger in the box and the black kitten tried to lick it. "Ah! Look at that. D'yer know, I might ask the RSPCA to let me 'ave this one. Be a real friend for this little one 'ere." He indicated the cat basket he'd put down on the floor. "They'd make a right pair—both completely black and only a few weeks between 'em." The client tickled the black kitten on his chest. "He seems to 'ave taken to me, doesn't he?"

"He does."

"Is it a boy or a girl?"

"I'm afraid I don't know for sure, but my granny used to say that a he always had a wider forehead even at this age than a she. What do you think?"

"If that's the case, then the black's a boy; look."

They compared the heads of the three kittens and came to the conclusion that yes, the black was a boy and the two tabbies were girls.

Stephie came back to say, "Rhodri says take them into his consulting room and he'll run over them. A job for Lynne, this. She knows how to make up the formula for them. She'll get them to drink if anyone can; she's done it before. If they're hungry, they'll probably take to it straightaway."

When Kate rang the RSPCA and explained the situation, the reply was a groan. "Oh no! You won't believe this, but we've just taken on board one hundred and forty-two cats and kittens from a place that bred cats for science. They've been closed down and we've got them all. We've sent twenty of them to another RSPCA home and even then we're packed to the doors. There is no way that we can take any more on board, there's literally no room at the inn. Could you possibly keep them till they're ready to be adopted?"

"Well, I'll have to ask our practice manager; see what she thinks."

"After all, they are in good hands, aren't they? Couldn't be better, come to think of it. We'll be ages, you see, adopting out this lot because they're not used to being handled and we've a lot of work to do on them before they're ready. If you could manage them, we'd be very grateful. They couldn't be in a better place, could they?"

"No, you're right there. It's just that we're not geared for long-term care, but I'll see what I can do."

"We'd be more than grateful, believe me. If you're in need of advice or some such, do please ring us back, won't you?"

"Will do."

"We shall be forever in your debt. If it really is impossible, then we'll take them—if push comes to shove, you know. Keep in touch."

By lunchtime, the kittens were warm and well fed and sleeping peacefully, cuddled in a thick blanket in one of the postoperative cages. Kate took her lunch in there and ate her beef sandwiches wishing she could have one of them for herself. They'd taken to drinking milk wonderfully well under Lynne's supervision. She certainly might not be a nice person to know, but she'd succeeded with the kittens in no time at all and Kate complimented her on her success.

Lynne shrugged her shoulders. "All part of the job. They're in good nick, actually. Been looked after OK up to now. Makes you wonder, doesn't it? Why did they get thrown out?"

"The black one's spoken for; the client who found them outside wants it. That leaves the two tabbies. Just wish I could take one, but Mia's allergic to fur. Brings on her asthma."

"Is it nice having a stepmum?"

"Well, my stepmum is like a real mother to me. I've never known my own mother, you see. Dad and Mia married before I was two."

"That's different, isn't it? Must be awful if you're fourteen, say, and your dad marries again."

Kate sank her teeth into an apple. "Mm."

Lynne opened the cage door and felt the kittens. "They're much warmer now. Right time-wasters, kittens are. So tempting to come and play with them and they need feeding all the time. Pity the RSPCA hadn't room."

"Imagine the work, looking after all those cats."

"They've all to be neutered too, you know, before they can adopt them out. The mind boggles."

Kate stood up to brush the crumbs from her uniform.

"Not on this floor, please."

"Sorry. I'll sweep them up."

"You will. This is postoperative—got to be scrupulously clean. And don't eat in here again."

"Sorry."

"So I should think. You've a lot to learn."

"I know I have."

"A lot to learn about manners, for one thing. Speaking to my brothers like you did. That Adam is a fool. A complete fool. Imagine not realizing they were finding him amusingly pathetic."

Kate, surprised by the sudden change of tack, said, "He's a kind man, that's why. He wouldn't act like that, ever."

"No, he's too wet."

"Your brothers are arrogant."

"So? Oxford and the City. They've something to be arrogant about."

"I'm surprised that with that background they know so little about good manners."

"They haven't got where they are relying on good manners, believe me."

"I can imagine."

"There's no need for your sarcasm."

"There's no need for you attacking me like this."

Lynne faced her, hands on hips. "What is it about you that annoys me? Your CV, for a start. What are you doing playing at being a receptionist with a CV like yours? Eh? Answer me that.

Two A's. You should be at university, not piffling about here. Well?"

"What I do with my A levels is my choice. How do you know anyway? I've never said."

Lynne tapped the side of her nose. "I have ways. Just keep out of my way. I don't like people who are well in with the management; it smacks of toadyism."

"I have never tried . . ."

"Lynne!" Joy stood in the doorway. "I am quite sure there is something better for you to be doing than gossiping in here. Kindly *move*! Sharp!"

Lynne made to leave.

Joy turned her attention to Kate. "And you, Kate, don't eat in here again. If your lunch hour is finished, please get on with your accounts. We don't want you getting behind with them, do we?"

"I'm sorry."

"Apology accepted."

Joy stood to one side to allow Kate to leave. The girl was flushed with embarrassment at her reprimand and Joy felt uncomfortable, for Kate hadn't deserved that, but in front of Lynne it was the only thing to say to make them equal. So Lynne had been snooping around in the files, had she? Excellent worker, none better, but as a person . . . The incident made Joy recall the missing money and she wondered if this spat between the two of them was a confirmation that it was Lynne who'd removed Miss Chillingsworth's one hundred pounds. Joy went to take a peep at the kittens. With business on the increase since their move to these premises, she rather felt the kittens were a burden they could well have done without. But one touch of their warm, soft furry heads and the sight of the little appreciative wiggle one of the tabbies gave as she stroked it changed her mind. Rather fun to have some healthy creatures to look after for a while.

For some unknown reason, Duncan came to the forefront of her mind. Joy looked again at the one that had wiggled its appreciation and she noticed that its stripes had a ginger tinge to them, which made it rather unusual. Since Duncan had sent the flowers to Miriam after his disastrous faux pas, he'd been slightly more mellow toward mankind. Maybe this kitten, whose ears she noted were attractively larger and rather more pointed than those of the other two, might interest him. She'd drop a few hints; see how he felt. Reluctantly leaving the warmth of the three kittens, Joy took her hand out of the cage and carefully clicked it shut.

"Can I have a turn?" It was Miriam. "Mungo told me at lunchtime, so I thought I'd come for a peep. Aren't they sweet!"

Joy unlocked the cage again so Miriam could see more easily. Tears filled Miriam's eyes. "The poor dear little things. Abandoned like that. How cruel."

Joy watched her gentleness and felt the love flowing from her toward the three kittens. "Miriam. I haven't said properly about Duncan. The flowers . . . they were his idea, not mine. When he stopped to think, he was appalled at what he'd said."

"He's been to see me."

"He has? He didn't say."

"The next day with the flowers. We had a cuddle and a kiss, and we're friends still. Somehow it helped me. He is such an understanding man."

"He is?"

"Oh yes. There's a delicacy about his feelings that is unusual in a man and he explained how it had all come about and, well . . . it helped."

"I see."

"He needs hugging, you know, Joy. I expect I'm telling you something you must already know, but he does; he needs hugging. At some time in his life he's missed out on it right when he needed it. Perhaps he doesn't know it, but I'm sure I'm right."

"I see."

Miriam stroked the kittens. "Very therapeutic, isn't it? Touching sleeping babies, even if they are furry ones."

Joy choked on her tears. "Miriam!"

Miriam turned to look at her, opened her arms wide and invited Joy to hug her. They stood, arms around each other, for a while not speaking, then broke apart as Miriam said, "I wish I could have one of them, but the risk of Perkins mistaking it for a rat is far, far too great. You won't have got homes for them?"

"The black one is spoken for and I'm wondering about having one for Duncan."

"Two down. One to go!" Miriam locked the cage. "Must get on. If you need help with feeding at the weekends, let me know."

"Rhodri says they need to stay together until they're six weeks; not right to separate them at this age."

"Of course. Yes. See you, Joy."

"And you."

Duncan had never said he'd given Miriam the flowers in person. Miriam was right; he did need loving and, to be absolutely frank, he wasn't getting it. Weeks went by and she scarcely touched him. Made his meals, did his washing, tidied the house, but loved him? Joy shook her head. What was worse, he'd known for years that she loved Mungo and in the beginning she'd never intended he should realize that fact. But he had and he did and he'd been right when he'd said it wasn't fair to Miriam. Yet Miriam had put her arms around her as one did with a close friend. Like a bolt of lightning the thought entered Joy's head that if Duncan had realized without being told, then possibly Miriam had too. That idea had never occurred to her before. But if she had realized, would Miriam have wanted to be a friend to a woman who loved her own husband? Wouldn't she have wanted to keep her at a distance to lessen the chance of losing Mungo to her? Of course she would, so obviously Miriam didn't know. Joy felt a great wave of relief wash over her.

So Miriam must never know. She'd have to be very careful in future, though, because breaking Miriam's heart would be too big a responsibility for her to take. Before she left, Joy took another glance at the kittens who were just beginning to stir. The one with the pointy ears looked up at her; its muzzy blue eyes had that slightly square look that kittens' eyes always have when very young, and there and then Joy lost her heart to it.

Duncan, somehow or other, was getting a kitten.

THE following week, Kate had a day off and was spending it in the shopping mall, choosing a birthday present for Mia and a wedding anniversary card for her and her dad. Well, it wasn't just for that reason. She also wanted to see about collecting some brochures for a holiday the next summer and, last but not least, she had a new textbook to buy for chemistry.

For Mia some new earrings. Kate went to the ethnic shop on the first floor of the mall and found instead of earrings a necklace, all fine silver, delicate and Indian, and she knew it would suit Mia and though it was dearer than she'd intended, she bought it. For someone as generous as Mia, nothing was too good. Kate wished she were wealthy so she could buy her a studio and some marvelously up-to-date equipment, and set her up for her miniatures good and proper, though it couldn't make her paint any better. Mia was on the brink of making a name for herself and Kate was very proud of her.

At street level the mall boasted innumerable card and gift shops and Kate went down the escalator to choose Mia's card and another for the anniversary. The mall had been furnished with several wooden seats, planned in cozy groups to give a kind of village green effect. As she passed through a group of seats, she spotted Miss Chillingsworth huddled in the corner of one, looking despondent. Kate had never noticed how old she was till now. "Why, Miss Chillingsworth! What a nice surprise."

Miss Chillingsworth looked up blankly at first, then recognition dawned. "It's Kate, isn't it? How are you, my dear?"

"I'm fine. How are you?"

"I'm fine, dear, thank you." Miss Chillingsworth looked anything but fine to Kate, but she didn't comment. "Not working today?"

"My day off. I'm working Saturday this week."

"You sound as if you enjoy it."

"I do. May I sit down?"

Miss Chillingsworth patted the seat beside her. "I'd be delighted. It's nice to have someone to talk to who's congenial. How are things at the practice? I miss seeing you all."

"We're terribly busy at the moment; one of the nurses is on holiday and we've got three kittens to look after. They're running about now and we've to be so careful because of Perkins. He reckons kittens equal rats and he's such an escape artist we have to watch him like hawks."

"Why have you three kittens to look after?"

Kate explained and while she did so a brilliant idea sprang unbidden into her mind, an idea complete the moment it was born. "It wouldn't be fair to separate them until they're a bit older, you see, so we have them for another two and a half weeks at least."

Miss Chillingsworth listened with growing interest. "How

kind you all are. So very kind. I've never forgotten Mr. Murgatroyd's little talk when . . . I lost Cherub. He was so good to me. I can see it must be hard work. That Perkins is a real character, isn't he?"

"He's a love, but so naughty and then, when you're cross with him, he looks up at you and you fall in love with him all over again. He's the only dog I know who laughs like a person. Miriam would love to have one of the kittens, but Perkins would very likely mistake it for a rat and then . . . I can't bear to think."

"That's what Airedales were bred for."

"What is?"

"Clearing riverbanks of vermin. Water rats and things." Miss Chillingsworth shuddered. "I can't bear the thought of him getting at a kitten and one couldn't be angry with him if he did, could one? He would only be obeying his instincts."

"Exactly. But it's getting more and more difficult the more active they become." Kate left a silence while Miss Chillingsworth had a think.

"Is there no one who could take them all home?"

"Not really. My stepmother has asthma and she's about the only one who is home most of the day. All the others are out following careers and the like."

"Of course, that's the problem nowadays. You say they have homes to go to?"

Kate nodded and counted off the homes on her fingers. "Oh yes. The black one is going to the client who found them on our doorstep. One tabby, the one with ginger in its stripes, is going to Joy's husband and the other tabby is going to a cousin of Mr. Price's."

"If they hadn't, I couldn't do it. I can't replace Cherub just yet."

Hardly daring to breathe Kate said, "Couldn't do what?"

"Take them home till they're old enough. They could sleep in Cherub's basket by the stove and I could train them to the litter tray she used at night when she got older, and they could have the run of the kitchen, couldn't they?"

"Miss Chillingsworth, what a brilliant idea. You've so much experience with cats you'd be ideal. The practice would provide all the food, of course. We wouldn't expect you to have that expense. Would you really do it for us? We'd be so grateful and it would be so much better for the kittens."

Miss Chillingsworth nodded and beamed at her, and Kate continued, "I could kiss you."

So she did and Miss Chillingsworth kissed her back. "I haven't been kissed for years. Shall we go?"

"Right now?"

"No time like the present. We could catch the bus."

"I've got my car."

"All the better."

Kate left Miss Chillingsworth in reception and went to explain the whole idea to Joy in her office. Joy said, "But they're not all spoken for, that other tabby . . ."

"I know, but she daren't take on the job if any one of them is homeless, because she's not ready to have another cat yet. So I told a white lie. Remember, it's a cousin of Mr. Price's who's having the other one."

"Kate! Honestly!"

"It's in a good cause. She so needs something to throw herself into. Losing Cherub has been devastating for her; she's aged twenty years at least. We're sure to find someone willing to have one before long. Say yes. Please."

"All right, then. It would be a great help, wouldn't it? Clever girl!" Joy stood up. "We'll go for it." Together they went to speak to Miss Chillingsworth.

"Miss Chillingsworth! How very kind of you to offer to have the kittens. Come in the back and take a look. They've had their dinner and they're asleep at the moment. You'll love them when you see them."

The three of them had fallen asleep in a heap of fluffy toy mice and brightly colored squeaky toys, and looked almost unbelievably appealing. Miss Chillingsworth gasped with delight. "They are so sweet. Oh, my word! So sweet. Of course I'll take them. Gladly. The poor little dears, abandoned. I'll make it up to them, you'll see! How shall I get them home?"

Kate volunteered to drive her home. She loaded tinned kitten meat, milk formula and cat litter in the back, leaving Miss Chillingsworth to put the kittens in a carrier with their toys.

WHILE Miss Chillingsworth fussed around getting Cherub's basket out and finding a piece of blanket to line it with, Kate sat on a chair in the kitchen waiting with the cat carrier beside her. Poor Miss Chillingsworth. "Genteel poverty" were the only words to describe the circumstances in which she lived. Everything was tidy and extremely clean but so threadbare: The tapestry seat of the chair on which she perched had holes in it; the rug on the floor was patched to such an extent there was hardly anything of the original left; the curtains were so faded but when new had been of fine quality; the doormat was almost bald. It didn't take much intelligence to know that Miss Chillingsworth didn't always get enough to eat.

"There we are, Kate, my dear. I'm ready. Let's lift them out. I've put a hot-water bottle in the basket to make it feel like home."

The kittens tumbled out of the carrier and skitter-scattered on the shiny floor, their tiny claws finding it difficult to walk on. Miss Chillingsworth picked each up in turn, pressed it to her cheek, then plopped it down in the basket. Having been thoroughly awakened by the car journey, the kittens had no inclination to sleep, and they hopped out immediately and began to investigate.

"I'll bring the tins in."

By the time Kate left, Miss Chillingsworth had shed the years that Cherub's death had heaped on her shoulders and she looked up at Kate with shining eyes. "Thank you, Kate, my dear, I'm going to have such fun. You're a dear girl."

Kate left her kneeling on the floor, the kittens spilling around her skirts.

"So you see, Joy, we've done her a good turn. I'll call at the end of the week and see how she's getting on, and if it's all right with you, I'll take her some more tins and some more milk formula. There's no way she can be expected to pay for their food; she's so poor."

"The dear old thing. Good idea of yours. Now all we have to do is find a home for number three."

"We will, I'm determined."

Joy laughed. "If you've said you will, I know it'll happen. Off you go and get on with the accounts, Kate; you did a good day's work yesterday with the kittens."

"Thanks."

Kate took coffee out to Stephie and Joy on the dot of ten and stopped for a chat. Joy took her mug from Kate and complained it was too hot. "Here, look, I'll leave it there where Mungo can't see it."

Stephie began drinking hers immediately. "I'm ready for that. I do miss going in to play with the kittens, don't you, Kate?"

"I do, but as Lynne said, they were terrible time-wasters. Do you know anyone, Stephie, who might fancy a kitten?"

"I don't. But there's sure to be someone who has to have a cat put down in the next two weeks and that's the moment to strike."

"Sounds a bit callous, but I know you're ri—My God!" Kate felt the hairs stand up on the back of her neck; her scorching hot coffee spilled over her hand, but she never felt the scalding, for coming in through the door was . . . a man gone raving mad. A man hurling himself in through the glass doors, wearing a black balaclava and brandishing a billhook. Stephie screamed. Joy went stark white and Kate dropped her mug. Most of the clients screamed and, far quicker than it takes to tell, Graham and Rhodri shot out of their consulting rooms to see what was amiss.

The madman screamed, "Where is he? Where is that damned traitor? Just let me get at 'im."

The voice sounded familiar, but in the panic Kate couldn't place him.

"Just let me get my bloody hands on 'im, I'll bloody kill 'im."

Not one of them could find a voice, so getting no reply, the man surged around the reception area peering at each petrified client in turn, waving the billhook too close for comfort to their faces, but it was difficult for him to see, for the balaclava didn't allow both his eyes to look out at the same time. The clients were close to hysteria by now and seeing their fear made Kate find her voice. "Who is this person you want to kill?"

The madman veered back toward the reception desk and leaning over it, snarled, "That bloody Aussie! That's who!"

"He's out on call."

"I'll wait."

"Not with that in your hand, you won't. Give it to me." He made no move to hand it over. "I said give it to me."

The madman, responding to the authority in her voice, looked down at his weapon. "I'm not giving it up."

"You're not staying in here if you don't. That's an offensive weapon and I shall call the police if you won't hand it over."

"Call the police! Nay."

"Nay nothing. Try me."

The madman looked at this slip of a girl ordering him about and some of the humor of the situation hit him and the anger in him began to evaporate. "I'll wait, though."

Kate took the billhook from him saying, "You'll have a long wait, but you're welcome to sit down. Coffee?"

He nodded and Kate took Joy's mug from behind the computer and gave it to him. He sat on the chair nearest the door and though his hands were still shaking with his temper, he managed to drink from Joy's mug. "I can't forgive 'im for what he's done to me. I thought him and me was friends. Who needs enemies with friends like 'im. Stabbed in the back I've been." He sat, shaking his head in despair.

Stephie whispered, "Scott's coming back in any minute, with some urgent samples to be mailed."

Joy, standing with her back to the madman, asked, "Who is he?"

Kate answered, "From something Scott said, I think it's Mr. Parsons."

Stephie whispered urgently, "He'll be back any minute. What can we do?"

Joy queried, "What's Scott been up to, Kate? My God! It's not Blossom, is it?"

"Heaven alone knows."

Stephie said even more urgently, "He'll be here!"

Catching the sound of the Land Rover, Kate said, "That sounds like him now." She rushed out to the back to catch Scott before he entered.

They each arrived at the back door at the same time. Kate opened it and pushed Scott out, slamming the door behind her. "I think we've got Mr. Parsons waiting to see you. He's absolutely livid and swears he's going to kill you. He arrived brandishing a billhook, which mercifully I've got from him, and . . ."

Scott looked shocked. "A billhook? Hell!"

"He's furious. What the blazes have you done?"

Scott, his hands full of samples for the laboratory, tried to demonstrate his innocence with outstretched hands and almost dropped the lot. "Nothing. I haven't been near the place since I treated Sunny Boy's foot that time. What does he say I've done?"

"He hasn't."

Scott dithered on the step, trying to make up his mind what he should do. Ever one for a challenge he asked, "You've taken the billhook off him?" Kate nodded. "Good on you, mate. Then I shall face up to him. Here, take these samples. Joy knows where they should go. Tell her they're urgent." He happened to be still wearing the tie Mungo insisted on when he went on visits. He straightened it, pulled his collar tidy, tucked his shirt in and made sure his pullover was in order. Kate opened the door for him and tootled a trumpet call under her breath. Scott grinned, saluted her and marched inside to his fate.

In a loud, cheery voice he called out, "Phil! How nice of you to call. What can I do for you, mate?"

Mr. Parson's fury had abated, to be replaced by a moroseness so deep it was a wonder he could speak at all.

Scott went to sit beside him. "Do we need to go somewhere private?"

A quiet groan trickled around the waiting clients. Were they going to miss all the drama?

Mr. Parsons shook his head. "You know you said you could report me for selling milk illegal-like to the campsite and passersby and that?"

Scott nodded and was about to deny vehemently doing any such thing, but Mr. Parsons didn't give him the chance. "On reflection, I know it wouldn't be you, because we're mates, aren't we? You and me." Scott nodded. "Well, someone has. Some interfering sod has reported me and I'm in deep water. They spied on me and set me up and caught me at it. There isn't a better drop of milk anywhere in Britain than mine from my cows. Even the queen's cows couldn't produce no better. Natural, wholesome milk is mine, no modern messing about with it. My Blossom and me, we drink it every day of our lives and what's wrong with us?"

"Nothing. But I did say you wouldn't pass a single hygiene test, didn't I?"

Mr. Parsons lifted his head and managed to look at Scott with one of his eyes. "You did. But they're all 'ealthy, aren't they?"

"You're right there, Phil."

"You couldn't speak up for me, could you?"

"As a friend, there's nothing I would like better, but honestly, I have told you before about your lack of hygiene and I'm afraid that on that basis I would have to be truthful. I couldn't support your selling milk."

"Ah, well. I understand. It's only right. But I know it's good milk. I've got proof. There was a baby in the village not thriving, premature she was, and the doctors couldn't find a remedy for her. She was sinking, slowly I admit, but sinking. Her mother started giving her milk from my cows, in desperation I'll grant you that, and the blessed little thing began to put weight on and now she's running about like a good 'un. What better testimonial can you have than that?"

Scott shook his head. "None."

"It doesn't make sense. I'll be off. Where's my billhook? That sparky young lass took it off me. She's a grand girl, she is.

Spirit she's got, that's what I like in a woman. Spirit. Same as my Blossom."

Mr. Parsons took the billhook from Kate and gave her a wink—well, she thought he gave her a wink; it was difficult to tell.

"Bye-bye, Mr. Parsons. Nice to have met you."

"And you. At least I've livened up your morning."

"You have indeed."

Mr. Parsons wagged a finger at her. "You could do worse than that Aussie. He's a grand chap."

The big outer doors were shut this morning because of the cold and they all waited until he'd closed them behind him before they began to laugh. The laughter ripped through the reception area like a whirlwind, swirling and twirling back and forth, bubbling and frothing, clearing away the panic and the fear. Joy had to wipe her eyes and Stephie was taking great gulps of her coffee to help her pull herself together. "I have never witnessed anything like that before. Heck! Was I frightened! And you, Kate! You were so brave."

Joy agreed. "She most certainly was. I don't know how you dared to speak to him like that."

Suddenly Kate had gone weak at the knees and had to grip the edge of the desk to keep herself up. "Neither do I. I feel very odd."

Scott moved a chair up behind her and pushed her down on to it. "You're a heroine, that's what."

Graham and Rhodri sheepishly retreated into their consulting rooms, feeling less than manly at having allowed a mere female to take command.

"I think I'm going to be sick." Kate rushed out through the back. Scott suggested he follow her but Joy shook her head. "I'll go in a minute. Leave her alone for now." She went out from behind the desk to speak to the waiting clients. "Sorry about that. Everyone feeling all right?" She spoke to each in turn, offering them coffee or tea if anyone needed reviving. "It was a nasty shock for us all. I'll gladly get you something if you would like me to."

"He needs locking up. The thumping big idiot. Scaring the living daylights out of us! He's always been a bit cracked, even at school. Poor Scott. You all right, are you, Scott? You've Kate to thank. She didn't half stand up to him."

"She did. You should take her out tonight for a slap-up meal, to thank her."

"All in favor?"

They all voted in favor and Scott declared he had no alternative, but dare he take her out? Was he a match for such a tough sheila?

An elderly client, clutching a cage with a sad, almost featherless canary in it, suggested he could take her instead if he liked, if Kate was too much for him.

The clients were still roaring with laughter when Graham Murgatroyd opened his door and called for his next appointment. The elderly client with the canary stood up saying, "Another offer coming in. What it is to be in demand! Where are you taking me tonight, then, Graham?"

"I beg your pardon?"

They all laughed again.

"As I say, it's better than the theater coming here. You should sell tickets, Joy."

But Joy had gone to check on Kate.

Chapter

· 8 ·

There were words on the screen and she hadn't put them there. Kate leaped from her chair in fear. How could they possibly be there when she hadn't typed them in? She took a sideways look at the screen, too afraid to look straight at it.

TUESDAY. YOU'VE FORGOTTEN YOU'RE MY GIRL.
I'LL PICK YOU UP WHEN YOU FINISH AT SEVEN.
SEE YOU! DON'T BE LATE!

Kate paced up and down her tiny office. Back and forth. Back and forth. It wasn't Scott playing the fool, she knew that, because he called her his "sweet one," never using that controlling phrase "my girl," and he wouldn't do that kind of thing anyway, not Scott. Oh God! How had it got there? She hadn't seen Adam for weeks now, not since they'd met by accident at the mall. Goose bumps broke out all over her skin. Was it a coincidence that they'd met or had he been . . . ?

The door opened and the handle hit Kate in her back.

It was Joy. "Oh, I'm so sorry! I didn't expect you to be standing behind the door. I've found the printouts from last year you wanted . . . Why, Kate, whatever's the matter? You look as if you've seen a ghost."

Kate tucked her trembling hands into her armpits so Joy couldn't see how upset she was. "I don't feel very well."

"I can see that. Look, sit down. These figures can wait awhile. I'll get you a glass of water; stay there."

Joy held the glass out for Kate and she managed to stop shaking long enough to take a sip.

"Go on, take another. It always works and I don't know why."

"Thank you."

"Do you feel faint?"

"Not really."

"Then how do you feel?"

Kate looked up and wondered whether or not to tell. It was stupid. She'd got this whole thing totally out of proportion. How could Adam have put that on her computer? He had no access to it unless . . .

"Would you like to go home?"

Kate answered even before Joy had finished speaking: "No, thanks. I'd rather stay here. Dad's working and Mia's gone to an exhibition today, so there's no one at home. I'll be all right in a minute. Thank you." Kate tried half a smile but it didn't emerge properly.

Joy propped herself against the desk. "You're as white as the proverbial sheet. If you were to ask me, I'd say you were frightened. Or you've had a shock."

Kate shook her head. "Neither. Must be flu starting or something."

"Come on, Kate, I'm not a fool. I'm not being nosey; I just want to help."

"I know and I'm grateful. Please, I'm feeling better now. Thanks for the water."

"Very well. But I'm here to help, you know. Anytime."

"Thank you."

"Give me a shout. I'll be on the desk if you need me. I don't want to come across you in a dead faint over the keyboard, you know, so don't hesitate."

"I'll shout if I need you."

"Good. I'll leave the door open in case." Joy kicked the doorstop into place, gave her a generous smile and left Kate to her fears.

Tuesday. You've forgotten you're my girl. I'll pick you up when you finish at seven. See you! Don't be late! She hadn't imagined it. It was still there. Somehow he'd got in and done this when no one was about. There was too much going on all day for him to have done it when the hospital was open. So it had happened between about eight o'clock in the evening and eight o'clock in the morning. Occasionally a vet could be doing an emergency operation during the night if there'd been a road accident or something, but that was rare, very rare, so his chances of being observed during those hours were slim. Had he a key? That was unlikely too. Joy had a key, and Mungo Price and Miriam had keys, but no one else.

She had to delete it. But before she did, she'd print it out. It rolled out of the printer with her figures in the top half and Adam's words below typed in capitals and bold print so there would be no missing it. He'd been in here, sat in this chair, her chair, and done it. She'd left it with the screen saver on last night, so he'd known exactly where she'd last worked on the accounts and that she would see it immediately, simply by touching the mouse and clearing the saver. Well, there was one thing for certain: She wouldn't leave it switched on again. Never. But this wasn't the end of it, was it? The clock wouldn't stop ticking just because she'd swiped the screen clear of his words, would it? It would be seven o'clock at seven o'clock as sure as night followed day, wouldn't it? And he'd be there, waiting.

The memory of his hand tightening on her wrist, the grasping hand on her knee, the smell of onion on his breath . . . Her heart began racing as it had that night when she'd run like hell for the string of lights in Sainsbury's car park.

Adam's physical presence loomed in her mind so vividly that he could have been in the room with her. The comforting sound of Joy sympathizing with a client brought Kate to her senses. She'd been famous at school for her common sense and it asserted itself now. She was being completely ridiculous. Adam had something better to do than run about in the night gaining entrance to the office and typing threatening messages on her computer. After all, as he so frequently had said, he needed his sleep with the important job he held. She could hear him saying, "I've a big week on this week, got to get some early nights." Of course Adam, with his rigid timetable, his everything-by-the-book attitude toward life, wouldn't be tramping about in the night, would he? His mother would have something to say if he did. Kate laughed at herself. Hell's bells, she could be stupid, she could! She took the sheet of paper from the printer, folded it and put it in her bag.

She pressed the delete key and got on with her work. But somehow Adam's face kept coming between her and the screen. At one o'clock she should have gone home and then come back at four, but she didn't. She should have gone out to buy lunch but instead she asked Stephie to bring her something back. Her excuse was catching up on the accounts, but it was all fabricated nonsense so that she didn't have to leave the safety of the practice. Still, she had not resolved the question of what to do at seven. Inexorably the clock ticked on, and even though the evening surgery was very busy, the problem of Adam was ever present in her mind. Kate knew she musn't go out to the car park alone if his car was there. Then a thought occurred to her. "Scott's late back, isn't he, Joy?"

"Yes. Up to something, I suppose. He is such a naughty boy."

"Naughty he might be, but you like him."

"Oh yes! Such fun so long as you don't take him seriously." She looked curiously at Kate. "Feeling better?"

It was on the tip of her tongue to confide her problem to Joy when Scott burst through the back door calling, "Hi! Here comes the golden boy."

Joy and Kate burst out laughing. Joy spoke first. "Honestly, Scott! What are we going to do with you? Golden boy indeed."

"I am! I slave day in day out. I do more nights than anyone else for a start and I get all the rotten jobs, like Applegate Farm *again*."

"It was Sunny Boy, wasn't it, this time?"

"Sunny Boy. Yes. My God, a bull and a half! Why he keeps a bull I'll never know. A.I. would be much easier and cheaper than feeding that monster. He's like putty in Phil Parsons's hands, I swear, meek as a lamb, he is. One look at me, though, and his hooves are scraping the ground and his eyes are rolling. I tell you he'll be the death of me one day, he will."

Kate asked what his problem was.

"Infected foot, *again*. But you try getting a peek at it. Oh, mate! He's dynamite." He pulled up his trouser leg and showed them a huge, sickening bruise developing on his leg where Sunny Boy had kicked him. "Wonder he didn't crack my shin."

"Did you get a peek?"

"I did." Scott bowed elegantly, hoping for applause. "Any chance of Kate going early?" Ignoring the fact there were three clients still waiting their turn he added, "It's a quarter to and the place is empty."

Joy caught Kate's eye and raised an eyebrow. She nodded

and Joy said, "Just this once, and because it's you asking, she can go. She deserves to go, she's been working since eight this morning. I'll finish here."

Kate said, "Thanks. I do appreciate it."

Her relief at having someone to leave with was immense but short lived, because when they went out of the back door into the car park, there was Adam, sitting waiting. But what shocked Kate more than anything was that he'd changed his car; it was no longer that nauseating purple thing but a slimy kind of diarrhea color, one even more decrepit than his last. So he could have been following her and she'd never realized.

"What the merry hell is he doing waiting? Have you promised to go out with him?" One glance at her face and the panic registered there and Scott had his answer. "The sod!" He made to go across to him.

"Scott, don't aggravate him, please, for my sake." He picked up on her fear and stopped in his tracks. "Get in your car and lock the doors, then set off for home and I'll follow, and for God's sake keep control of yourself. I don't fancy facing Mia if her little joy has been involved in a road accident. Take care."

The journey home was a nightmare. There'd been an accident with a lorry carrying timber, which had caused it to shed its load across the road so the traffic had to be diverted, and the major road works close to home slowed her down so much that by the time she reached the house, only a very small part of her brain was controlling her driving and the rest was in complete terror. Scott had stayed stuck to her tail the whole time, twice going through the lights at red so as not to lose her. She'd no idea if Adam had followed them, but if he had, her father and Scott together would deal with him and she could get to Mia and safety.

Scott was parked and out of his car by the time she'd picked up her things and unlocked her door. "Come on. He gave up following us at the diversion. When we get inside, you can tell your dad all about it." He locked her car for her, took a grip on her elbow and led her up the path.

Kate flung her things down on the chair in the hall and called out, "I've brought someone home!"

Mia came into the hall from the kitchen. "Oh, hello! It's Scott, isn't it? Do come through into the back."

"If it's not an intrusion."

"Not at all. Have you eaten?"

"Not had a bite since breakfast."

Mia was horrified. "That's disgraceful; you're neglecting yourself. You'll eat with us." Having got over her surprise at seeing Scott, Mia looked properly at Kate. "Kate! You look dreadful. What's the matter?"

"Nothing at all. Really. It's me being daft."

Mia gave her a hug and said, "We'll eat first, then you can tell me. It's soup and salad tonight, Scott, because I've been out most of the day. Will that do?"

"Of course; it sounds great."

Mia called upstairs, "Gerry! We've got company. Scott's arrived, from the practice. Come on down and open a beer for him." They heard Gerry's muffled voice call a cheerful "OK" from the attic and in a moment his feet pounding down the stairs.

Mia confided to Scott, "He keeps his train set up there."

Gerry shook hands with Scott, pumping his hand up and down with great energy. "Good to see you, Scott. What a pleasure. Kate, love." He offered her his cheek for a kiss and said, "Not got 4X, Scott. Will John Smith's do or would a lager fit the bill better?"

"A John Smith's, please. Mia says you have a train set upstairs."

Gerry's face lit up. "I have indeed. Are you an enthusiast?"

"No. But that doesn't mean I wouldn't like to see it."

"Have we time, Mia?"

"No."

"Let's sit down, then, and we'll have a go afterward. You'll have a surprise." Mia laid an extra place and got the glasses for their beer, keeping an eye on Kate at the same time, for she knew things weren't right, but it wasn't until Scott sat back after he'd rounded off his meal with two slices of Mia's apple pie that she spoke up. "Well, then, Kate. You've not eaten much and you've said even less and I'd like to know, and I'm quite sure Gerry does, what the matter is."

Both Gerry and Mia gave audible gasps of astonishment when Kate told them about the message on her computer. When she added that Adam was there waiting for her when she and Scott went out to their cars, Gerry said, "That's it. That is it. He has finally overstepped the mark. Gerry Howard can take so much and then *finito!*" He banged his clenched fist on the table and made the cups jump. "I can't believe it of him. He's sat here and eaten meal after meal at our table, been a guest in our house and this is what he does. You were right, our Kate, to say he wasn't for you, absolutely damn right."

Mia said in a quieter than usual voice, "I'm not very clever where computers are concerned, but how did he get a message on to yours? How did he do it? I mean, did he have to touch the keyboard to do it?"

Kate nodded.

"You mean he gained entry to the building, sat in your chair and then typed it?"

Scott answered her question with a nod, adding for good measure, "I've always said he's a nutter."

Gerry applauded his assessment. "You're damned right. I never suspected that side of him, did I, Mia?"

"You did not, Gerry. Question is, what shall we do about it?"

Scott snorted his anger at Adam's behavior and suggested, "Beat him up?"

Gerry opened his mouth to agree with him, but Mia got in first. "I find it hard to believe that Adam is behaving like this; it is so out of character. I mean, what was he doing in the mall on the day you bumped into him if he has that promotion? There's no way he would step so far out of line as to be missing from work. Has he actually *said* he's got the job?"

Kate thought for a moment and recalled his words. "It was me who said, 'You've got the job,' and he agreed with me; he answered, 'You said it.'"

Scott nodded. "That's right; I was there. He didn't actually *say* he'd got the job."

"There you are, then. There's one thing about Adam, he never lies."

"But that doesn't mean he didn't stay put in the job he already had, does it? I mean, he must still be working. He's certainly spoken about his job as though he is," Kate said.

"Oh yes, of course. Silly me. You're right, of course. Just me letting my imagination run away with me."

Kate, keeping her eyes on the table for fear of giving away how worried she was, went on, "What's worse, he's changed his car, hasn't he, Scott? So he could have been keeping watch on me and I haven't realized because I was on alert for his old purple one."

Mia said quietly, "It gets worse by the hour."

Mia's heartfelt comment pierced Scott's habitual bravado and he stayed mute while he studied his situation. Why on earth was he, a free-thinking, free-as-a-bird chap, involving himself in this? According to his lights, any self-respecting twenty-seven-year-old Aussie partway through the ritual blooding of working his way around the world didn't stop in one place more than six months. It wasn't done, it didn't fit the picture and eight months would be up before he knew it. He looked across the table at Kate, caught her glance as she looked up and he swallowed hard. She was quality, was Kate. Real quality. Not some common or garden sheila to be picked up and dropped when he got bored. Kate smiled at him, a sweet, nervous smile, and he smiled back. If he wasn't careful . . .

Gerry, who'd been doing some deep thinking while they'd been speculating, burst out with, "Nevertheless, Mr. Price ought to know that Adam's gotten into the building. We'd be guilty of conniving if we didn't tell him what we know."

"I'll tell him tomorrow."

"Tomorrow, my girl, either Mia or I will take you to work and bring you home. Scott can't always be about when you need him. You're a good chap for seeing to Kate tonight, Scott, and I want to thank you man to man for looking after her." Gerry stood up and shook Scott's hand.

"There's no need for that, Dad. I can manage."

"Till we know the facts you'll do as I say. Tell them your car's in need of serious repair and they can't find the parts. Anything but have you traveling about on your own. You agree with me, don't you, Scott?" Gerry gave him a meaningful look and Scott took the hint.

"I most certainly do. If there's an evening like tonight, Kate could ring you and I'd bring her home and save you the journey. My hours are unpredictable, so I can't promise . . ."

"You're being ridiculous, Dad; Adam wouldn't hurt a fly. We all know that. I'm perfectly capable of seeing myself home. I won't be carried about like a child."

"You will."

"I won't."

"You will, Kate, because I say so. It was bad enough that night you had to run away from him. Heaven alone knows what he might do next."

Scott's ears pricked up at Gerry's words, but Mia shook her head at him and he said nothing except, "The train set?"

Gerry jumped to his feet, eager to show off the pride of his life, and they disappeared upstairs. Kate and Mia knew that would be the last they'd see of them for at least two hours.

"I NEED to have a word with Mr. Price, Joy, this morning. His first appointment is at ten. Do you think he might see me before then?"

"You're not wanting a reference, are you? You're not leaving?"

"No, I'm not, but I do need a word about something. Can I tell you all about it later?"

"Of course. I'll give him a buzz right now and schedule you."

"Thanks."

Mungo came downstairs at nine o'clock to find Kate in the accounts office entering the previous day's veterinary calls in the computer. He closed the door behind him and sat down on her spare chair. "Well, now, Kate, I understand you need a word with me."

Kate dreaded having to tell him. In her small office his aura was striking, and she felt him to be too big for the available space, but she had to inform him clearly and concisely without any silly girlish panic. So she began at the beginning and told him about their estrangement, and how Adam had obviously got into the practice building at some stage. Out of her handbag she took the printout she'd done and handed it to him to read.

"If he hadn't trespassed, I would never have told you, because obviously it's a personal matter, but he has and my dad said I must."

Mungo read it and commented, "It couldn't be someone here having a joke?"

"I don't think so. He uses the expression 'my girl,' which is a favorite of his. I'm sure it was him and of course he was here to meet me like he said he would, but Scott followed my car home for safety's sake and Adam lost us at the road works."

"Mm. I'm most concerned about this for your sake. It's not at all pleasant. There's also theft or destruction to be thought of. If someone is very determined to get at the drugs, nothing we can do will stop them, besides which there's the operating equipment and such. We've a lot of money invested here, you know. Do you think he's likely to do it again?"

"He's behaving so out of character I really don't know what he'll do next." Some of the horror of it overcame her and tears came into her eyes. "It's making me feel dreadful; it's like being stalked."

"It *is* being stalked, make no mistake. Have you spoken to him about it?"

Kate shook her head.

"No, perhaps that's wise. You don't happen to have a photograph of him, do you?"

"A photograph? For the police, you mean?"

"Not yet. Have you met Johnnie?"

"Johnnie? No."

"He cleans for us. Most often he cleans at night, but sometimes he takes a turn and has to come very early in the morning instead and get it all done before we open up. Johnnie King his name is. He's deaf and it will make it much easier to explain what we suspect if I can show him a photograph. This Adam must have come in while he's been here, you see, and he must be told not to let him in."

"How can you explain if he's deaf?"

"He lip-reads and I use sign language too. Known him for years. He's a great chap. He does a good job, doesn't he?"

"He does. It's always immaculate."

"Exactly. I admire him. He gets on with his life, earns a living, doesn't expect preferential treatment and cares for his father in the bargain." Mungo took her hand. "Has your dad had a word with this Adam?"

"No."

"I think he should. I shall tell Joy; leave it to me. Don't tell the others; best not for now." He got up to go. "Oh! Photograph?"

"Tomorrow, will that do? Scott knows, though, because he was with me last night when I was leaving, like I said."

"I'll tell Scott to keep mum. Take great care of yourself, Kate. These situations can escalate in no time at all." He patted her hand, gave her one of his radiant smiles and made to go, saying before he closed the door, "Joy will murder me if anything happens to you. She thinks very highly of you."

At home, Mia spent the morning painting. This one was for an exhibition she'd been invited to put on in the major library in the town. Small potatoes, really, in the scheme of things but important to her. It was of Kate as a little girl. She'd used her facial features several times and the results had always sold well. She could put her in any century and somehow she always fitted the bill. This time the neckline of her dress was that of an early nineteenth-century girl about seven years old. People often assumed that her paintings were of real people because they looked so full of character, so taken from life. Mia liked it best when she wasn't working to order from photographs because it meant she could use her imagination; photos were so limiting artistically.

Thinking about photos brought to mind the one Kate had chosen to take to the practice that morning. Of Adam on the harbor at West Bay with Kate. "Cut yourself off that photo before you give it to Mr. Price," Mia had said in the car on the way. "I don't want you on it with him. How could he be doing this to you? He must have gone mad."

So Kate had cut herself off with some nail scissors out of Mia's bag and Mia had wished it was as easy to get rid of Adam for real. He was tenacious, certainly, and obsessive. Two characteristics Mia hadn't much of a fancy for. No one seemed to be alarmed by the fact that he appeared to have so much time for wandering about during the day. So why did he? No job, that's what. Obviously. Being so self-obsessed, he couldn't tolerate such a letdown. He hadn't got the promotion and he'd been sacked, and there was no way he would admit it, especially in front of Scott. Mia frowned. She'd find out. Yes, she would. She'd ring his office and ask to speak to him. That would give her the answer. If a receptionist said, "I'll put you through," she'd put the receiver down quickly, but if he had been sacked, they'd also give her the answer. Either way she would *know*.

The excitement of her little scheme made her hand jerk and a streak of the red she'd been using for Kate's lips ran across her face and made it look as though Kate had been knifed from lip to ear. Mia was horrified. What had she done? Was this a sign of what was to come? She quickly picked up one of her tiny blades and scraped the blood-red away before it began to dry. Once her portrait had been put to rights, Mia put down her brush.

She poured herself a drink of water and sipped it to make sure her voice wouldn't be croaky when she spoke. Mia practiced out loud what she would say. "Could you put me through to Mr. Pentecost, please? Adam Pentecost." Or "I want to speak to Adam Pentecost, please." Or "I'm replying to Mr. Pentecost's call." If they asked who it was, she'd give a false name; call herself Betty Lomax. That was it. Right. Here we go. Before she dialed the number, she questioned which answer she wanted. Did she want "Yes, I'll put you through" or "I'm sorry, Mr. Pentecost no longer works here?" Preferably the former because then perhaps he would seem less of a danger; if it was the latter, then . . . "Could I speak to Mr. Pentecost, please?"

"Mr. Pentecost? I'm sorry, no one of that name works here anymore."

"But he must; he suggested I ring."

"I'm sorry, he left last month."

"Can you tell me where he works now, then?"

"Sorry, I'm not able to divulge any personal details."

"It must have been sudden; it's only a matter of a few weeks since he suggested I ring him. Such a very nice man, he seemed." Mia let a kind of throwing-myself-on-your-mercy tone enter her voice, a tone inviting confidences, and it worked.

"Truth to tell, he was dismissed. Instantly. A kind of 'thank you but no thank you' and he left that afternoon. Worked here since leaving school. He'd fully expected to be promoted but instead . . . well . . . curtains. Terrible shock."

"I'm sure it must have been. Thank you anyway for your help; you're most kind."

"Not at all. Good morning." And she was off, answering another call, no doubt.

But Mia was left worrying. She put away her painting. It was no good trying to do such minutely delicate work when she was upset, because all she'd do was what she'd done already: make it look as though Kate had been attacked. She thought of herself as a perceptive person and sat in front of the Rayburn, considering what should be done next. He ought to be warned to leave her alone, but by whom? The police? Gerry? Scott with his beat-him-up attitude? But would Adam ever *do* something serious? Maybe it was all fantasy and quite harmless. But somehow it wasn't harmless, was it? Not anymore, not after leaving a message on her computer. And he was guilty of deception of the highest order, giving the impression he'd been promoted.

He couldn't face up to the reality of being sacked. How cruel people were nowadays. What a blow to a man, or a woman come to that. Instant dismissal. But at least Adam hadn't a wife and children, and a huge mortagage—he was footloose and fancy free. Oh no, he wasn't! He was obsessed by Kate.

She leaned back in her chair and thought about Kate; the nineteen years of caring more and more as each year went by. She'd been a handful always, on the go right from the moment she was on her feet. Into everything, talking in sentences long before most children did and so loving, her dear little Kate had been. So loving. Still was. Mia picked up her bag and took out the piece of the photograph Kate had cut off that morning in the car. The wind was blowing her hair and she was laughing. Mia had a sentimental moment while she sat there admiring and loving. If anything ever happened to her to stop the laughter, to spoil that lovely face, she'd . . . If she peered closely at it, she could see Adam's hand, left behind on Kate's shoulder. Angrily she hunted for the scissors in her bag and snipped off the hand. There. Nothing of Adam left. If only it would prove as easy in reality.

"Hello!"

"Gerry! Is that you?"

"Who else!"

He stood in the doorway. "Forgot my lunch." He spotted the obvious distress on her face. "What's up, Mia? What's happened?"

"Adam lost his job. He didn't get the promotion."

"But he said . . ."

"He didn't actually, you know; it was Kate assuming he had and he let it ride because he couldn't face up to the fact that he'd been sacked. A man like him with such an opinion of himself, and yet so scared of life he couldn't abide change or spontaneity of any kind, wouldn't be able to, would he? Such a blow to his ego, besides being a terrible shock. Now he has nothing to do but hang around after Kate."

"How do you know all this?"

"I rang his firm. Asked to speak to him."

"Mia!"

"I found out what we wanted to know, though, didn't I?"

Gerry picked up the photo of Kate from the table and studied it. "What can we do?"

"I think you should go and see him. Kate mustn't, but you could."

"Me?" Gerry didn't see himself as a diplomat or, if he'd thought about it, as a James Bond either. "Me? What would I say?"

"You'd think on your feet; you're good at that. I won't have something happen to Kate simply because we did nothing to help her. If he should get at her . . ." Mia wept, her shoulders shaking with her fear.

Gerry put his arm round her. "Come on, Mia, it won't come to that. Of course not. We're getting things out of proportion."

Mia blew her nose loudly and choked out the words, "Go, please go and see him. Tell him. Please. I mean it."

To pacify her, he agreed to go. "But not right now. I'll go after work, tonight."

"Thank you. I know you'll say the right thing." Mia took his hand in hers and squeezed it. "You know how much I love her."

"I do. I've always been grateful for that. More than grateful."

Mia cheered up after he said that and went into the kitchen to make Gerry his lunch. She called out, "I forgot about your lunch with taking Kate to work. Ham all right?"

"Fine." He'd call on Adam tonight.

But instead, he went straight from their house to Adam's. If the fellow was out of work, he'd likely be at home, wouldn't he? There'd be no point in Adam's hanging about waiting for Kate at this time of day and the sooner it was faced up to, the better, in his opinion.

He'd never been to Adam's house, though Kate had pointed it out to him. The terrace of stone cottages stretched right from the riverbank to the council park—a quiet, secluded lane with desirable cottages, some smartened up and modernized, others as they'd been for a century and more.

He found number fifteen and pulled up outside. It was so entirely clean, it was hard to believe that Mrs. Pentecost hadn't been out since dawn scrubbing down the outside walls and polishing the windows. Not a spider's web or a speck of dust anywhere; not a single patch of flaking paint. The net curtains lined up like soldiers on parade. In the window boxes were winter pansies, their faces turned to the autumn sunshine, planted with such precision he doubted they'd ever dare to die. There was something unnerving about the exactness of it all. Something almost . . . Gerry couldn't find the right word but *obsessive* crept into his mind.

He got out and went to rattle the brass knocker. At first he thought they weren't in, but then he heard footsteps. The door opened a few inches and a face very like Adam's came into view.

"Yes?"

"Good morning. I'm Gerry Howard. I've come to see Adam."

The door opened wider. "Oh, you're Kate Howard's father?"

Gerry nodded.

"He's at work."

"He is?"

The door opened wider still. "Come in. Come in. You can leave a message."

The chill of the house struck Gerry as soon as he walked

in. Because it was a cottage entrance, the front door opened straight into the living room and it seemed he'd walked into an immaculately kept shrine. On every well-polished surface stood photographs of Adam in all stages of his life: the naked baby on the sheepskin rug, the toddler playing with his brightly painted wooden engine, the schoolboy in his too-big blazer, the teenager in athletic kit holding up a trophy, and in pride of place on the mantelpiece was Adam in cap and gown. *Oh God!* thought Gerry. *If I hadn't had Mia to keep me in check, I'd have had Kate all over our sitting room too.* Mrs. Pentecost went to a drawer in a table under the window. "Here, write on this." She didn't have to root about in the drawer to find a piece of paper as Mia would have had to do, because all there was in the drawer was a writing pad and a pen.

She handed them to him and waited.

"I've nothing to write; I wanted to see him."

"But I said he isn't here. He's at work. He won't be home until half past six at the earliest. That promotion he got is keeping him so busy, but then what can you expect when a young executive is climbing the ladder of success? They have to put in all the hours, haven't they?"

Had Mia got it wrong, then? "You must be proud of him."

"I am. It will be lovely when Kate and he marry and we all live together in the one house."

When what she'd said had registered, Gerry cringed with disgust at the future planned out for his Kate.

"We went to look around one the other day, Adam and I. Bigger than this, of course, as suits an executive. I shall have company all day and someone to look after me then. I'm so looking forward to it. I'm not in good health, you see."

Gerry dared a stupid question: "Kate like it, did she?"

"She's going at the weekend with Adam. Just the two of

them. You know what it's like when you're in love. You don't want a doddery old mother with you, do you?" She smiled coyly, asking him to deny her dodderiness.

Gerry got the distinct impression as he looked at her that she was no more decrepit than he himself. "I see. Kate hasn't said."

"I think Adam's keeping it as a surprise."

"It will certainly be that. Look, I'll call back tonight if I may—catch Adam in then."

"I'll tell him you're coming. Oh, he won't be in, though. It's Tuesday, so he'll be going tenpins bowling with Kate. He'll be picking her up at your house."

Gerry began to think he might be going insane, but swept along by her self-delusion, he entered into her crazy charade. "Of course, I'd forgotten it's Tuesday. I'll see him tonight at our house, then. I was thinking it was Kate's night for seeing her tutor." As soon as the words were out of his mouth, he knew that was the last reason he should have given, because word for word it would be relayed to Adam and he'd know what Kate had decided.

Gerry shook Mrs. Pentecost's hand and levered himself out of the door. Standing on the pavement, he felt such a rush of relief to have escaped he was almost skipping. "Bye-bye, Mrs. Pentecost. Nice to have met you."

Gerry drove away down the street a little, then pulled up and dialed Mia on his mobile. She wasn't in, so he left a message: "It's me. I've called at the house and he wasn't in, but she was and she's crackers, I'm certain. Please, Mia, pick up Kate tonight, won't you? I'll explain when I see you. I might be late, but I'll do my best. Bye, love. Keep the doors locked when you get home, just in case."

Who was deluding whom? Was his mother aware Adam was out of work and, knowing what a blow it was to him, going along with his deception for his sake? Or had he deceived her so completely that she truly believed he had been promoted and was working all hours? Did he, then, on Tuesdays get his ludicrous tenpins bowling outfit on and set out as though calling for Kate? If so, the matter was far more serious than he had ever imagined. What a tragic mess the pair of them were in.

Gerry had to swerve to miss a car pulling out at a traffic circle, which forced him to put his mind on driving and work. He'd deal with it all when he got back home. Had Gerry foreseen the events that would take place that night because of his unwitting revelation that Kate was having tutoring, he would not have thrown himself with such vigor into persuading a new outlet to take his superb collection of biscuits specially put together for the Christmas trade. They were so tempting that he could eat a whole box himself straight off.

College of the Ouachitas

Chapter

· 9 ·

That same afternoon Kate was scheduled to go to Miss Chillingsworth's to pick up the kittens. But having been taken to work by Mia, it was Miriam who volunteered to drive her there.

"She's really quite poor, you know, Mrs. Price. Genteel poverty, Mia would call it. But she's a total dear and absolutely thrilled to have been so useful to us. She's done a good job. They're all toilet trained, which is brilliant."

"There's no need to apologize for her, Kate."

"I'm sorry, I didn't mean to."

"Right turn here, is it?" They'd reached the traffic lights by the church.

"That's it and then second left. These houses are lovely, aren't they? I'd like to live in one of these. Kind of stately and Victorian."

"Rather large for Miss Chillingsworth."

"Much too large, but I think it's the house she grew up in and it's hard to leave."

"I can understand that. Clinging to memories." Miriam

went silent for a moment and Kate didn't know if it was because she was concentrating on driving or if her last three words had given her food for thought. "Here we are. What number did you say?"

"Twelve. Prospect House. That's it there."

Miriam applied the hand brake and asked if she should come in or wait. "Oh, come in! She loves company."

Miss Chillingsworth was at the door almost before the bell had stopped resounding through the house. Overcome with embarrassment when she saw Miriam, she declared, "Why, Mrs. Price, what an honor! I'd no idea. Do come in."

"Kate's car is being repaired, so I've brought her. I'll wait if you prefer."

"Not at all. Come in, do."

She led the way down the hall toward the kitchen. Their footsteps echoed on the bare wooden floorboards and Miriam wondered if the floor was bare through choice or necessity, and thought more than likely it was the latter. There were pale square and oblong patches here and there on the wallpaper and it occurred to her that pictures had been sold to make ends meet.

"Here they are!" Miriam exclaimed. The kittens were playing king of the castle on an old wooden apple box in the middle of the kitchen floor. They'd grown almost beyond recognition. "Haven't they grown! The last time I saw them they were scarcely toddling and look at them now. Twice the size and twice as confident. You've worked miracles."

Miss Chillingsworth was delighted by Miriam's praise and clapped her hands with pleasure. "You think so? It's been a privilege to look after them and I'm so grateful to have had the chance."

"You're grateful! It's we who are grateful, isn't it, Kate?"

"It most certainly is. We'd never have been able to give them such a lovely time. They're wonderful. I just wish I were taking that one home."

"But they're all spoken for, you said."

Hastily Kate agreed. "Yes, they are. I was only wishing. As I said, my stepmother has a tendency to asthma anyway, so anything furry is out."

Miss Chillingsworth showed instant concern. "Of course, you said."

"Here, look, I've brought the carrier. Let's get them in."

She could tell this was the moment Miss Chillingsworth was dreading, so it was best to get it over with briskly. Kate was so relieved to have got away with her slip of the tongue, because though they hadn't anyone for the third kitten, not for the world would she tell Miss Chillingsworth. She knew in her bones that the time was not ripe for her to be taking on a kitten of her own.

"Oh, I've got tins left. I'll get them for you."

"I'll be putting them in the car while you do." Kate slipped out down the hall and left Miriam to wait for the tins.

Miss Chillingsworth emerged backward from the pantry with half a carton of tins and a bag of cat litter in her arms. "Here we are."

"Thank you for all your hard work. We couldn't possibly have done such a good job. Thank you for all your time and patience."

"Not at all. I've enjoyed myself. Helped to fill a gap, you know."

Miriam smiled at her and Miss Chillingsworth felt warmed by it. "You're all such lovely people at the practice. I do miss seeing you."

Tears welled in her eyes and Miriam sensed the pain that

was Miss Chillingsworth's. "If we should have kittens in need of loving care again, could we perhaps rely on you?"

"Of course. Gladly." She was eager to close the door and Miriam made her retreat as swiftly as she could, realizing that Miss Chillingsworth would not want to break down in front of her.

Kate turned to look at her as she settled herself in the driving seat. "I don't really know what it is to be lonely. Her loneliness makes me terribly sad."

Miriam said, "Clinging to old memories is what is making her life so difficult. If she sold it, she'd get a tremendous price for that house, and she could buy a much smaller one and live comfortably on the residue. That's the sad bit about it all." She started up the engine and moved off. "We all have a lesson to learn from her predicament, haven't we?"

Kate nodded and except for the mewing of the kittens in the back, there was no further sound in the car until they arrived at the practice.

Waiting for them in reception was the client wanting the all-black kitten. "You've got them, then? My word, haven't they grown." His choice licked his finger as he poked it through the bars. "See, he knows me already. Bless him. I'm calling him Midnight."

Joy had come out to see Duncan's Tiger. "Here they are. Haven't they grown? I can't believe it." She and the client enthused over the kittens together.

Kate lifted the homeless one out of the carrier and took it into the back. She was nursing it on her knee, wishing she could take it home, when Scott returned. He crashed in through the back and caught sight of Kate through the open door. "Kate, my sweet one! How's things?"

"OK, thanks. Do you want a kitten?"

"No, but I know a man who does. Phil Parsons. Someone has poisoned his cats. Poor chap's heartbroken. Unbroken line since his grandfather's days and all gone. I just wish I could catch the sod who's done it."

"Are you pulling my leg?"

Scott shook his head. "Of course not. I'll ring him if you like."

"Please. I'd be so glad to find it a home. But come to think of it, will he take care of it?"

"He may be a farmer with abysmal standards of hygiene, but yes, he will and Blossom certainly will. I'll do it now, right away. We'll take it to them when I've finished and you can see for yourself."

Since Scott had no more calls and Kate finished at four that day, the two of them set off with the kitten in Scott's Land Rover.

"One thing I must say is if they offer you a cup of tea or anything, make up whatever excuse you can think of, but do not in any circumstances drink anything at all. Their kitchen is disgusting and the risk of food poisoning is extremely high."

"Are you certain this is a good idea? I don't want the kitten to die."

"Believe me, it will survive. All his animals do despite the lack of cleanliness. They develop their own immunity." Scott checked the crossroads and glanced at her. "You're special. Know that, do you?"

"Don't be ridiculous and you're being tooted at, so make a move."

"So I am. Why do you always rebuff personal comments?"

"To be honest, I don't usually, but at the moment Adam has completely put me off making relationships with anyone at all." Kate looked out of the window and then turned back to Scott. "You're a lovely person and I do enjoy your company. You're such fun, but the timing's not right. I'll be all right when I've got Adam out of my hair."

"That bloody man. Let's go out on the town tonight, shall we? Forget all about the Adams of this world."

"Can't. Chemistry tonight; it's Tuesday."

"Tomorrow night, then?"

"I'd love that."

Scott braked hard, switched off the engine, put a finger under Kate's chin and gave her head a quarter turn so that she faced him. He studied her features, smiled at the apprehension he saw there and kissed her lips with none of his usual demanding eagerness. "I don't know why it is, but I kiss you quite differently from others."

"It's not very polite to mention all the others you've kissed. It's quite spoiled it for me."

"I'm sorry, but I have to be honest with you."

"Not that honest, surely?"

The kitten began to struggle against being clamped between the two of them.

"Let's go. Got your boots? You'll need them."

"Of course not. You could have told me."

"Good excuse for me to carry you, then."

Which he did. Through the sludge and the mud right to the farmhouse door. She refused to allow herself to be influenced by the smell of his skin or by the manly scratchy feeling of his jacket against her cheek, but it did feel comfortable and welcome, and she thought about Adam and realized he'd never appealed to her physically the way Scott did. In fact, when she thought about it, there had never been anything physically appealing to her about Adam at all. The kitten began to fight against being imprisoned in her jacket and her claws came out.

"Ow!"

Scott laughed. "So the ice maiden has feelings after all."

"I do indeed. The kitten is scratching me. Could you put me down?"

He stood her down on the doorstep, opened the door and shouted, "Mrs. Parsons! It's Scott." They went in.

Blossom Parsons was standing at her cooker stirring something in a pan, which smelled absolutely revolting. Phil was seated in a chair where the heat from the fire drew forth his habitual body smell and distributed it around the kitchen. Kate had difficulty in resisting the impulse to put her handkerchief to her nose.

Scott took off his hat and said, "We've brought her and this is Kate, holding her. You won't have met Kate, Mrs. Parsons."

Blossom lowered the light under the pan and came across. "We've been a whole week without a cat. Isn't she lovely?" She took her from Kate and lifted the kitten to her cheek, burrowing her nose in its fur and luxuriating in the feel of its softness. "Aren't you a beauty? An absolute beauty! Six weeks, you say. She's well grown for six weeks."

"She's had a lot of care," Kate said.

"I can see that. Look, sit down, I'll make a cup of tea. Kettle's boiled already; you won't have long to wait."

"I'm so sorry, but I have evening class tonight and I'm pressed for time. Thanks all the same. But I would be glad to pop over to see the kitten from time to time."

"Any time you like. Scott can bring you and we'll have a cuppa and a good natter. What do you think, Phil, about her?"

Phil, wearing his balaclava even indoors, said, "I'm that pleased to have a cat again. She'll be a bit before she starts catching rats, but I reckon she'll do all right once I've taught her what's expected."

Kate almost blanched at the thought of what Miss Chillingsworth would have to say about this state of affairs—one of her precious charges catching rats! Lying out in the sun and being fed delicious meals of cooked chicken and fresh salmon would be more what she had in mind.

"What will you call her?"

Mrs. Parsons looked coyly at Scott. "I did think of Scott."

"But he says it's a she."

"Cats don't know that, do they? A name's a name to them." Again there was this coy, inviting look and Kate remembered how Joy had said half the women in the county fancied Scott.

Kate laughed. "You're right. I hadn't thought of it like that."

Mrs. Parsons plumped the kitten down on Phil's knee and went back to her pan. "I'll take good care of her. Cats are my most favorite animals. They get treated like royalty here."

Kate found it hard to believe, in the circumstances, but she recognized the love in Mrs. Parsons's voice and had to leave it there and hope for the best.

Scott winkled them out of the situation by reminding Kate of her evening class. "So we've got to go. I'll bring Kate to see you in a while. Good night, little Scott." They left Mrs. Parsons to stirring her stewpot and Mr. Parsons to cuddling little Scott, who had snuggled down on his lap oblivious of the smell and was preparing to go to sleep, warmed by the fire and soothed by the gentle stroking of Mr. Parsons's thick, swollen fingers.

"I'll drive you home. Are you eating first?"

"I am."

"I'll wait, then, and take you to your tutorial."

"No, please, don't do that. I can't allow it. Mia will take me. She'll sit in the car and listen to the radio till I come out."

"You're still not driving your car, then?"

"Dad said not. But he'll calm down in a few days and I'll be a free agent again."

"He's right to be cautious." He bent down, scooped her up and transported her back to the Land Rover.

"This fresh air smells good. Are you sure we've done the right thing, bringing the kitten here?"

"It won't have the pampered existence of most surburban cats, but it will live an interesting life more suited to a cat and you can't ask more than that."

"She fancies you."

Scott sighed. "I know; that's why I call her Mrs. Parsons and never get within a yard of her if I can avoid it."

"It's a terrible burden for you to carry, isn't it?"

His eyebrows raised, Scott asked her what she meant.

"Having all these women taking a shine to you."

"I don't know what you're talking about."

"You do. And you love it."

"Have you taken a shine to me, whatever that might mean?"

"I just might."

Scott thumped the steering wheel and caused the Land Rover to swerve.

They both laughed and he drove her home with more style than safety. They were still laughing and talking when he pulled up outside Kate's house and it wasn't until he heard her sharp intake of breath that he realized something was very wrong.

"What is it?"

"That's Adam's car parked in front of us."

"What the hell's he playing at now?"

"It's Tuesday, tenpins bowling night. He must think we're going bowling!"

"He can't possibly, can he?"

"Is he sitting in his car? Can you see?"

Scott peered as best he could through his windshield, but because of the shadows he couldn't make up his mind as to whether Adam was there or not, so he leaped out and went to see. Adam wasn't sitting in his car, so he must have gone in. *Now what? Bloody hell!* He got back in his Land Rover and said, "He's not there. That's your dad's car in the drive, isn't it? I mean Mia isn't in on her own, is she?"

"No, it's his office car, so he'll be in."

"What the blazes is the nutter playing at?"

Kate gripped her seat with both hands, unable to cope with what she knew inevitably would have to be faced.

"If your dad's there . . ."

"What can he be doing?"

"Let's go find out."

Kate clutched hold of Scott's arm. "Please, no!"

"We can't sit here all night. You need your books for your tutorial. Anyway, perhaps your dad needs some help."

"I can't face Adam."

"I'm with you. I won't let any harm come to you. Believe me."

"If I face him now, do you think we can sort him out?"

"Of course." Scott sounded confident, but in truth he couldn't begin to imagine what might be going on in that lovely friendly kitchen.

"All right, then. But I'm so frightened for Mia and Dad."

"Well, you and I make a good team, and there'll be four of us to his one."

"You don't think he'll have brought his mother, do you?"

Scott snorted his amusement. "Of course not! Why should he?"

He opened the door and went around to Kate's side to help her out. "Here, take my hand and hold on tight."

Kate pulled her hand away from his. "No, if he sees us holding hands, he'll think we're . . . friends."

"We are."

"Yes, but you know what I mean. No, we won't hold hands. Let's go in as if we don't realize he's there and see what happens."

"OK, then."

Kate opened the door and called out cheerfully, "It's only me. Scott's here too. He gave me a lift home."

Both of them sensed the tension in the house the moment they walked in. Panic seemed to hang in the very air, but Kate flung down her bag and coat on the hall chair as she always did and marched into the kitchen. For all the world as though time had been turned back four, five weeks, there sat Adam at the kitchen table with her dad and Mia. A strong smell of burned vegetables came from the pans standing on the cooker. A frying pan held crisply burned onions and liver. Adam had a mug in front of him, the tea in it untouched and the milk in it a cold eddy on the top.

But this wasn't the Adam they had known. This Adam had a nerve twitching in his cheek, which contorted his face every few seconds. This Adam had beads of sweat on his top lip and clenched hands, and a patch of sweat between his shoulder blades showing through his beige tracksuit.

"Hello, Kate! It's Tuesday, so I've come to go bowling." The tightly controlled, precisely enunciated sentences were the words he invariably used each Tuesday, but they sounded very different. This time they were a threat. He hadn't said, "And you'd better come with me or else," but the words hung about on the end of his matter-of-fact statement.

Kate caught Mia's eye and picked up on the very slight warning shake of her head. Gerry looked paralyzed with apprehension. She had to say it. "I can't, not tonight." Adam took a sip of his cold tea. "You may as well know. I'm having some tutoring sessions to help me improve my chemistry grade, and there's one tonight."

"You'd better get your meal or we shall be late. I've booked our lane, you see, for half past seven as usual."

"Can you not hear what I say?"

"I'm feeling in good form tonight. I shall be able to give you a run for your money. I'm really looking forward to beating you." He rubbed his hands together with apparent glee.

"I'm not going."

"Mia! Get Kate her meal. I hate having to rush." Adam's cheek twitched rapidly.

Mia's voice sounded as though she was in the later stages of strangulation. "She's already told you she isn't going."

Gerry spoke up, having found his courage now he had Scott to support him. "There's no one orders my wife about, so you can stop that straightaway. Kate is not going bowling. We've told you and now so has Kate. Now clear out . . . and . . ."

Adam banged on the table with his fist. Some tea in his mug splattered out onto the tablecloth and the stain rapidly spread. "We always go bowling on Tuesdays and that is what we are going to do. Bowling. Right! I've booked the lane and we're going." His cheek twitched violently.

Scott decided to enter the discussion. "See here, mate, Gerry's asked you to leave, but I notice you're still here. Now bug— clear out. Or do you prefer me to throw you out?"

There was no reaction from Adam at all. It was as though Scott weren't even in the room. "I'm afraid I've let my tea go cold, Mia. I'd like a refill while I wait for Kate."

Scott said loudly, "Right then, mate. O-u-t spells *out* and out you are going."

He grabbed Adam by the collar of his tracksuit and heaved him to his feet.

Gerry leaped up with the intention of helping Scott with Adam's departure.

Mia got to her feet shouting, "Be careful!"

Kate opened the kitchen door, assuming that Adam would not resist. But he did. He lashed out at Scott, striking him with a frenzied thrust of his elbow on his mouth and splitting his lip. Incensed, Scott proceeded to manhandle him out of the kitchen and down the hallway, with Gerry urging them on from behind by ramming both his fists ferociously hard against Adam's back. Between them they managed to get him to the front door. It looked like they were losing the battle while Scott struggled to open the front door, but Scott hung on tightly and finally rid them of Adam by planting his safari boot on Adam's backside and shoving him so that Adam sprawled full length on the path. Gerry slammed the door shut and locked it behind him.

Mia shouted as she followed them through from the kitchen, "His car keys! He's left his car keys!"

"Give them to me." Scott snatched them from Mia's hand, pried open the letter box flap and flung them outside onto the path. The snap of the letter box shutting broke the spell of terror.

Between gasps Gerry, bending over with his hands resting on his thighs, said, "My God! . . . You arrived just in time . . . The fella's mad . . . completely mad . . ."

Mia flung her arms round Kate. "Oh, Kate! I was so scared. I thought our end had come."

They hugged and kissed each other in breathless relief.

Scott dabbed at his cut lip and grinned at them. "Good day's work there. You did right not to tackle him on your own, Gerry. He's dangerous."

"What I can't understand is why he completely ignored everything we said. Before you came, Mia and I both told him you wouldn't be going bowling, but it was as if we hadn't spoken. He breezed in, calling out as he always used to as though it were only last Tuesday you'd been out together. He's finally cracked, he has, and with a mother like he's got, it's hardly to be wondered at."

"Dad! When did you meet his mother?"

Gerry explained Mia's telephone call and his morning visit to their cottage, and told of his scalp prickling when he went in and the odd unlived-in feeling the cottage had, and of how mad she was. "They deserve each other, they do."

Mia, still clinging to Kate, said, "He frightened me."

"And me." This from Scott. "He's going to do something dangerous, he is. See that muscle twitching?"

"Could hardly miss it, could we, Mia? It was like that when he came in. We didn't cause it."

"Let's go and sit down again; and I'll get your meal for you, Kate."

They trailed into the kitchen after her, glad of something positive to do. Gerry peered at the crusted contents of the frying pan with a look of distaste on his face. "I shan't ever want liver and onions again."

"Neither shall I." Mia, lifting the lids off her burned vegetables, said, "I don't think I fancy you eating it either, Kate. What shall we do?"

Scott had an idea. "I spotted a fish and chip place down the road. Why not let me go and get some for all of us? That is, if you don't mind me eating with you."

They welcomed the idea. Gerry prepared to get out his wallet, but Scott pooh-poohed him. "No, this is my treat and after we've eaten, I'll take Kate to her class. Save you a job, Mia."

Mia said, "Well, that's very kind. Thank you for your help tonight, Scott. We shall be forever in your debt."

Scott took a bow and headed for the hallway. They heard the door open and as swiftly close. He reappeared in the kitchen saying, "I'll wait a moment, if I may. He's only just stood up."

Gerry asked, "You mean he's still lying there?"

"Looks like a neighbor's just helping him up."

Kate went to the bay window of the sitting room and discreetly peeped out. The neighbor was helping Adam down the path and Adam was moving as though he were sleepwalking. She watched him get into his car and sit doing nothing, then his head went down onto the steering wheel with a jerk time after time, so hard he could almost be thought to be trying to fracture his skull. Her kind heart kicked in and she wished that she could love him as he wanted, and that he were more appealing, and more confident and more . . . well, anyway . . . He wasn't and he never would be. Not for her, anyway, and in a strange, cockeyed way his desperate actions strengthened her resolve to get to college whatever huge amounts of effort it took her. Not for her a wasted life.

The others joined her and watched through the net curtain until finally he drove erratically away and they were all left feeling distressed about him but at the same time glad to see him gone.

Scott took it upon himself to cheer them up. "Right! I'll get the fish and chips, and be back in a flash."

Mia asked him not to bring cod. "Anything but cod. Shall we have wine, Kate?"

"You can. I won't. I need to keep a clear head for my tutorial."

Scott dashed away, and Gerry and Kate sat down at the table while Mia searched for an appropriate wine in the cellar. "You know, Kate," Gerry said, "it always surprises me what a nose Mia has for wine. I don't know where she gets it from."

"Or her painting. Where does she get that talent from? What did her family do, you know, what were they? She never mentions them."

"Orphan. Brought up in a council home. She loathed it;

that's why she never talks about it. I can't understand how she turned out so special. Because she is, isn't she, Kate?"

"Oh yes, and not only to you and me. Other people love her too. Except Adam never did. He thinks she's odd, which she isn't. Funny that, when you think how odd he's become."

Gerry paused with a fork in his hand and he waved it in her direction. "When I think about it, he's always been odd at bottom. I can't imagine why I ever thought him right for you. I have to ask this; does he make you afraid?"

"He does now. You read in books about people being in denial and I think that's what he is. He's denying what's happened because it quite simply isn't acceptable to him that he's lost his job. Without the security of it, you see, he has fallen apart. I reckon his mother knows he's lost his job, but she won't face up to it either."

"God! She's a queer one and not half. I know it gets me annoyed sometimes when I can't find something I want because Mia is so untidy, but I'd rather have that than have it like his mother does."

Mia appeared out of the cellar, holding up a bottle of wine. "I'd forgotten we had this. It's a Miranda Estates Unoaked Chardonnay; should be good with fish. You'll like this, Gerry. I haven't enough time to chill it, but we'll have to put up with that. Look at the time! You'll be late, Kate."

"She's not to be there for half an hour, Mia. Doing well for you, is she, your tutor?"

"Dad! She couldn't be better and when it gets nearer the time, I'm going to go twice a week. She's determined I shall get an A, and so am I."

"Good girl."

Scott came back with piping-hot fish and chips, and by the time they'd finished off their meal with cheese and biscuits and fresh fruit, their good humor was restored. So Kate went off to her tutorial in high spirits—life couldn't be better, she thought.

But in the early hours of the morning she woke, trembling and afraid, with vivid pictures in her head of destruction and death and skeletons—a nightmare just like those she had had as a child. Her first instinct was to rush for comfort to Mia, but before she could act upon it, Mia was standing by her bed. "Kate?" Their arms were around each other even as she spoke.

"I've had a nightmare like I used to. I'm so frightened."

"I know. I know. So am I."

They hugged each other in silence until both felt comforted.

It was Mia who spoke first: "Your dad insists you still mustn't drive alone, so I'll take you and collect you every day. I promise. Somehow we'll sort it, love. Gerry and Scott between them, they'll sort him. You'll see."

Chapter

· 10 ·

Joy put her head around the door of Kate's office and asked, "Are you all right? I thought you looked a bit down when you came in."

The look Joy got in response to her question persuaded her to close the door and sit down. She watched Kate fiddle with her pen, make a pretense of shuffling some papers to her satisfaction, and waited for her to reply.

Eventually Kate answered her: "After we'd taken the kitten to Mr. Parsons, Scott took me home . . ."

"And . . . ?"

"Adam was there, for all the world as though nothing had happened and it was Tuesday and we were going tenpins bowling."

Kate told Joy everything—each detail of what had taken place—and the relief was enormous.

"My dear, it must have been horrific."

"It was. When Dad went to see him, only his mother was there and she said that we were getting married and buying a house and she was coming to live with us."

"Oh, dear! Oh, dear! I don't know what to say. They must have gone completely crackers. How does your father feel about it?"

"He's worried sick and so is Mia and so am I."

"It's the stuff of nightmares."

"You see, apart from trespassing here, he hasn't done anything we could tell the police about. Sitting in someone's house drinking tea isn't a crime, is it?"

Joy shook her head. "I'll talk to Duncan about it. He sees life from a different angle from most people. He may well come up with an answer. Meanwhile, keep your chin up and take extreme care not to be alone anywhere."

"I will. Is Duncan enjoying the kitten?"

"He most certainly is. We had guidelines about not in the bedroom and mustn't this and mustn't that, but all that's gone down the pan. Tiger rules the roost."

"You don't seem to mind."

Joy laughed. "Somehow I don't, no. The kitten gets through to Duncan in a way human beings can't. He said last night that he couldn't understand why he'd never had a cat before. He says cats are private people and so is he, so they match beautifully."

Kate smiled. "I'm so glad he's pleased. I think Tiger will have a very different kind of life from poor little Scott. She's lined up for rat catching. But Scott thinks that's a good life for a cat."

"It is, I suppose, more natural anyway. Is Scott behaving himself? Oops! That's none of my business. I'm sorry, I shouldn't have asked." She got up off the chair and went to open the door. Looking back at Kate, she said, "In view of Adam's getting at your computer here and what happened last night at home, which shows he's getting worse, I wonder if the staff should know, then we can all be on the *qui vive* just in case."

"No, definitely not. Lynne and Stephie would think the whole situation ridiculous and it wouldn't do my image any good at all."

"You're right, it probably wouldn't. I'll press on."

As she left, Kate said, "And for your information, yes, he is."

"Surprise, surprise! He must be losing his touch."

"The perfect gentleman."

"My word. Do you sometimes wish he weren't? Sorry!" Joy's eyes lit up with fun as only hers could. "Shouldn't have said that. But let's face it, he is a charmer, isn't he?"

"Oh yes. And he's proud of it."

"He is; you're right. Keep your chin up about that other, you know."

SCOTT would have been highly gratified to have known he was being discussed in such terms by Joy and Kate. But at the time his name was being mentioned, he had other more important things on his mind. Phil Parsons had called him out to see Sunny Boy once more. The foot infection had decided to erupt again and, according to Blossom Parsons's muddled message on the practice phone, it was worse than ever.

An animal in pain was anathema to Scott, and he loathed not being successful in curing the bull. There was nothing more certain to destroy the vet/farmer relationship than calling time and again and coming up with one solution after another, and none of them being successful. Still worse, the farmers hated the subsequent bills. He'd done all the right things. He'd scoured his brain for reasons and solutions, and each time he thought he'd succeeded, within two weeks the whole problem had flared up again.

Crossing the yard to Sunny Boy's stall, he decided to call in Mungo for a second opinion that very afternoon if he wasn't operating. At least it would impress Phil, who was rapidly losing faith in him, and no wonder.

Phil was waiting for him, perched on the stout four-foot-high wall of which the stall was made. "Scott!" He nodded his head at Scott. "He's in agony this morning. It's not fair to 'im. I need an answer."

"I'm very sorry, Phil. I've decided we should have a second opinion. If you agree, I'll ask Mungo Price to come and have a look."

"Well, at least he has a brain. I'm beginning to doubt you have one."

"Now, Phil, I feel bad enough about it without having a fall-out with you as well."

"Sorry. But 'im and me are mates. I've had 'im since he was born. Born here, he was, in this barn on Christmas Day five years ago. An absolute fluke, he was. I knew the minute I saw 'im he was special." He hopped off the wall and watched Scott putting on his protective clothing, experience of Sunny Boy having taught him that there was a high chance of being covered in filth before the exercise was over.

Scott sprang up onto the wall, not taking the risk of drawing the bolts on the stout gate and possibly having Sunny Boy charging out and running him down. He dropped slowly down into the stall so as not to startle poor Sunny Boy, who was standing with all his weight on his three healthy legs, with the fourth touching the ground tentatively.

In accordance with his strictly imposed rules, Scott went to say good morning before examining Sunny Boy's foot. He stroked his huge knobbly forehead, admiring the almost mahogany color of his head, which contrasted so strikingly with the snow-white of his nose and jaws, and spoke softly to him. "Now, old chap, things not going so well for you today, eh? Well, never mind, your uncle Scott's come to make things better."

The only reply he got was the stamping of Sunny Boy's good front feet and a roll of his eyes. The snort that followed appeared more threatening, but Scott delayed moving to his rear for a split second while he . . .

Sunny Boy took that as Scott's tacit agreement that he wanted to be tossed.

In less than an instant, Scott was lifted from the ground and rammed hard against the outside wall of the barn. The pressure on his ribs and especially his lungs was enormous; the thrust of Sunny Boy's great head having emptied Scott's lungs of air, he hadn't even the breath left to shout to Phil to take action. All six feet two of this proud Australian son was rendered totally helpless.

Hanging there, with his spine in a vice and his feet dangling six inches above the ground, it seemed an age before Sunny Boy suddenly released him and Scott fell down against the wall, heaving great gulps of air into his starved lungs. Whereupon Sunny Boy decided that since Scott appeared to be lying there inviting further action, he would oblige. His great head, with half a ton of bull behind it, butted Scott's body time and again.

Scott could hear Phil shout, "You bloody great sod, you!" There came the sound of Phil landing with a thud on the floor of the stall and instantly Sunny Boy lost interest in Scott, swung around despite the confined space and went hell for leather for Phil, snorting and pawing the ground. Phil leaped out over the wall in one swift balletic movement and Scott, while Sunny Boy's attention was absorbed by wondering how he'd missed Phil, went just as swiftly as Phil over the wall and then collapsed, painfully breathless and in agony from head to foot, on the stone floor.

"My God, Scott! I'll kill the bastard. He went for me. Me! Who's tended his every need since the day he was born. So help me, I'll kill him."

"He didn't get you, though, did he?" Scott tried to sit up, but the pain was horrific. His ribcage felt shattered and the searing agony of his stomach and thighs where Sunny Boy's head had landed so emphatically was beyond endurance.

Sunny Boy was still snorting and stamping, and Scott muttered some ugly curses he'd heard the hands on his father's sheep station using since his infancy.

Phil shouted in admiration, "By Jove! Them sounds damn awful foul. You'll have to explain the meaning of them to me when you're feeling more like yourself. Can you get up?"

"No."

"I'm getting Blossom."

"I'd rather you got me to hospital."

"Bad as that?"

"Has he ever tried to gore you?"

Phil shook his head. "Never. I've never had a cross word with him until today. He must be in terrible pain. I'll get the ambulance."

"You won't. This Aussie boy is not going in any wimpy ambulance. Take me in your truck, but ring the practice first and tell them what's happened. Someone'll have to do my calls. Kate will sort it."

Phil ambled off, his balaclava even more askew than usual.

Scott lay still, wallowing for the moment in self-pity. Then he heard the *shlap-shlap* of Blossom's fashion boots on the cobblestone yard. He groaned.

Dressed more suitably for a brothel than a barn, Blossom

paused in the doorway for a moment and then came in, over-flowing with sympathy. "Scott, you darling boy. I heard you groan; you must be in agony. Phil's phoning the practice." She knelt down on the stones beside him and, taking hold of his head, pressed it to her chest. "Where does it hurt the most?"

"You name it, it hurts."

"He didn't stamp on your vital regions, did he . . . ? I mean you're not going to be impaired in any way? I wouldn't like to think . . ."

"Fortunately for the Spencer line, no, he didn't."

Blossom pressed a hand to her chest. "That's a relief. I wouldn't like to think that Sunny Boy was responsible for inca-pacitating you in that area, as you might say. There, now, lean against me and we'll get you up. Phil's bringing the truck as close as he can."

Scott, unwisely—but in the circumstances it was unavoid-able—accepted Blossom's help and slowly heaved himself to his feet. The throbbing pain caused him to almost faint and Blos-som had to take his whole weight for a moment. "Sorry."

"Don't apologize. I'm only too glad to be of help. I have some arnica in the house. It's excellent for relieving bruising. Could I rub some on your chest? It would help."

Scott shook his head. He decided to pull himself together. He simply was not behaving as a real man should. Bracing himself against the excruciating pain he knew was inevitable, he straightened up and headed drunkenly for the door.

The journey to the hospital passed by in a blur. He'd never realized just how many bumps and holes there were in major road surfaces. Finally, he surrendered to the ministrations of the hospital staff, feeling less than himself and certainly not in charge of Scott Spencer, Australian extraordinaire.

He woke later that day to find Joy sitting beside his bed. Scott struggled to make himself more comfortable but groaned horribly and gave up trying. "What's the damage? Do we know?"

"They've x-rayed *all* your vital parts and the news is you've cracked three ribs on your right side at the front and two on the left. Apart from that, no other breakages. Heavy bruising just about everywhere, but no internal damage to vital organs so far as they can tell at the moment. Everyone sends love and hopes you'll soon be feeling better."

"I'll go home, then." He made an effort to sit up and blanched with the pain it caused. "Well, perhaps not at the moment. I'll give myself another half hour and then see how I feel."

Skeptically Joy said, "That might be an idea. Do you realize how close to being killed you've been? Eh?"

"Hang that. Sunny Boy is in grave need of attention. His left hind foot is torturing him. I was going to ask Mungo to go and see him this afternoon."

"He's been."

"He's not in the next bed, is he?"

Joy laughed and Scott tried but failed. "No, he isn't. He's too wise a bird to get himself trampled by a bad-tempered bull. He sent Phil in first."

"Wise man. So . . ."

"When he got there, he found that a huge abscess had formed and he's lanced it, got rid of loads of pus and gunk, given him a massive dose of antibiotics and painkiller, and is going back tomorrow."

"Thank heavens. I never got a chance to look, you see."

"Might as well tell you, Phil's thinking of getting rid of him. Sending him to the abattoir. Can't believe he went for him when they are, well, were, such chums."

"He mustn't. Tell him he mustn't. Sunny Boy was in terrible pain. No wonder he went for me, it served me right for not curing him straightaway. Promise me."

"I promise. We've sorted your work till the weekend—well, at least Kate has—so you've no worries until Monday and we'll see what you're like then."

"I shall be fully operational, believe me."

"For heaven's sakes, drop the macho pose, Scott. It's the biggest wonder in the world we're not sending for the undertaker right now. Just behave yourself. The news of your accident has stunned us all. Half the county will be in here before the night's out and when you do leave the hospital, you're coming to our house to recuperate. Duncan's at home most days and he's an excellent nurse, despite all evidence to the contrary. He knows just when not to fuss."

Scott eyed Joy for a moment, weighing up her offer, and thought about his bare, comfortless bachelor flat with little food in the cupboards. The idea of returning there was very unappealing, so he decided to give in. "I shall be delighted to accept. And thank you."

Joy stood up. "I mean it; I'll speak to the nurse on my way out." She leaned over the bed and kissed him. "You're a dear boy. I'm glad you've survived; it could have been so much worse. Kate is coming in later when she finishes. That'll be nice, won't it?"

"She's not driving herself, is she? She mustn't."

"No. She's not. Mungo's bringing her. He's coming for a full briefing on the whole affair."

"I must be ill if *el supremo* is coming to mop my fevered brow." Scott pulled a dreadful, tortured face, sucked in his cheeks and crossed his eyes.

"You must be on the mend." Joy blew him a kiss as she disappeared through the cubicle curtains. She returned, grinning wickedly. "There's a line of nurses forming at the ward door to attend to you. Make the most of it; Duncan's not nearly so appealing. Au revoir."

. . .

Duncan was proving to be an excellent nurse. He had the instinct to know that Scott didn't want to be mollycoddled but that he did need caring for. The shock of the accident had to some extent at first masked the pain of the cracked ribs and the bruising, but now Scott was grateful for painkillers and even looked forward to the next dose when the relief they gave him was wearing off. Consequently, he slept a lot and Duncan left him to it.

By Friday afternoon Scott was downstairs and sitting in Duncan's study in front of the fire, with Tiger snuggly cuddled on his knee while Duncan worked at his computer. It was very companionable being with Duncan. His long silences were not isolating but comforting, rather, and Scott found himself relaxing more and more. He'd be back at work on Monday, though. A chap could get too used to this kind of life. No soaking-wet days, no mud, no filth, no cold, no missed meals, only warmth and solace. Yes, he could quite take to it. He stretched a little, but it disturbed Tiger, so he stopped halfway through the stretch. In any case, it would have been definitely uncomfortable to do it properly. Scott glanced at the clock. Past lunchtime. Should he offer . . . no, he'd wait for Duncan. He dozed and only came to when he heard Duncan coming in with lunch.

"Tomato and basil soup. That sound all right?"

"Excellent." Scott released Tiger and she jumped down and went to her little basket that Duncan had placed close to the fire. "Thank you. This kitten will be getting soft."

"Never mind. Bread?"

"Yes, please. Her sister will be out rat catching before she's much older."

"Good luck to her, that's what I say."

"Looks cold out."

"It is. Been out to feed the chickens. Much too cold for either man or beast. Don't you sometimes long for the sun and the heat? How long is it since you left home?"

"Eighteen months or thereabouts. I do today, funnily enough."

Duncan fell silent and concentrated on his soup. He cut himself another slice of bread from the loaf he'd balanced on the end of the bookshelf and continued eating in silence.

Scott drank up the last of his soup, spread a little more butter on the remains of his bread and munched on it. A big log on the fire slipped and rolled over so that its bright-burning red face turned toward him. The sudden increase in warmth reminded him of home, of the shimmering heat hitting him in the face the moment he stepped out of the air-conditioned house onto the veranda. The endless vista of land stretching and stretching away to the far horizon. The hot, hustling reek and clatter of the shearing sheds and the relentless day-in, day-out back pain at shearing time. The leathery aroma of his saddle and the stink of his sweat after a day's riding. Best of all he remembered the startling ice-cold shiver of the first beer when the heat had reached a hundred and you thought you'd die if you didn't get it all down in one long pull. But he'd had to get his wanderlust out of his system, otherwise he'd have been restless the whole of his life. Maybe now was the time . . .

Duncan took hold of Scott's soup mug and wrested it from his fingers. He took the remains of the bread into the kitchen and left Scott and Tiger to sleep.

Defrosting on the worktable was a chicken whose neck he'd wrung, and which he'd plucked and cleaned and put in the freezer along with three of its sisters some weeks before. Duncan tested it to see if it was ready for the oven. While he prepared the casserole he thought about Scott. There'd been a very wistful tone to his reply when he'd asked him about home. He'd better warn Joy that Scott could be getting itchy feet, as they all did. Though why anyone should prefer to burn up in the intense heat of Australia he couldn't begin to imagine. Give him a hill to walk up, a summit to reach on a crisp, bright, frosty day. For enriching the soul it couldn't be improved upon. He looked out of the window at the hills. Not today, though; the air was damp, and the sky full of clouds. Even so, it would be better than scrambling his brains into oblivion working out his current computer problem.

Scott came to stand in the doorway. "Has Joy told you about Kate's problem?"

"She has."

"Do you have any ideas? She's being stalked, you know, and it's beginning to eat away at her."

"At the moment, no."

"Her parents are making sure she never goes out by herself, but what more can they do?"

"Nothing. They'll have to hope his problem goes away."

"Gerry blames his mother."

"Mothers get the blame for most things that happen to us, especially the bad things."

Scott laughed. "I wish in a way he would do something we could report to the police, then at least they might put the fear of God into him and he would stop. He's obsessed."

"Aren't we all?"

"Are we? Are you?"

"My obsession is myself, though I'm working on that at the moment." He gestured to the chicken and the casserole dish. "Hence all this effort."

"Tell me, what's mine, then?"

"Scott Spencer."

"Hold it there, mate! Is that how I seem to you?"

"To everyone. Obsessed with your sexuality, with your macho image, with the admiration of women, with your need for approval, with being an Australian male and living up to it . . ."

"Hell, Duncan!"

"You did ask."

"You don't pull any punches, do you, mate?"

"You did ask."

Scott began to get angry. "Are you always like this? Because how the hell Joy puts up with you I do not know."

Duncan wiped down the worktable and ignored Scott.

"Well, how does she?"

"None of your business."

"I'm fond of Joy. She's great and she's helped me a lot. But I feel sorry for her, coping with your kind of person day in day out."

"She chose *me."*

"Not the best day's work she's done."

"You would think like that, Scott."

The pain Scott was suffering added malice to the tone of his voice. "Have you absolutely no consideration for other people's feelings? Time someone shook you out of your little cocoon and you entered the real world. Joy's a treasure, though obviously you don't appreciate that." Scott hitched himself against the doorjamb to ease his pain and sensed that as a guest in the house he'd gone too far.

Duncan turned to look at him properly for the first time since their conversation had begun; his eyes bored into Scott's with an unnerving intensity. "Being a guest in our house does not give you the right to poke about dissecting our marriage, so kindly put your scalpel away, if you please. You've no God-given right to be so judgmental."

"Huh!" It was the cold, unemotional way that Duncan went about his attack that angered Scott. It made it more calculated, more cruel. "Don't know what I've said to bring all that malice out of you. If you feel like that, I think it better if I leave."

Duncan shrugged his shoulders. "Your choice."

"You're damn right there. I'll be off, then."

"Fine. Be seeing you." Duncan put the chicken casserole in the oven, walked out of the kitchen and returned to his computer.

Scott slowly climbed the stairs. He hadn't intended their conversation to end with his leaving. He'd only asked for a different angle on Kate's problem and then he'd brought all that down on his head. Intellectuals irritated him; you never knew where you were with them. Give him a straightforward fella like Phil Parsons; you knew where you were with him even on one of his belligerent clays.

Duncan's analysis of his personality had touched him on the raw and angered him. Who the hell did Duncan think he was? He'd damn well order a taxi and be gone before Joy got back. He looked at his watch. One of Joy's perks was never having to work the late shift on Fridays, so she'd be home in an hour. Best be gone before she arrived. His Land Rover would be back at the practice and he always carried spare keys, so he'd collect it, go and shop for food and then go home and see to himself all weekend—and stuff the lot of them.

He scribbled a thank-you note for Joy on the back of an envelope he found in one of his pockets, left it on the bedside table, flung his belongings in his bag and went downstairs to order his taxi, the weight of his bag reawakening his pain.

The taxi pulled into the practice car park and there, waiting with its doors wide open, was an ambulance. Scott gingerly heaved himself out of the backseat, paid the driver and went to put his bag in his Land Rover. He was going to drive off without making contact with anyone, but the unusual sight of an ambulance at the practice stopped him. He walked across to the back door to find Bunty being wheeled out, eyes closed, ashen faced. He stood back so as not to get in the way. The ambulance doors shut and someone he took to be Bunty's mother came out and got into her car to follow the ambulance.

Scott stood for a moment, weighing what to do. It most certainly was not the best week he'd had. What to do? The only right thing was to go in and find out.

Joy was standing at her desk, her hands resting on it, her head bowed.

Scott tapped lightly on the door. "Joy?"

She looked up, her eyes unfocused and weary with anxiety. "What are you doing here?"

"On my way home, but that's another story. I saw Bunty."

"So you did. Close that door. Better sit down."

"I'll stand, thanks."

Joy pulled up her chair and sat on it. "I've had some difficult afternoons in my life, but this one has capped all." She drew in a deep breath. "Unfortunately or fortunately, it depends where you're coming from, Bunty is having a miscarriage. Something tells me you might be responsible."

"God! Has she said so?"

"No."

"Why should it be me?"

"A glance here, a laugh there. I'm not blind and I know what you're like; you love the buzz of being attractive to women. I can't doubt you get carried away with only the slightest encouragement."

Scott wished she hadn't said that. It reminded him of the scene in her kitchen and what she would learn when she got home. Truth, he'd always stood by the truth; lies got you nowhere. Wasn't it Walter Scott who said, "Oh, what a tangled web we weave / When first we practice to deceive"? Today, it seemed, was a day for truth. "It could be, but I asked her and she said, no, she wasn't pregnant."

Joy shook her head in despair. "Well, she is, was, rather. Poor girl."

"Indeed, poor girl. If I am responsible . . . well . . . it takes two."

"That's your vindication, is it?"

"I'll sit down."

Joy looked at him and saw the lines of pain in his white face as he seated himself. "Not your week, is it?"

"No, and I've fallen out with Duncan and left."

"That's not difficult. He could pick an argument with a saint."

"I've really upset him."

"Let's not go into that right now."

"If it is me . . . Will you find out for me?"

"I'll try, but girls can be very funny about babies and such. There are all sorts of complicated reasons and emotions for not coming up with the truth."

"I see." Scott eased himself up out of the chair. "I'll be here Monday if it kills me."

"Sorry things have gone badly for you. I'll make things right with Duncan."

"Thanks. See you Monday. I *did* ask her and she said no she wasn't, so what can a chap do?"

"Not do it in the first place, young man."

Scott allowed himself a rueful smile.

The tone of Joy's voice hardened as she said, "None of my business, but I warn you, take care of Kate or else." She wagged her finger at him. "I mean it."

Scott didn't answer, but he paused for a moment, saluted her with a single finger to his head and a nod, and left.

He'd intended spending the entire weekend by himself, pottering about, sorting his washing and generally pulling himself together after his disastrous week, but at about eight o'clock on Saturday evening he heard a car pull up outside. The entry phone buzzed and when he answered, to his delight he found it was Kate.

"It's me. I've come to cheer you up. Can I come up?"

"Kate! Of course you can."

"Mia dropped me off. Open up. It's cold."

He pressed the entry button. "Third door on the left, first floor. Number eight."

"I'll be there."

"See you."

He was so thrilled to see her he held his arms wide open and she went into them and they kissed. Kate hugged him as close as she dared, given his cracked ribs, and he responded by showering her face with kisses. "You've no idea how glad I am to see you. My self-imposed isolation was beginning to drag. Sit down. Drink?"

"Yes, please. I've heard all about your walkout from Joy's. Why ever? I find Duncan so easy to get on with."

"I trespassed on his married life and he objected. He told me a few home truths that got me annoyed and we suddenly didn't hit it off."

Kate asked what the home truths were, but he wouldn't tell her. "Not likely. You might agree."

"He's very perceptive."

"In a twisted kind of way."

"Was he right?" Kate had a grin on her face, which began to irritate Scott.

"Look, subject closed."

"Oh, dear! He has touched you on the raw. OK. I won't ask anymore." Almost as an afterthought she added, "I've been with Joy to see Bunty this afternoon."

Scott looked her straight in the eye. "How is she?"

"Home tomorrow. Rather low. None too happy. Despondent, only to be expected. Asked how you were, after your argument with Sunny Boy, you know."

"Did she?" Scott fiddled with his glass, downed half his lager in one go and inquired, "Anything else?"

"Oh, nothing, really. Joy seems to think . . ."

"I'm responsible."

"Something like that." Kate had to ask. "Were you?"

"It was before you came and yes, I could have been, but I asked and she said no."

Kate nodded. "I see."

"She's actually lost the baby now, has she?"

"Oh yes."

There was silence for a while and then Scott said, "I told her I wouldn't have married her."

He didn't like the sarcastic undertones of Kate's reply. "Oh, great. That was a very good idea. Very comforting and so supportive."

"I'm ashamed, really, but I don't feel anything for her. Marriage would have been disastrous."

"Ah! Right."

"She was as much to blame. How could she expect a red-blooded male not to respond to her overtures? If anyone was seduced, it was me. You modern girls don't give a chap a chance to say no."

"Oh! You poor thing."

"Kate!"

"Time you grew up."

"Please don't you fall out with me too; it's more than I can take this week."

He looked so genuinely upset that Kate decided to change

tack. "You're not thinking of going in to work on Monday, are you?"

Scott nodded.

"It's far too early. Be different if you had an office job. Sunny Boy's due for another visit on Monday."

"Well, Zoe could do that. Or Rhodri or Valentine. They could pretend he was a dog. Let them get kicked or trampled."

"You are down, aren't you?"

"Give us a cuddle; that'll do the trick."

Kate moved to the sofa and sat close to him. "Is it Duncan?"

Scott nodded.

"Well?"

"I'm not telling you." He took hold of her hand. "It must be the pain. I'm not used to it."

"It *is* Duncan, isn't it? He can be quite ruthless, I understand."

"It's his coldness I find difficult to take. It makes what he says that much more hurtful."

Kate sat back to appraise Scott. "I've never seen you so introspective."

"Stop using long words; it's too much for a simple Aussie like me." He grinned at her, pulled her close to him and kissed her. Several times. "I needed that."

"So did I." She pulled herself away from him and said quietly, "I don't know why you always put on this act of being tough."

"Sorry. It's how I am. Kiss me again. Please."

Which she did, gently and appreciatively, savoring the sensation, finding it new and enthralling.

"I bet that nutter Adam has never woken anything in you, has he?"

She drew away from him again. "Why spoil it with reminding me of him?"

"Sorry. I can't believe he could go out with you for two years and never manage to excite you."

"That, Scott, was how I wanted it. In any case, I'm not into relationships here, there and everywhere. It's not my scene."

"Not even with me?"

"Not even with you." She stood up. "I know the other girls think I'm a prude, but I don't care. It's a decision I've made and I'm sticking with it. I'm not going to finish up like Bunty, thanks."

"I see. I don't want that either, not with you, you're different. I was just feeling in need . . ."

"Of a boost."

Scott smiled up at her. "I admire you for standing by your principles."

"Good. We understand each other, then."

"How are you going to get home?"

"Mia's gone to visit a friend and she's coming back for me in about an hour."

"Stay here, then." He patted the cushion beside him. "Sit here and we'll watch TV and I promise to behave myself. Boring though it might be."

She laughed. "I do like you very much indeed, you know that, don't you? I think I must have fallen under your spell."

"Most women do."

"Honestly! Your ego!"

Her comment reminded him of Duncan and he sobered. "I like you too, perhaps too much for my own good, but there you are." He switched on the TV set and they sat holding hands and occasionally smiling at each other, watching an old American cowboy film until the doorbell rang and it was Mia.

She came up to sit for a few minutes. "I'm early. My friend was just going out for the evening. My fault, I should have given her a ring first. Nice flat, Scott. I like it. Feeling better? I didn't think you'd be home so soon, perhaps Monday at the earliest."

Scott caught Kate's eye and then answered with a noncommittal "Thought they'd like the weekend to themselves."

They chatted idly for a few more minutes and then Mia got up to go. "Take care of yourself, young man, and if you're not right on Monday, take a few more days off. Go back too soon and you'll only make things worse. Bye-bye."

"Bye-bye, Mia."

He kissed Kate gently on her lips and ran a caressing finger along her cheekbone. "Good night, thanks for coming."

"Good night. Take care."

Mia drove Kate home carefully, only too well aware that Adam was following them. She didn't tell Kate that he'd been sitting outside Scott's flat all the time Kate had been visiting and that all she, Mia, had done was position her car where she could watch Adam without him knowing. When she saw him for the second time decide to open his car door as though getting out, she'd started up her engine and driven back into the road as if returning from somewhere. Adam had swiftly shut his door when he saw her and slumped down in the driving seat to avoid being noticed. But he couldn't deceive her, even though he'd changed his car for the second time.

Chapter

· 11 ·

No one quite knew how to treat Bunty when she returned to work. Did they sympathize or did they behave as though the miscarriage had solved a lot of problems for her? The one with the most need to clear the air was Scott, and he found her at lunchtime eating her sandwiches sitting outside the back door on an old bench, which had been put there temporarily when they'd first moved in and had never been moved.

"Can I sit down?"

She didn't look at him. "It's a free country."

"Feeling better?"

"Ditto?"

"Yes, thanks, and you?"

"Well, Scott, I think they say in these circumstances 'as well as can be expected.'" Bunty took another bite of her salad sandwich and continued looking up at Beulah Bank Top.

Scott stared at it too. "I'm sorry it happened."

"I'm not. Didn't fancy bringing a child up on my own. It's no picnic."

"I don't expect so."

"Wouldn't have had an abortion, but fortunately for me it made its own mind up."

"I see."

Bunty chanced a glance at his face. "You were right. It wouldn't have worked anyway."

"Marriage, you mean?"

"That's right."

So the baby must have been his. Scott felt an upsurge of emotion, a sudden fierce joyousness at this proof that he could fulfill his male role to its full potential. His elation showed on his face and he almost leaped to his feet to shout "Eureka!"

Bunty, with a quick glance, caught sight of his look of delight. Carefully folding up the plastic bag that had held her sandwiches and gazing up at the hills again, she said, "It wouldn't have been the right basis for marriage to have saddled you with someone else's baby, now would it?" She stood up and, without giving him a chance to answer, walked to the back door, opened it and disappeared inside.

Scott's ego plummeted to new depths. Women! How could any man ever begin to understand the workings of their minds? Was she being a tease to punish him? Was she that liberal with her favors? Did she see his delight and decide to get her revenge on him? Or was she so hurt at his reaction to her pregnancy that she wouldn't allow him the pleasure of believing he'd fathered a child? *Was* he the father? Maybe he would never know. The main thing was he had no responsibility now toward her or to a child, so he was still free as air. Well, not quite, there was Kate, who wouldn't stay out of his mind.

He sat there for a while, thinking about her, until he grew so cold he had to go inside. As he turned to make his way in, he caught sight of a car coming to a halt at the top end of the tarmac, a curious bilious yellow, it was, with a soft beige top. Some people's taste! He strode in without looking back. He'd see if Kate was free to make him some coffee and then get on with his calls. As he passed the operating theater door, Bunty rushed out of it in tears and fled into the staff toilets. Mungo, in his full operating kit, came out after her. "Seen Bunty?"

Scott pointed to the toilet door. Mungo nodded and shouted, "Joy! Where are you?"

Scott left him to it and went to find Kate, but she'd gone off at one, so he made his own coffee and went his solitary way to his afternoon calls. If he hadn't been so cold and had stayed out on the bench awhile longer, he would have seen Adam get out of the bilious yellow car, ready for a walk on the hills.

Joy had had a challenging afternoon. Bunty had gone home after her tears, leaving Mungo with no one to assist him in the theater, so Joy had had to leave Lynne by herself on reception for the afternoon and get gowned up to work with Mungo. It had been some time since she'd had to fill in on the operating side and she was under stress the whole time, worrying about letting Mungo down, or worse, causing the animal, whose quality of life Mungo was hoping to improve, to die.

It was a very delicate operation on a cat whose leg had been shattered in a road accident, and the constant reference to X-rays, handing of implements and the final framework of pins and screws to keep it all in place while the bones had a chance to heal ended with Joy feeling completely done in when Mungo finally declared he was satisfied. At the same time, though, it brought back splendid memories of how they had worked together in the early days; and the old welcome feeling of working as a team and the closeness of their relationship of those days filled her with pleasure, and for the moment both Duncan and Miriam were forgotten.

"Done! Thanks, Joy. Thanks for stepping in. Quite like old times, eh?" He patted the cat's head as Joy took it off the anesthetic, saying, "There we are, Muffin, it's all up to you now. I can't do any more. Tea in your office for old times' sake? Yes?"

"Yes. That was brilliant. You don't lose your touch, do you?"

"Neither do you."

"Was I nervous! But it all came flooding back."

"What about Bunty, then?"

"Early days."

"I'd be sorry to lose her. She's the best nurse we've got. The two Sarahs are excellent, but Bunty has the edge. She's very intuitive."

"I know. I'd hate to lose her too. The girl's all mixed up and no wonder.

"Is it Scott?"

Joy shook her head. "I honestly don't know; she hasn't said. He says she says it isn't him, but . . ." Joy shrugged her shoulders. "Give her time. I'll put Muffin in intensive care. Tea in my office in five minutes?"

Mungo nodded.

When they'd settled down to drink their tea, Joy said, "If Bunty doesn't come back, though I'm sure she will, I can help out till we find someone else. Kate is so good. She got reception and accounts under her belt in no time at all. Far too good for the work entailed. Sometimes I wonder why she's here."

"So do I. This tea's welcome. She's never said anything, has she?"

"No. Not a word and I'm not going to ask. As long as she works well, that's all that concerns me. Except . . ." She put down her cup. "Except she still has the problem of that idiot Adam stalking her. It's really preying on her mind. Her parents insist, quite rightly too, that she never go anywhere without being driven by either Scott or them. Not fair her life should be so curtailed by the man."

"Maybe he'll cool off in a while."

"Let's hope so."

Mungo stood up, reached across her desk, cupped her chin in his hand and kissed her. Combined with the feelings stirred in her by working with him in the operating theater, the hint of fervor in the pressure of his lips served to awaken the longings she'd had for him for years.

When he straightened up, he looked at her for a moment and then said, "Got to go. Miriam's got a surprise planned for me. You've not lost the old skills, Joy. It's good to know you could still be my right-hand woman if need be. Thanks again. Keep in touch about Bunty. I'll look in on Muffin when I get back." Mungo treated her to one of his beautiful warm smiles, which thrilled all who were privileged to receive one, and her heart jumped into her throat and she couldn't speak. She wiggled her fingers at him and let him go without a word.

Damn him! Damn him! His kiss had been a reward for helping him, nothing more, nothing less. Would she never learn that it was Miriam he loved, not her?

Having been reminded all over again of the bitter truth, Joy drove home in no mood for one of Duncan's silences. But he wasn't there. He'd gone walking and, unusually for him, he'd left a note to say he would be home in time for his evening meal. By his computer was a thick pile of printout sheets, so finally he must have solved his problem. She wished she could solve hers.

Duncan came home tired and hungry, but he'd obviously kept an eye on the clock because he was in through the door half an hour before the meal was ready. "Quick shower and I'll be down." He smiled at her and blew her a kiss.

Joy pulled a face. What had she done to deserve that? Maybe he really was trying to make an effort to improve things between them. She went to get a bottle of wine, because she knew she needed to make an effort too, if only to erase the guilt of what Mungo's kiss had aroused.

Duncan didn't speak until after he'd finished his first course. He sat back replete. "That is the kind of meal a man needs when he's been walking in the hills. Was I hungry, was I!"

Joy toasted him with her glass. "I see you've solved your problem. Loads of printouts."

"I have. That was why I needed to walk, clear my head. Which it did. Do you fancy going out? A drink or something?"

Startled by this departure from the norm, Joy hesitated and then suggested: "Cinema?"

"OK, then. I'll check the paper when we've finished."

"Duncan . . ."

"Mm?"

"Oh, never mind."

"You've started, so you must finish."

"You seem happier. More relaxed."

Duncan thought over what she had said. "I'm trying to be more considerate. To you. After my run-in with Miriam, I saw the error of my ways."

"Ah! You did?"

"Why the hell should you care about me? When ever do I do anything at all to deserve you? Never. So I decided to be more . . . attentive." He gave her a wry grin. "It's hard, unaccustomed work for me, but I am giving it a whirl."

"I'm glad. It's been an uphill struggle."

Almost too casually Duncan asked, "How's Mungo today?"

Joy jumped guiltily. "Mungo? Why do you mention him?"

"I can see that look in your eyes that consigns me to the wilderness. It's very hard to bear, Joy, and hasn't helped at all. I'm so jealous of that man."

Ashamed, Joy said, "However *I* might feel, you can rest

assured that nothing, absolutely nothing, will separate Mungo from Miriam, believe me. The battle is with myself and myself alone. Most of the time, ninety-five percent of the time, he's just someone I work with and then something happens and the balloon goes up. It's time I packed it in."

"Your job, you mean?"

"No, not my job, I couldn't do that; I love it too much. No, letting Mungo stir me up. I'm a sentimental old idiot at bottom and I've got to put a stop to it. The trouble has been that you didn't make any effort to redress the balance, if you see what I mean. Slowly but surely I've become your housekeeper and that's not what I want, but it's what I've got. You gave me nothing here, so I've clung to what remained of Mungo, but if I look it squarely in the eye, nothing remains except a good working relationship built up over a lot of years."

There was a long silence while Duncan made sense of what she'd said. He sipped his wine, finished his pudding, stared out of the window and finally said, "I've loved you since the day we met, but my feelings have been strangled by yours for Mungo. I can understand how it came about. He is a most adorable man, but you weren't even fair to me when we married, were you?"

His question hung heavy in the air like some kind of overpowering incense that even opening a window would not disperse. Joy lifted her head and stared straight into his eyes. "After all these years, what makes you come out with that right now?"

"My own self-searching. I'm guilty too. My cramped emotions haven't helped. You're right about my offering you nothing to keep you. As you said, that damned computer is to blame. But you're not being fair to Miriam either. Does she know how you feel? Have you ever told her?"

Joy was appalled by his question. "Of course not. I wouldn't dream of breaking her heart by telling her. That's a dreadful, terrible thought."

"She's very perceptive. Maybe she's realized; picked up on that special smile you have for him?"

Joy flushed with horror at his question. "What special smile?"

"Well, you can't see your own smile but even a congenital idiot could. I bet the staff at the practice have guessed."

The possibility that they might have guessed was too dreadful for Joy to contemplate. Did they all know and were amused behind her back? Talking about it? Contemplating her chances? *Oh God! No! Of course not.* He was saying it to upset her. She'd never given away her secret, not by so much as a touch or a look. Of course they didn't know.

"Go on, be honest, Joy. Haven't you ever wished he was me when we used to make love?"

There was that cold, analytical tone in his voice, the one which probed without emotion or thought for his victim. But his eyes told a different story: they were pleading for reassurance. If she lied, would he guess? What if she told the truth?

She chose her words slowly and carefully. "Honesty being your watchword, there were times to begin with when, yes, I wished you were Mungo. Just sometimes. Not for a long time, though. But I'm bound to you by something invisible. There's no escape. I couldn't be without you and I don't know why . . . if that's any help."

"And me to you. I'm bound by I know not what. Maybe it's a passionate love we've both of us smothered with neglect. Since we are coming out in the open about ourselves, how about telling Miriam? You might be cleansed of him then."

"I can't do that. I couldn't! I couldn't stay at the practice if I did. For heaven's sake."

"In that case, then, maybe the more straightforward thing to do would be to give your notice."

"Is this an ultimatum of some kind?"

Duncan didn't answer immediately. When he did, he simply said, "Just testing." He got up from his chair and went to stand at her side. His mood had changed as quickly, as if he'd flicked a switch. She looked up at him and scrutinized the somber face with its deep-set eyes and sad, gentle mouth. With more desire than she had experienced in an age, she wanted him to kiss her.

"Taken slowly in small doses, one step at a time, there's hope for us, isn't there?" For the second time that day her chin was cupped in a man's hand. Briefly he touched her mouth with his.

"Oh yes!" And suddenly she felt there was. She took his hand from her face, kissed the back of it and pressed it to her cheek. "Let's sit in front of the fire. Leave the table for now."

They both moved to sit in the easy chairs before the fire. They were silent for a while, each running over in his and her own mind the conversation they'd just had. Then, out of the blue, he said, "Met a chap today. Strange chap."

In the silence that followed, Joy said, "That'll make two."

"Yes, but *I'm* not weird."

"What was he doing?"

"Walking and, like me, trying to make sense of things. He's barmy, if you ask me."

"Tell me."

Joy put another log on the fire and settled herself to listen. Duncan, eyes half closed, remembered his meeting with the man.

THERE'D been at least another mile to go before he would reach the summit and he'd decided to find somewhere out of the wind to sit to eat the bread he'd brought with him. He could never be bothered with making fancy sandwiches, so he'd picked out a roll from the freezer and a lump of cheese from the fridge and chosen one of those Cornice pears he loved out of the fruit bowl. He knew that by the time he was ready to eat, the roll would have defrosted and be fresh and soft and rich smelling, just how he liked them. He'd taken a couple of bites from it when a man came into view wearing, for some curious reason, a second-rate business suit and nice shoes, with a beige-colored anorak to keep out the cold. He hesitated, watching Duncan from where he stood on the sheep track. Duncan saw the twitch he had in his cheek and thought, *Here we go; a nutter of the first order.*

Having resolved his computer problem, he had room to feel full of concern for mankind, so he shifted along the boulder he was sitting on and invited the chap to take a pew. "You can share my roll and cheese if you wish."

The man patted the pocket of his anorak and said, "Got my own." But he accepted the invitation to sit beside Duncan and the two of them sat in total silence, eating their lunches and enjoying the view.

When Duncan pulled a can of beer from his pocket, the chap looked at it enviously. Duncan offered it to him. "Have a drink; you're most welcome."

But he rejected the offer, so Duncan, never one to make the effort to persuade people against their wishes, emptied the can himself.

"I prefer lager."

Duncan wiped his mouth on the back of his hand. "I'm a beer man myself."

"I see."

They sat a further while in silence, looking at the view, each wrapped in his own thoughts. Eventually Duncan said, "I'm heading for the top. Coming?"

The chap shook his head. "I've never reached the top, never had the courage."

"What's courage to do with it? It's a simple matter of putting one foot in front of the other."

The chap stood there, trying to make up his mind. "I suppose it is. Do you mind?"

"I did ask you."

"Right. I will. You lead on." He crumpled the wrappers from his lunch and was about to stuff them into a crevice of the boulder when he saw Duncan carefully storing his empty lunch bag and beer can in his jacket pocket. So he did the same.

They strode up the rest of the way, following a sheep track, and when they reached the top, Duncan went to his favorite sheltered spot to rest. It was only a small dip alongside the track, but it kept the worst of the wind off and he liked the idea that in the depths of the night sheep would be huddled here. It made him feel at one with them. The two of them found it rather a squash but Duncan, being so at peace with the world, had not minded.

"Married, are you?" the chap had asked almost immediately.

"I am."

"I live with my mother."

"Cramps your style, doesn't she?"

The chap shook his head. "Haven't got any style to cramp."

"You should have, a chap your age."

"Your mother. Did she cramp your style?"

"My mother scarcely noticed I existed. The occasional pat on the head for doing well at school constituted the extent of her sortie into parenthood."

The chap thought about this and observed, "That's better than being smothered like me. Are you out of work? I just wondered with you being about during the day."

"I'm a computer programmer and I work at home. I've just finished a big project, so I'm free for a few weeks."

"I see. Do you come every day?"

"I shall for two or three weeks till the next project."

"I might see you, then." His cheek twitched furiously and his head jerked in tune with it. "Would you mind?"

Duncan did mind, but he could see the chap's need. "Not at all. Look out for me." Duncan watched him walk away down the hill, shoulders bent, hesitant, jerky, twitching, and thought, *Poor devil.*

"So that was all that happened and I expect I'm stuck with him for the next few weeks."

Joy asked, "Did he tell you his name?"

"No. Didn't seem like that kind of a relationship."

"He sounds in need of someone to talk to."

"Aren't we all?" Duncan slid from his chair and hitched himself along the floor till he reached Joy. He rested his back against her legs and she set about putting his untidy hair to rights. "We all need someone."

Joy left her hand resting on his head and stared into the fire. "We do."

"We'll give the cinema the elbow, shall we?"

"I'd forgotten."

"Getting too late anyway. Do you mind?"

"No. We can always go tomorrow night if there's anything decent on."

Induced by the good food and the warmth of the fire, Joy and Duncan sat there for more than an hour enjoying each other's company. Halfway through, Tiger came in to investigate their silence and chose to climb on Duncan's legs, planning to tease him into playing with her, but she, too, succumbed to the warmth and the quiet between them and eventually gave up persuading him to play when she fell off his legs onto the carpet, going to sleep beside him with his hand caressing her ears. It was the first evening for a long time that the house had been so at peace with itself.

THE next day it seemed that peace had been restored at the practice too and Joy was looking forward to a busy, enjoyable day. Bunty had returned, apparently determined to ignore her upset of the previous day; Graham and Valentine were in the consulting rooms; Zoe and Scott out visiting the farms; Lynne was covering reception with help from Kate, who was doing the accounts as and when the pressure lessened on reception. Mungo had several clients coming that morning and Joy herself was going to tackle the roster for November.

She'd settled at her desk with everyone's holiday requests lined up at the side of her computer, focusing her mind on her task, when she heard the sound of argument. Her head came up and she listened hard. Lynne's voice was strident and uncompromising. Kate's voice placatory. What was that Lynne said? ". . . too bossy by half . . ."

She couldn't hear Kate's reply, but there again came Lynne's voice, raised even higher: "You're not telling me what to do. You've a long way to go before you know this job as well as I do, so you can pipe down."

Joy could hear the tone of Kate's voice but not distinguish the words.

There was Lynne again, shooting her mouth off: "Miss Perfect, are we? Little white hen that never lays away. Huh!"

Joy shot out of her office and into reception, ready for action. Between clenched teeth and sotto voce she said, "What is the matter? I can hear you in my office. Have some consideration for the clients; they can hear every word. This is disgraceful."

Neither Lynne nor Kate answered her.

"Well, I'm waiting." One of the phones rang, but the two girls were too busy glaring at each other to answer it. Joy dealt with the problem, answering the telephone as though nothing were amiss, changed someone's appointment on the computer and then turned to them again. "Well, I'm still waiting."

Lynne decided to get in first with her side of the story. "Kate has sent Zoe halfway across the county to an emergency when Scott is only four miles away and could easily have gone on his way to his next call. I told her she shouldn't have and she told me to mind my own business." Lynne pointed to herself, continuing, "I've been here long enough to know what I'm doing. She comes and thinks she knows it all in five minutes. Well, she doesn't. She doesn't know anything."

Joy turned to Kate. "Well?"

"Scott especially asked to be given plenty of time at his next call. The farmer's really been kicking up a stink about things and saying he's thinking of moving to another practice if they don't improve, so I thought it best, seeing as he has such a full list today, that he stick to his schedule, and Zoe, who's cutting down on her number of calls because of the baby, could fit this emergency in quite easily. That's all."

"I see. Lynne does have a point."

"I most certainly do. That Scott thinks he's indispensable and she"—pointing at Kate—"favors him no end. It's ridiculous. Scott this. Scott that."

"That's not true."

"And if we're really getting down to the nitty-gritty, who's she anyway? With her A levels and that, she thinks herself something very special. Oh yes! But look at the mistakes she's made . . . that money, for starters."

Joy pricked up her ears at this. "What money?"

"Miss Chillingsworth's."

The moment she said it, Lynne appeared to regret it and Joy picked up on that. "What about that money?"

"She lost it, didn't she?"

"Well, she didn't actually lose it. It turned up."

"Careless, though, wasn't she? Not quite part of the goody-goody image, that kind of mistake."

"Lynne, I get the distinct feeling you know something you haven't told me. Do you know where the money disappeared to and how it came to materialize again? Because if you do, you'd better come clean right now. Kate, stay here. Lynne, my office." Joy jerked her head toward the back. Lynne hesitated for a moment, then followed but not before she'd deliberately trodden on Kate's foot as she squeezed past.

Joy, who knew her staff and was a past master at dealing with difficult ones, had the truth out of Lynne in the sweetest, kindest way before they'd been in the office five minutes. "So you took it, hid it, put it back when I read the riot act, all for what?"

Lynne avoided looking her in the eye. Instead, she stared out of the window. "She really gets my back up. Too clever for her own good, she is. What's more, she was very rude to my brothers. Oxford graduates, they are, with top jobs in the City, but it made no difference to her. She told them off. I mean! Who does she think she is?"

"Did they deserve it?"

"No. Well, yes, perhaps they did. So I saw what had happened, that she'd forgotten Miss Chillingsworth's money, and I thought I'd teach her a lesson. I wasn't going to keep it, you know, I wasn't stealing."

"I never for one moment thought you were. I shall overlook the incident this time, but if ever anything of this nature occurs again and you are involved, then . . ." Joy drew her forefinger across her throat and made a strangulated sound. "As you know, I always mean what I say and I would not hesitate to give you the sack immediately, on the spot, with no time even to collect your belongings. Kate is a good worker and with all the sickness and whatever we've had recently, I don't know where we would have been without her. You're a good worker too. None better. You're quick, polite and helpful to the clients, pleasant to work with and that's how Kate is too. That's how I run this practice, with happy, hardworking people who get on well with one another and who put the clients and their pets first. As for those brothers of yours, they are only human beings after all."

"If you were in my shoes, you'd have been taught they were gods. Public school and university for them; comprehensive for me because it wasn't worth educating me and that's how it's been all my life."

Joy smiled at her. "Then it shouldn't have been. Lynne Seymour is worth her weight in gold. Off you go and send Kate to me, please."

Before she opened the door Lynne, not quite sure how she'd finished up apologizing, said, "I'm very sorry. Thanks. It won't happen again."

"Of course not."

Joy had made up her mind while she'd been talking to Lynne that she'd ask Kate outright why she was working there. Lynne was absolutely right: Kate was out of place as a receptionist and Joy had always known that, but hadn't faced up to it until now.

"Sit down, Kate. I've had a word with Lynne and she's apologized and said she hid the money out of spite to get back at you. Her reason being that you'd been rude to her brothers, but more so because you were too clever for your own good. Her words, not mine. Which I've always known you were. So the question I have to ask is why are you here?" Joy had no intention of letting her leave the office until she had a satisfactory answer, so she sat with arms folded, waiting.

Kate knew there was no escape; the question had to be answered and you didn't tell fibs to Joy because being the kind of person she was, she'd know immediately that you were lying. She looked at Joy's lovely, kind face, at the curly blond hair framing that face and most of all the bright-blue eyes full of honesty, and said, "I'm a failed vet. Well, not really. Actually, I got two As at A level and the third one I only got a grade C, so I didn't get a place and I was so bitterly disappointed that I took this job as being the nearest I could get. Looking back on it, it was a stupid, stupid thing to do, but it felt right at the time." Kate shook her head. "No, it wasn't a stupid thing to do because I love it and enjoy every minute of my time here. But . . ."

"Yes?"

"They have said that if I get this third grade A, then they will have me. So I'm having tutoring in chemistry every week and taking the exam in the summer. Fingers crossed I shall get in."

"What a wonderful surprise!" Joy got up, went around her desk and kissed Kate. "I am delighted. So pleased to hear that, Kate. Brilliant! You'll stay with us until then?"

"If you'll have me. I know I should have been more straightforward with you at the beginning, but I was so badly upset by it all and Dad would keep going on about my trying again, and I kept saying no because I'd worked so hard and couldn't face . . . I could hardly bear to think about my failure, let alone talk about it."

"What made you change your mind?"

"Scott mainly, I suppose. But also Adam, who was so resist-ant to my trying again because he wanted us to get married that he kind of stiffened my resolve, as you might say. I should have come clean when you offered me the job. I am sorry."

"I'm glad you got yourself together again. It would be churlish of me not to wish you every success. If at any time you want to go out on a call in your spare time, just say so."

"Thank you, I'd like that."

"I think you should let the others know when the opportunity arises, just to clear the air. Meanwhile, you're reception and accounts, so you'd better get back to it and please do your best to keep the atmosphere pleasant for all concerned. I value Lynne just as I value you, and Stephie and all the others. Thank you for being honest with me."

"Thank you for letting me stay on."

Joy sat back in her chair and pushed her fingers through her hair. *Would you believe it? Kate hoping to be a vet. Well, well.* She should have guessed. She'd make a lovely vet; she truly would. Such a pleasing girl. A girl she would have liked to have had as a daughter. When she'd married Duncan, he had declared he didn't want children and she was so distraught at Mungo's marriage to Miriam that at the time she hadn't cared two hoots about anything except easing her broken heart. She'd always known that Duncan had loved her deeply when they'd first married, but she'd been the cheat, longing for it to be Mungo when she and Duncan made love and him realizing it, and finally allowing her obsession to spoil everything for them. Well, now it was too late for children but perhaps not too late for the two of them to make a real marriage of it. Duncan was making an effort and so too must she.

Joy went to the mirror in the staff restroom and gave herself a frank appraisal. Not bad for fifty-three next birthday—skin still clear and unwrinkled, eyes still bright, not a single strand of white hair showing, figure slightly full but comely. She imagined Duncan standing beside her. Did people ever notice that he was nine years younger than her? Not really. He looked gaunt and older than his years with his hollow cheeks and his deep-set eyes, and that stoop from bending over his computer all these years. She'd better keep herself in trim, though, in case this was her decade for beginning to show her age. Where would she be if a few weeks' striding up Beulah Bank Top every day restored Duncan's good looks and revitalized him?

THAT night Duncan told her the second episode of the story of the man in the beige anorak. "He must have watched me yesterday and seen which way I'd come because as soon as I reached the stile where Beulah Bank Top really begins he was there, leaning on it, waiting. He looked cold, as though he'd been waiting quite a while. I climbed the stile and we set off, him behind me because the path is narrow there. I know it sounds odd, but we walked almost all the way to the top with-out speaking. I stopped in my favorite place and so did he, and we shared the boulder and ate our lunches in silence. Today he'd brought a can of lager. I looked at him and smiled, saying nothing.

"'You don't say much,' he said.

"'Neither do you,' I replied.

"He stared into the distance.

"I said, 'I'm willing to be quiet if that's what you want, or you can talk if you wish.'

"He waited awhile and then looked hard at me. 'My prob-lem is I have no job. I was elbowed out by someone we all nick-named Motormouth. Lot to say but did very little. I was sure I'd get the promotion; I told everyone I would. Which was stu-pid.' He eased the knees of his business suit so they wouldn't crease. 'That's why I'm wearing this suit. I've not told anyone I've lost my job. I go out of the door each morning, dressed for work with my lunch in my briefcase and a wave to my mother.'

"'You mean she doesn't know?'

"He nodded. 'She doesn't know, and I can't tell her.'

"'Can't tell her? Why ever not? What the hell!'

"'If you knew my mother.' He said that so vehemently I was nonplussed. 'I don't know what to do.'

"'Get another job?'

"'I'd never get one that pays as well. I've so few skills.'

"'There are companies crying out for loyal, hardworking, reliable staff. I bet you could get a job tomorrow.'

"For a moment I saw a glimmer of hope cross his face and then it disappeared. 'You're nothing without a job.'

"'Right at this moment I don't know if I shall ever work again, but you can see it isn't bothering me.'

"He looked me square in the face. 'Is it?'

"'No. Because I've every confidence that the world is my oyster. There's work out there for everyone if you're a trier. I bet right now, somewhere, you are just the man someone is wishing they could employ.'

"'Really?'

"'Oh yes. Then you can go home to your mother and tell her that the promotion you got didn't fulfill your expectations and you decided to get another job.'

"'I could?'

"'Of course. She doesn't have to know, does she? There are things mothers shouldn't be told.'

"'There are?'

"'I nodded. 'Oh yes.'

"'I see.'

"'I can't say the twitching stopped, but it lessened.

"'I'm ready for the top, are you coming?' I asked.

"'Yes, I am.'"

Duncan fell silent, so Joy asked, "Is that it, then? Didn't you say any more?"

"No. He left me at the top and I watched him walking away with a firmer stride, not so jerky, you know."

"Well, send for Duncan Bastable, freelance psychiatrist. Let's hope it works."

"I hope so for his sake."

"And you still don't know his name?"

Duncan shook his head.

But Joy had a niggling thought that she wasn't putting two and two together.

Chapter

· 12 ·

"Hello, Scott here. Is Kate about?"

"Yes."

"Get her for me, there's a darling, Lynne."

Lynne slapped the receiver on the desk and went to find Kate. "It's lover boy, wants a word." She spoke abruptly with something of a sneer on her lips.

Kate went to the desk and picked up the phone. "Hello, Scott. Got a problem?"

"I'm on my way to Applegate Farm. I wondered if you'd like to come with me? You finish early today, don't you?"

"I'd love to. I'll be ready to leave in about half an hour."

"I'll pick you up. I've got to go past anyway. See you, sweet one."

Lynne watched her from the comer of her eye. "Got a date?"

"No. Just going with him on a visit."

Lynne nodded her head, remarking sarcastically, "Oh, of course, the budding vet."

"OK, Lynne, enough. It is in my own time."

"I know. Just wish it was me."

"I wish it was too."

213

"No, you don't."

"I do. I genuinely do if that's what you'd like."

"No hope of that, I'm afraid. Science wasn't exactly my favorite subject at school."

"What was?"

"English."

"Ah! Well."

"Exactly." A client came to the desk and their conversation had to be put on hold. By the time they resumed it, Kate was waiting for Scott to appear.

"In any case, I couldn't be doing with all that muck and mess. Operations would turn my stomach, believe me."

"Good thing we don't all want to do the same things. There's always college or evening classes. Maybe you could improve your grades or something. Find a whole new career."

"Perhaps. I'll think about it."

They heard a banging on the back door. "That'll be Scott. See you Monday, Lynne." Kate picked up the boots she'd borrowed from Joy and went out.

"Fling your boots in the back. I'm running late; get in." Scott rode hell for leather along the country roads, up hill and down dale at a furious pace.

Kate had to protest. "Scott! Please! We're going to have an accident."

"Sorry." He slowed a little and took the next comer at a steadier pace.

"What's the matter?"

"Tired of the cold, that's me."

"We all get tired of the cold and then as soon as the hot weather starts, we all complain. English people are never satisfied where the weather is concerned."

"You're right. But somehow it feels depressing. Oops! Sorry!"

Scott swung the wheel over quickly to avoid their going head first into a ditch.

"Please, Scott! Your driving is going from bad to worse. Slow down!"

"OK, OK."

"Look, here's the turning."

The Land Rover slid to a halt just past the road to Applegate Farm. Scott reversed a few yards, then pulled on the steering wheel and maneuvered into the opening to the lane.

"You'll have to pull yourself together, or were going to have an accident."

Scott slowed right down to a crawl and then drove into the side. Switching off the engine, he turned to face Kate and said, "It's no use. I've got to say it."

"What?"

"I think I might have fallen in love."

"With whom?"

"Who do you think?"

"I don't know, do I?" Kate stared out of the window watching the wind blowing through the tattered winter grass. He wasn't going to mess up their whole relationship with some wild statement of undying love, was he?

"You."

"Me?" She turned back to face him. "I think not."

"If you don't know it's you, how can you say you don't think so? It's not logical."

"No, it isn't. But you don't."

"I think of you night and day."

"You don't, Scott."

"I do. You're the first girl I've ever met who occupies my thoughts all the time." He leaned forward and placed his lips on hers, kissing her with great gentleness. "See?"

"I'll tell you why I occupy your thoughts all the time, shall I?"

Scott nodded.

Looking directly at him Kate said, "Because you know I have no intention of falling into bed with you at the first opportunity. My resistance has to be overcome and that's a challenge for you, and that's what makes you think of me all the time, not love."

"Kate! That's not fair."

"The truth isn't always fair." Not for the world would she tell him how much she longed to make love with him.

"I've always said you were different from the others."

"Is that what you told Bunty? That she was different?" If she wasn't careful, it would show.

"No, I did not. I told you it was mostly her fault. No, that's not right. It was fifty percent me, of course. She tempted me and I was feeling . . . well, I was feeling a mite homesick, would you believe, and I was looking for comfort. But that night she was that woman in the Bible. Jezebel."

"Oh, dear! Poor Scott." Until she met Scott, she wouldn't have known how to play a shameless woman like Jezebel, but now she would.

"Look, why won't you take me seriously?"

Kate looked at her watch. "You're running late. Mr. Parsons will have something to say and Blossom will be anxious." Her old headmistress firmly believed that it was the female side of a relationship that dictated how far and how fast it went, so here she was, firmly applying the brake.

"Please don't mention Blossom Parsons in the same breath as you and me. I may be . . . well . . . overfriendly with certain people, but I do draw the line at Blossom."

"Drive on." Some instinct, deep down, warned her to keep

him at a distance because nothing but terrible hurt could result from falling in love with Scott. Maybe she was already in love, maybe not, but Kate knew she was right. Beneath his complaints about the weather she sensed a longing for home and she knew he'd be gone one day without so much as a backward glance.

"What is Mr. Parsons's problem?"

"Scouring."

"I trust you mean one of his cows?'

Scott laughed. "Yes. It's Christabel. We can't stop it. Kidneys, you know. She's no use to him as a commercial proposition—she's far too old—but he can't bear to see her go. He's such a sentimental fool; I just hope he'll face up to it today without too much stress."

"I like Mr. Parsons."

"So do I. He's great. He'll never make a fortune, but there you are. Right, boots. Please." As he reached into the footwell of the passenger seat to get his own boots, he made it an excuse to kiss her.

"Scott!"

"You sound like a schoolteacher."

"Well, someone has to keep your urges in check."

Scott grumbled as he struggled to put on his boots in the confines of the driver's seat. "No heart, you haven't, none at all. Hard as iron."

"I have a heart all right, but it's not yours for the taking." Tempted by the vulnerability of the nape of his neck, she kissed it before he straightened up.

"Wow! She's kissed me!" He pretended to fall out of the open door with the shock, and stood in the lane looking up at her, grinning. "Come on, then, you temptress. Let's be having you."

They strode across to the cow barn amicably, sidestepping as best they could the filth that, despite his constant promises, Phil had never cleared up. He appeared like a specter through the gloom of the barn, almost colliding with them as they entered. "She's down. Went down an hour ago; that's when I rang. That's it, isn't it? I can't get her up."

"Let me look. I did warn you two days ago that the stuff wouldn't cure it, Phil. At her age there isn't much hope. I did say. You'll have to brace yourself, mate."

Scott took out his stethoscope and bent over Christabel to give her a thorough examination. He shook his head. "We could put a sling under her and get her up between us. Kate is pretty strong and if Blossom helped us . . . But I really don't think . . ."

Phil took out his handkerchief and pressed it to the gaps in his balaclava. Blossom appeared in the doorway. "I heard you come. All up, is it?"

Scott nodded. "It would be kinder, you know. Her heart's . . . you know . . . what with that and the kidney problem . . ."

Blossom burst into noisy tears. Phil desperately tried to smother his sobs, but they wouldn't be stilled. Between them he said, "She's been my favorite all these years." He looked at Kate. "She knew me, yer know. Knew me, she did. Bless her. Came when I called."

Kate weighed in on Scott's side, saying as gently as she could, "I understand how fond you are of her, but you'd be doing her the best of all kindnesses by letting Scott put her to rest. You can rely on him. He wouldn't put her to sleep a moment too soon. For her sake, it feels almost cruel to prolong the decision."

Phil Parsons looked at Kate from inside his balaclava. "You're right. I can't let her suffer, can I? That's not the way a friend would behave. I'll just have a moment with her before you . . ."

Kate and Scott went to stand in the yard. Quietly Kate said, "This is dreadful. Are all farmers like this?"

"No, not all. No farmer likes having an animal put down, but Phil takes it all so personally. They're his friends, you see."

"I'll be crying next."

"Lean on me, sweet one, you can cry on my shoulder."

"OK, then. Thanks for the offer."

"Scott!" Phil shouted from inside. "All right. Let's get it over with." He burst out through the door and marched without looking back into the farmhouse. Blossom teetered after him, her high heels slipping and sliding on the cobbles of the yard. Over her shoulder she hissed, "Get it done, and quick, before he changes his mind." She followed him into the house.

"Well, we'd better get on with it. You and me."

"Tell me what to do." Kate went to Christabel's head and stroked her forehead.

"I think the situation calls for an overdose of anesthetic." When Scott came back with the syringe and the bottle of anesthetic, Kate unexpectedly felt ill at the thought of watching this dear old friend of Phil's take her leave. But she continued stroking her head, kneeling down in the straw to get closer. She cuddled Christabel's head with her arms while Scott prepared the syringe.

"Watch! Take note." He plunged the needle into Christabel's vein and almost in an instant she was gone.

They both went to the farmhouse door intending to say they were leaving. It was open and Scott put one foot inside and called out, "It's done. All quiet and peaceful. She's out of her misery. We're going now, all right?"

But Blossom would have none of it. "Come in, even if it's

only for a moment. Phil's having a whiskey. Would you have one too? In the circumstances, you know. Please!" They couldn't ignore the pleading tone in her voice.

Scott glanced at Kate and she nodded. After all, at least the whiskey might be wholesome if nothing else was. She supposed that not even Blossom could do damage to whiskey. So they went in and found sparkling crystal glasses awaiting them on the cluttered, dirty kitchen table.

"Only a small for me; I'm driving. Same for Kate; she's not used to it."

Blossom handed them their glasses and, picking up her own, toasted Phil. He was slumped in his favorite chair by the fire, lost in gloom, his balaclava askew, his handkerchief pressed to it.

"Twelve years I've had Christabel. Twelve years. Never a mite of trouble she's been. Eight calves she's had. Eight. Mother of Sunny Boy, yer know, and for that alone she's special. I won't tell him tonight; best not till morning. It'll only upset him, yer know." Sorrowfully he shook his head.

Choked by the depth of Phil's sorrow, Scott muttered, "Quite right." He braced himself and found words of comfort. "She's had a good life, though, Phil. There's nothing on your conscience where she's concerned, is there, Mrs. Parsons?"

She shook her head in reply. "Treated like royalty she's been."

What she'd said reminded Kate of little Scott. "Where's Scott? I'd like to see her."

"Scott? Oh, the kitten. On our bed, I expect." She went to the bottom of the stairs and shrieked, "Scott! Scott!" In a moment little Scott came running down the stairs, a bundle of energy and well grown for her age. She wrapped herself around Kate's legs, then Scott's and then jumped up on Phil's knee. She arched her back and flirted her tail, inviting him to stroke her. Phil nuzzled her with his forehead. "Christabel's gone, old love. Did you know?"

The three of them stood in silence, watching him. Scott broke it by suggesting it was time they were off. "Thanks for the whiskey. Sorry and all that. Take care."

Kate swallowed the last of her whiskey and said, "Good night, Mr. Parsons, Mrs. Parsons."

"Good night and thanks." This from Blossom because Phil was too full of grief to reply.

Before Scott unlocked the Land Rover, he stood Kate against the driver's door and kissed her. She put her arms around him and hugged him tightly. They kissed a few more times and then stood holding each other close. "Scott, I was almost crying in there. It won't do for a vet, will it?"

"Why not?"

"Maybe I shouldn't be one."

"Of course you must. You handled yourself brilliantly. Is it the first time you've put an animal down?"

Kate nodded.

"It won't be the last, you know. It's all part of the job. You never do it unless it's completely necessary, the one and only course of action. It's never pleasant, but it has to be done."

"I know, but Mr. Parsons was . . ."

Inexplicably, Scott was suddenly pulled away from her, and almost hit the ground but managed to save himself.

"Who the hell!" Scott turned and found he was being gripped by . . . *Oh God! No!* It was Adam, wild with temper.

"She's my girl! My girl, do you hear! I could kill you!" Adam grabbed Scott by the neck of his jacket and tried to whirl him away down the lane, but he had not bargained for Scott's superior strength.

Scott slid out of his jacket and made a stand. Taking hold of the front of Adam's anorak with both hands, he hauled him to a halt. Face-to-face, Scott snarled, "What the blazes do you bloody well think you're doing? Eh?" Eh?" Scott shook him viciously, making Adam drop the jacket in his desperate effort to stop his attack.

Kate shouted, "Stop it! Stop it!" trying to put an end to Scott's violent shaking. But Scott wouldn't stop. He shook Adam till his head was rocking backward and forward like a rag doll's, his breath pushing in and out of his lungs with great grunts.

"We've had enough of you, do you hear? Stalking Kate. It's to stop. Now. Now, I say!" Scott released him. The two of them paused for a moment, both breathing heavily.

Kate went to stand between them and, summoning up some of the power she'd felt when Mr. Parsons had gone to the practice with his billhook, shouted, "Please, Adam. There's to be no more of it. Just go home."

"Home?" His Adam's apple leaped up and down in his throat with his agitation. "Home? There's nothing for me there. Nothing at all. If you'd just agree to marry, everything would be right."

Peering at him, Kate could see the desperation in his demeanor. "But I can't marry you. I can't love you; I said so."

Adam jerked his head at Scott. "There was love between us before he came. I know there was."

"No, Adam, not really, we were mistaken."

"I wasn't. *I loved you.*"

"I was mistaken, then."

Scott intervened. "It still doesn't excuse stalking Kate. Have you any idea how frightened you made her? Dogging her footsteps every day. Following her like you've done tonight."

"I needed to know what she was doing. I couldn't allow you to . . . I wanted to watch what you were up to. I wouldn't have *harmed her.*"

"She didn't know that, did she? Have you nothing better to do?"

This silenced Adam.

Sensing his agony at the idea of speaking aloud the dreaded words, but realizing he'd be all the better for admitting it, Kate quietly said, "I'm sorry you've lost your job."

Having the words spoken out loud in front of his adversary was the final humiliation for Adam. Just between the two of them he could have confessed his predicament but not in front of the damnable Aussie. He brought back his fist and pushed it with all his meager might into Scott's face. But Scott was too quick for him and dodged the blow. It spent itself against the Land Rover and made Adam hop with pain. He hugged his hand to his chest and achieved an appearance of such ridiculous helplessness that Kate was more upset by it than she wanted to admit. He looked so defeated that she went to put her hand on his arm in sympathy, but he brushed it off.

The pain of his hand and the heaped-up despair of the last few weeks mounted up and he spat out, "Glad, are you? Satisfied? Yes, I have to confess I have lost my job. Not only did I not get my promotion, but I also got the sack. Imagine. All my hours of dedication and wham!" By mistake, blinded by his suffering, he banged his injured hand on to the door of the Land Rover again and suffered even more pain. "Oh God! That hurt! I was chucked out! Not even time to say good-bye. They kindly forwarded my belongings!"

"I'm so sorry. Your mother, how has she taken it?"

Adam looked at her with burning, angry eyes. "I haven't told her yet."

"But . . ."

"I know! I go out every day ready for work and . . ."

"Oh, Adam. Tell her. That's what mothers are for."

"Not this mother."

Scott decided to put an end to all the sympathy. After all, Adam had made her life a misery and here she was, after Adam had attacked *him*, feeling sorry for him. Pugnaciously he said, "Well, if you don't mind, I'd like to get home. Do I take it there won't be any more following of Kate, then?"

Kate would have preferred a more kindly approach from Scott. "Scott!"

"Well, Adam, do I have your word for it?"

Adam ignored Scott and looked at Kate, taking in her lovely face and the sympathy in her eyes and wished—oh, how he wished—he'd behaved better than he had. He swallowed hard, knowing she'd see that pathetic Adam's apple of his bobbing up and bobbing down. What he felt was a sense of total outrage that someone whom he considered his property was in a closer relationship than he had ever been and with a man who surpassed him in almost every aspect of his life. His looks, his charisma, his appeal, his qualifications, his . . . "There'll be no more following of Kate."

Scott was determined he wouldn't get away with it too easily and decided to finally humiliate him by treating him like a child. "Say you're sorry, then, like a good boy."

"I am sorry, Kate. I should never have done it. I was just so . . ."

"I know. It must have been terrible. But tell your mother. You can't keep this deception up forever, you know."

He shrugged. "Mothers don't have to know everything. I'm going to get another job before I tell her. The money's running out anyway."

"That's it. You show her. I reckon she's not nearly so frail as she makes out, you know. Stand tall. Move out." Kate smiled up at him. "Move on."

Adam gave her the nicest of smiles. "You could be right, but she'll go mad."

"Let her. It's your life."

He rattled about in his pocket for his car keys. "I won't say good-bye, Kate; I'll let you know what happens." Adam set off down the lane toward his parked car. Kate and Scott looked after him in silence.

Scott put his arm around her shoulders. "Well, well."

"Poor Adam. What a night! What with Christabel and him . . ."

"At least that's the end of his following you. I really do think he meant what he said. Don't you?"

"Oh yes. Adam's always straightforward."

"I don't think sneaking about following you around is straightforward."

"Well, he wasn't in his right mind then, was he?"

"Where's my jacket? Ruined, I've no doubt." He bent down to pick it up. Fortunately, it hadn't rained for a few days and the jacket was dry. He dusted it off and put it back on again.

They both felt deflated by the evening's events and all Kate wanted to do was go home and eat. Without Scott. Just with Mia and Dad, and to tell them her news. "Take me home. Please."

"Get in."

As it turned out, Gerry was at one of his model railway meetings, so there was only Mia at home. "Scott not coming in, then?"

"No. Only me. I'm ready to eat.

"Two minutes." Mia looked at Kate and, seeing the stress in her face, opened her arms wide and folded her in them. "There! There! What's happened? You look upset."

Kate drew away from her. "As we were leaving Applegate Farm, Adam appeared."

"Adam!"

"Adam. He went for Scott and they had a kind of mini-fight."

"Oh, Kate!"

She told Mia word for word what had happened, ending her story with "I'm so glad it's all over."

"So am I. Thank God for that. Here, sit down and eat, you'll feel all the better for it. I don't think I could have taken much more, never mind you. And you say his mother still doesn't know."

Kate nodded. "I think he's going to get another job and then tell her what happened. I felt ever so sorry for him."

"Well, you would." Mia patted her hand. "That's just like you." Mia got halfway out of her chair to reach across the table to kiss Kate. "Too kind by half."

They smiled at each other and Kate continued eating in silence with Mia watching every mouthful. When she'd finished, Kate put down her dessert spoon, drank the last of her tea and said, "Mia."

"Yes."

"I never say how much I appreciate all you do for me. You're not my mum, but you are, if you know what I mean."

"It's a pleasure. I loved you the moment I saw you."

"When did you first see me?"

Mia drew her cup of tea out of the way and rested her forearms on the table. "You were six months old when I moved in next door. A year old when your dad and I married."

"But I thought . . ."

"Do you really want to know?"

"Yes."

"I mean really, really want to know?"

"Yes."

"Your dad should be here."

"Tell me all the same."

"You're right. It would only upset him and you've a right to know at your age."

"He's never told me, you know, not what really happened."

"First, did you know your mum and dad weren't married?"

"I didn't know that."

Mia nodded. "It's true. Where they met I've no idea, but when I moved in next door, he was on his own with you. Are you sure you're ready for this?"

"For some reason I am. I've got to know. Things are kind of moving on with Scott and I feel I need to have things straightened out before . . . before I take any steps."

"Moving on with Scott?"

"Kind of. I think."

"Well, he's a lovely young man and if he suits you . . . Here goes, then. Your mother had walked out when you were two weeks old and left your dad to get on as best he could."

Kate gasped with surprise. "I thought she'd died. I always thought she'd died. You mean somewhere I have a mother? A real mother?"

Mia felt stabbed through the heart by Kate's excitement and wished she'd never agreed to tell. It was too hard for her to take; she should have waited for Gerry. "Yes. But she's never been in touch since. He told me he'd tried every avenue he could think of to find her, but he never did. Before I knew where I was, I was helping him to care for you. I'd just left a savage marriage and the sight of you so beautiful and innocent, so bright and happy and kind of gurgly, gave me back my faith in the world. Just touching you helped to heal my wounds."

Mia stopped speaking and gazed into the distance, obviously enjoying once more the happiness the baby Kate had brought her. She sighed briefly and went on with her story. "I'd only been here about two months when my pig of a husband was killed instantly in a car accident. I didn't think immediately: oh, well, that releases me from my bondage. Relief, yes, but not any thoughts of being free to get married again. I'd had enough of that. Your dad and I bumbled along for a few months looking after each other, like people do. I had you to myself when he was at work and the whole arrangement worked out very well. One thing I loved was taking you out in the pram, because people thought you were mine and I wished you were. We were bathing you ready for bed one night when Gerry said, 'Why don't we?' Why don't we what? I thought. 'Get married,' he said."

"Oh, Mia, not the most poetic of proposals."

They were holding hands by now and Mia squeezed Kate's and laughed. "No, it wasn't and I point-blank refused. Poor Gerry, he didn't know where to look or what to do. We didn't love each other, you see; we only came together because of you. He never mentioned it again, but he was less forthcoming, more abrupt in his manner. Then one day, clear as light, I saw that if I didn't marry him, I'd lose you."

"Did you propose to him, then?"

Mia nodded. "I did. We acknowledged that we didn't love each other, but we agreed we *liked* each other and that for now we'd make do with that. He said he couldn't live with me because it wouldn't be decent for his daughter to be brought up in circumstances like that and I agreed it wouldn't. So we married."

"All because of me?"

"It suited us both, don't forget. He needed someone and so did I, and we both needed you."

"You seem to love him now."

"That all happened after we married. It's not the most romantic marriage in the world, but we rub along very, very nicely together and I've no regrets."

"I see."

"It's much much better than nothing and I've got you." Mia hesitated. "Haven't I?"

"You know you have. For always. It's you who brought me up. You are my mother as far as I am concerned. But my biological mother, you never knew her?"

Mia's heart sank like a stone and she looked away. "No. Your dad told me it wasn't part of your mother's life plan to be tied down to a baby and the routine it entails. How she ever came to be involved with him I don't know. I don't think she was his kind of person."

"Has he any photographs of her?"

"I don't know; I never asked. She had a career, you see. We mustn't blame her, must we, because we don't really know her circumstances, do we?"

Kate didn't answer her question and then, out of the blue, asked, "How do you know if you love someone enough to marry them and follow them to the ends of the earth?"

"If you're asking that, then you're not in love."

"I see."

"You're thinking about Scott?"

Kate nodded. She poured herself another cup of tea, but it tasted cold and she pushed it away. "One day, I know for sure, he'll be going back to Australia, because sometimes he talks about it with such longing. Then the mood passes off and he's Scott again, being daft and lovely and such fun. Trouble is, I doubt if a permanent relationship is in his mind right now. But he's so lovely to be with and he claims he's fallen in love with me. Then I remember about Bunty, and was her baby really his or not? He'd have left her with the baby, you know; he told her so. He was prepared to walk away and that worries me about him. But all the same . . ."

"There's one thing for certain: Adam would never have done for you. Never in this world."

"No. I told him to stand tall and move on. It's his mother who's ruining his life. She's so domineering."

"Do you think he will?"

"I hope so." Kate pushed her chair away from the table and stood up. "Must go, got chemistry to do." As she left the room, she turned back to say, "One day I'll ask Dad about my mother. It doesn't make a bit of difference to you and me, but I'd still like to know about her. Mothers aren't always the best of people to bring one up, are they?"

Mia smiled with relief. "Not always."

Chapter

· 13 ·

S cott came in at the stroke of eight o'clock and since not a single client had arrived, he leaned over the desk to kiss Kate. "There couldn't be anything sweeter than kissing you at this time in the morning. Considering how early it is, you look stunning. How're things? You must be feeling better after clearing the air yesterday."

"Oh, I am! I drove myself here this morning. My first taste of freedom has quite gone to my head. How is my knight in shining armor feeling this morning?"

"All the better for seeing you. Give me another kiss."

"Mm."

"Love you. Love me?"

"Don't know."

"Ah! There's hope."

They became absorbed in their kissing, she on one side of the desk and he on the other. Their elbows leaned on it so they could reach and they didn't notice that Joy had pushed open the heavy outer door and was standing watching them through the inner glass doors. So this was what they got up to. She had to smile, for she could see the attraction of Scott and of Kate, and it was a pleasure to see their delight in each other. But these were business premises and . . . the phone began ringing. Immediately, Scott started to pull away, but Kate put both hands behind his neck and kept him kissing. When the phone had rung four times and Kate still hadn't answered it, Joy opened the glass door and said, "Answer that, please, Kate."

They broke apart, startled by the sharpness of her tone, but more so because both of them were embarrassed at being discovered.

"Barleybridge Veterinary Hospital, Kate speaking, how may I help?"

Joy stalked straight past the two of them and went into her office. She put her coat in her cupboard, placed her bag beneath her desk and went to unlock the back door.

When she returned to her office, Scott was waiting for her. He was holding up both hands, signifying surrender. "All my fault, Joy. Sorry! Not in working hours and all that."

"There's something heartening about young love."

"There is?"

"Oh yes. Got your list?"

Scott nodded.

"Then off you go."

She couldn't help but smile at the surprise on Scott's face. He'd expected a telling off and hadn't gotten one. It was none of her business, in truth. What the staff got up to in their spare time was their affair. All the same, she'd have a cautionary word with Kate when the right moment presented itself. Or would she? Maybe not, the girl was no fool. Joy could hear laughter in reception and smiled to herself. He was such a rogue, was Scott. If she'd been younger, she'd have fancied him too, just like Kate. She went to check if the two Sarahs had come in yet and left Scott and Kate to enjoy their romantic moment.

A draught blew through from the back right around Scott's legs. It was Rhodri opening the back door, intent on making an early start. He bustled in, rubbing his hands. "It's cold today. Morning, Scott. Morning, Kate. How's the old love life, Scott? 'Spect the old cracked ribs have brought a halt to it, eh?"

Scott feigned surprise. "You're asking me about my love life? What about yours? After what I saw last night, mate, I should be asking you."

Rhodri blushed.

Kate drew closer. "Go on, then, what did you see?"

"Outside the Fox and Grapes. About eleven. My God, you should have seen! Talk about the old Welsh charm. These Celts!" Scott pretended to fan himself and then to swoon.

"Shut up!" Rhodri might have said shut up, but at bottom he looked pleased that at long last his private life was a subject for conversation. "Kate doesn't want to hear."

"She does," said Kate.

"Look! There's a simple explanation. We'd been out. I'd put Harry Ferret in the back in his cage and forgotten to close the second catch, and hey presto, while we were having a drink the little devil escaped, so before Megan and I could drive home I had the little blighter to find. Couldn't start up with him running loose. So that's what you saw."

Scott simply didn't believe his explanation. "Well, I've heard some cracking excuses for a rough and tumble in the back of a station wagon, but that's the best yet. Wait till I see Megan. I'll ask her. She'll tell me the truth."

Kate was laughing so much at the embarrassment in Rhodri's face she couldn't answer the phone when it rang, so Scott answered it for her. When he'd finished speaking, Rhodri said, "You'll do no such thing."

Scott now feigned indignation. "I shall. We'll see if Megan blushes any redder than you've done."

"I've explained what we were doing. Anyway, eventually we found him curled up asleep in the spare wheel. Took us ages."

"I bet! When are you going to make an honest woman of her?"

Rhodri sobered. "Don't know. I want to get married, but there's her father."

Kate's eyes opened wide with surprise. "Get married! You've known her barely three months."

"Get married and then tell him," Scott advised.

Rhodri shook his head. "No no, that wouldn't be right."

Kate asked whose life it was, but Rhodri didn't answer. Scott and Kate winked at each other as he walked away to see if the mail had arrived.

"Poor blighter!"

"Did you really see them . . . you know . . . in the back of his car?"

"Pulling his leg, though they did look suspicious. Must go. He shouldn't let other people stop him from doing what he wants with his own life. I bet the old dad wants Megan to look after him in his old age; that's what it'll be. Selfish old basket. What time do you finish today?"

"With any luck about seven."

"Pick you up."

"OK. Where shall we go?"

"Don't know, but we'll eat."

"OK."

"See you then."

KATE spent the afternoon between one o'clock and four shopping in the mall for something special to wear that evening. Adam being finally cleared from her mind seemed to have given shape to her feelings for Scott and she knew now for certain that he meant an awful lot more to her than she had hitherto dared to admit. And it wasn't just his looks, though they were fantastic in themselves. It was his whole attitude to life that she found exciting. His drive, his humor, his laughter, his mind and the serious side to him, the side that approached his job with such professionalism and feeling.

She studied her reflection in a shop window and remembered the gentleness of his kisses and the feel of his arms around her. Oh Christ! She sounded like a heroine in a cheap women's magazine. But it was true; she did like his physical presence and she did wish . . . Cold reason asserted itself. So he goes home to Australia, then what? Because he would, there was no doubt about that, and where would that leave her? Kate brushed aside her contemplative mood and went into the shop to buy something, anything that would give her a lift. As Stephie would say, a bit of retail therapy does wonders for the spirits.

SHE and Scott had decided to eat in a little Italian restaurant in the shopping mall and were on the point of ordering when Scott's mobile phone rang. "Excuse me. Hello. Scott Spencer speaking." Kate watched him listening to his caller, and admired the way his hair grew and studied the look of frustration that crossed his face as he listened. He really was the most beautiful man. She could fall for him in a big way. In fact, if she was honest, she had already done that very thing. He snapped the phone off and pushed it into his pocket.

"Look, you stay here and eat. I'm going to be some time."

"I thought you weren't on call."

"I'm not. Mungo is, but he's got two calls, both for difficult calvings, and he can't do them both at once. So I'm going." He stood up to leave. "Who'd be a vet?"

"Me for a start. I'll come. Can I?"

"If you wish. I'd be glad. But aren't you hungry?"

"We can both eat when we've finished; they'll still be open. Is it far?"

"No. Come on, then."

The farm was only a three-mile drive away and as soon as she stepped out onto the flagged yard, she saw it was the exact opposite of Phil Parsons's. The yard was floodlit and she could see that every barn and stable door, every window frame, was painted an immaculate marine blue. Each window pane shone, and huge terra-cotta pots holding ornamental bushes stood between the doors wherever a space could be found. If it hadn't been for the sound of a horse stamping in the stables, Kate would have imagined that no animal was permitted in this hallowed place.

"Through here." Scott led the way under an arch between the stables and immediately they were in another yard with a long cowshed running down the length of one side. Scott shouted, "Hello! Chris!"

A short, sturdy man appeared from what looked like a small office calling out, "Hi, Scott! Am I glad to see you. I was just ringing again to make sure you were on your way. In here. Aren't you going to introduce me?"

"Sorry. This is Kate; got a place at vet college. Wanting some experience. Kate, this is Chris, his lordship's stockman."

"Hi, Kate. Here she is. Been straining for far too long and making no progress at all. I've had my hand in to see if I can straighten it out, but she's straining so hard I thought my hand would be crushed. But for God's sake, hurry her up before we lose it and her."

The heifer was a lovely Guernsey with melting brown eyes full of distress. She was standing on lavish straw bedding and looked as though she had given up on life. Scott went to her head and had a word with her, stroking her, lifting her lips to see the color of her gums. "You should have called me earlier."

"You know his lordship's opinion of vets."

"I do. Bucket of water and soap. Warm. Please."

Scott stripped to the waist, put on his calving trousers and apron, washed his hands and arms, and tried inserting an arm to sort out the calf.

"No good. Straining too hard and there's not much room in there anyway. I'll give her an epidural."

Kate couldn't help but admire his approach: businesslike and yet so calm and compassionate.

"But we'll lose her if you don't hurry up. Put ropes on it and we'll pull it out." Chris was obviously becoming seriously agitated by Scott's delay in taking positive action.

"If I give her an epidural, she'll stop straining. That'll give me room to sort out the calf and then gently, gently we can pull it out. Otherwise, we'll tear her and have more problems than we had to begin with. Believe me."

Scott calmly injected the heifer at the base of her tail and then stood back to wait. "Kate, go get the ropes for me, will you?"

Kate sped away through the arch, found the ropes and went hurrying back, desperate not to miss a thing. By the time she got back, the heifer had relaxed and the fearful exhausting straining she'd been doing had ceased.

"Thanks. Now we'll see what we can do."

"Bloody well get a hurry on, will you? I don't want to lose this heifer."

"Neither do I, Chris. Neither do I." Scott inserted his arm, and Chris and Kate watched in silence. "One leg tucked back; that's the problem." He grunted and pushed and pulled and then said, "There, that's sorted. Rope? I'll put it around the feet

and then we'll have the other for its head and in no time . . .
That's it. Look, Kate, we can see both the feet already and its
nose. Rope." He was silent for a minute, struggling to get the
rope positioned correctly around the calf's head. Then very
slowly and steadily his pulling began to have an effect and the
calf's face appeared. "Put a finger in its mouth, Kate. See what
happens."

To Kate's amazed delight she felt the calf make a kind of
half attempt to suck her finger. "Why, it's trying to suck, and
it's all warm and wet."

"Good, then." He grinned at her pleasure. "We've got a goer."

Chris grew agitated at what he considered to be too much
delay. "For God's sake, Scott, hurry up or we shan't have. You're
being too casual. You'll be asking for afternoon tea next. Get
it out."

Calmly Scott answered, "All in good time. Now, Kate, hold
the head rope and slowly and *steadily* pull when I say."

Kate did.

Panicking, Chris shouted, "She's going down!"

"Push some more straw her way. Quick!"

The heifer was down and after some more steady pulling,
the head was out and the body followed in no time at all. With
a sudden *sploosh* the calf was lying on the straw. All panic forgotten, Chris breathed a sigh of relief. "Thank God. And it's a
heifer! Isn't she grand?" He got a handful of the bedding and
wiped the calf's face and nose with it.

Scott knelt and gave the calf a quick checkup, saying, "Great
little thing, she is. She's a real beauty. Come on, then, mother,
take some interest in your calf." Scott took off the ropes and
dragged the calf around to the heifer's head to encourage her to
pay it some attention.

Kate had to laugh because the mother gave the calf such
a look of surprise it was almost comical. Then, very tentatively,

as if instinct was overcoming her amazement at what she had produced, the mother gave the calf a lick. It made little noises and was rewarded by being licked more vigorously. Scott stood watching for a moment, and then quickly immersed his hands and arms in the bucket of water and washed himself thoroughly.

"I'll just make sure everything's OK inside."

After he'd examined her and decided the heifer was fine, Scott moved the calf a few feet away from her.

Kate didn't understand his reasons and protested loudly. "Oh, Scott! Don't do that. You'll upset her."

"I want her up before I leave." Believing that the calf was being taken away from her, the mother hastily got to her feet and moved a few steps to bring her close again, nuzzling and licking her offspring as soon as it was within reach.

Kate was totally overcome. So this was what it was all about. This moment. This birth. This lovely creature born safely because of a man's skill. She didn't think she'd seen anything more beautiful in all her life. Such a precious moment, she'd remember it always. She was privileged, that's what she was, privileged. She paused for a while to watch the delight the cow had in her young.

By the time she'd had her fill, Scott was hosing down his calving trousers at the tap outside in the yard. She watched him take them off and hang them on a stable-door catch to drip. The bucket of warm water he used for swilling his arms and hands.

Chris banged him on his bare back. "Thanks for that, Scott. Whiskey to celebrate?"

Scott nodded his thanks. Kate handed him the towel Chris had provided. He grinned at her. "Great, eh?"

"Absolutely. I'm dumbstruck. Are all Guernsey calves as beautiful as that one?"

"Mostly, yes. Brilliant vet his lordship's got, eh?"

Kate laughed. "Is the owner really a lord?"

"Indeed. Tightfisted as hell, he is. Except where his horses are concerned."

"I don't remember anyone being called out to his horses."

"Uses an equine practice. Can't trust them to people like us!"

"Huh! If he'd seen you in there with that heifer, he would. It was like a miracle. So wonderful."

"Such loyalty." He shrugged on his jacket, put his hand on her shoulder, studied the rapt expression on her face and saluted her with a kiss. "Come and get your whiskey. Is that all right?"

"Yes."

By the time she returned to the passenger seat and Scott was backing out prior to leaving, the whiskey had hit her empty stomach with a bang. The euphoria she'd felt at witnessing the birth, rather than wearing off, was increasing: Kate felt on top of the world; there was nothing she couldn't achieve. She glanced sideways at Scott and loved everything about him. Now her admiration of his skill with the calving was as nothing compared with her absorption in his physical magnetism. Her headmistress's homily was ditched as belonging to another age, nothing to do with a new century and the new woman she had become.

He turned to smile at her while he waited to pull out onto the main road and put a hand on her knee intending to give it a squeeze, but Kate put her hand over his and held it there. When he was ready to move off, he pulled his hand out from under hers reluctantly. Scott didn't speak again until they came to the crossroads where he needed to choose between the mall and food or collecting her car first.

"Which?"

"Collect my car? Please. First."

"First? Right. Will do."

They drove in silence until they reached the practice. After Scott had pulled on the hand brake, he turned to face her and at the same time switched on the internal light. "There, I can see you better now. Your face! You should have seen it. A successful calving never loses its excitement even when you've done it a hundred times and more. There's nothing to compare, is there?"

Kate shook her head. "Nothing. It was just . . . well . . . just *so* special. There's nothing like it in the whole world. One day I shall have skills like yours; I'm determined."

"I thought as much."

"How on earth do you sort out twin lambs, for heaven's sakes? All heads and feet and legs and things? How do you know what belongs to which?"

"Try lambing on a Welsh hill farm at dead of night with a freezing wind and icy sleet with it; believe me, you learn pretty sharpish what's what."

"Have you done that?"

"Just as a temporary for a few weeks before I went to Devon and then on to here. I worked for a Welsh farmer Dad met when he came over to a conference once. Never again. They deserve every penny they earn, farmers like him. I thought I'd never get warm again." Scott put an arm around Kate's shoulders and bent to kiss her. She welcomed him more eagerly than she had ever done, wrapping her arms around his neck, caressing his tongue with hers, pressing him to her, warming to a passion she had not shown before.

Though taken by surprise, Scott still managed to match passion for passion. His hands were roving over her, undoing buttons, enjoying the feel of her smooth skin, the rise of her neck from her shoulders, the sharp angle of her collarbone, the . . . Perkins barked furiously as he raced from the back door toward the Land Rover. He clamored to get in, leaping up, scraping his claws on the door, racing around and around, furious at finding someone in the car park when at this time of night it was his territory and his alone.

Miriam was with him and she tapped on the driver's window. "Be quiet, Perkins, it's Scott and Kate. Be quiet, I say. Hi, you two. Sorry."

Scott wound down the window while Kate pulled herself together.

"Hi, there, Miriam. Mungo not back yet?"

"No. It's a Caesarean, so Bunty's gone out to give a hand. Twins. Yours was easy, was it?"

"Just needed straightening out, then it popped out nice and easy. Brought Kate to collect her car, then we're going to eat."

"Sorry to take up your free evening, but there was no alternative."

"Not at all. Someone had to go."

Miriam peered into the cab. "All right, Kate? Good experience?"

You couldn't be resentful with her. Not with Miriam. "Marvelous! Thanks."

"Good. I'm glad. Be seeing you. Good night."

She went off up to the top of the car park with Perkins and disappeared into the darkness.

"I love you, Kate. Go get your car, follow me and we'll have that meal. I'm starving."

"So am I." She looked at him full face and laid a gentle hand on his cheek. "I love you too."

"If Miriam hadn't come . . ."

"I know."

"Would you have . . . you know."

"Oh yes. With you."

"I'm honored." Scott leaned across and opened the door for her. "She'll be back; we'd better go. Love you."

Reluctantly Kate got out and went to her own car. She'd come so close. So close. She did love him, then. She must, to have wanted him so much. What a night. If she were fanciful, she would have classed this as a night when there'd been a turning point in her life.

She waited until he'd reversed and was facing the exit, then put her car into first gear and followed Scott to the mall, and thought about following him across the world.

They ate back at the Italian restaurant, then each drove home, mulling over the memories of their meal, the touching of hands, of minds, of souls—Scott, overcome with concern at the way their relationship had taken off, Kate filled with joy, unable to contemplate a life without him.

SHE began work next morning full of energy, after a blissful night's sleep due to a long day but more so because she was in love with Scott. He was at the back of her mind all the time and filled the whole of it if there was a lull. She couldn't wait for him to come in this morning to collect his list of calls.

Stephie noticed how happy she was and asked the reason.

"I went to a calving with Scott last night. It was brilliant. Absolutely incredible."

"And was that all?"

"Oh yes! Well . . ."

"Yes?"

"We had a meal afterward."

"And . . . ?"

"Nothing."

Disbelieving the possibility of going out with a man like Scott and nothing happening between them, Stephie said, "Oh, come on! Give us the rest."

"There wasn't anything."

"So what's the cause of your sparkling eyes this morning and the moments when you're in another world?"

"You're talking nonsense."

"Can't wait for him to come in?" Stephie giggled. "Watch out, you don't want to do another Bunty."

Kate could have smacked her face for her. She was filled with outrage. How dare she? How dare she compare the unique beauty of what Scott and she felt for each other with what had happened to Bunty? In any case, Bunty had never actually said the baby was his. How dare she?

Before Kate managed to come up with a stinging reply, Miss Chillingsworth came into reception carrying a cat basket, and Kate had to brace herself to be polite and interested, and leave the stinging reply for later. She certainly wasn't going to let her get away with a remark like that.

Kate put every ounce of enthusiasm she could muster into her greeting. "Why, Miss Chillingsworth, what a lovely surprise! You haven't got a new kitten, have you? How exciting!"

"No, dear, I haven't. I have a cat. It's a stray. I'm very upset, actually, I've come early on purpose because I think it's about to die."

"Oh, dear. I am sorry. Tell me."

"There's been a cat about for ages. Then this last week it's been looking lost and forlorn, but I didn't want to start feeding it, thinking it belonged to someone. And I did suspect she was pregnant. I asked around if anyone knew whose she was, but they're all too busy to bother with me and my problems. However, I didn't see her for a day or so, then I did and I noticed she was walking awkwardly, as though she was in pain."

"Have you got kittens in there, then?"

"Oh no! Then I heard mewing last night very late and I

plucked up my courage and went to look and she was crouched in a cardboard box I'd put out for the bin men. She was in such a sorry state, and it was beginning to rain, so I picked her up very carefully and took her inside. She's very poorly. It would be cruel to leave her without help, so . . ." Miss Chillingsworth took a deep breath. "I know I shouldn't have done it because she isn't mine, but someone had to do something so I've brought her for Mr. Murgatroyd to see. It's very urgent, I'm sure."

Kate lifted the lid a little and peeped inside. It didn't need much intelligence to see that the cat was desperately ill. "He isn't here until eleven today."

"Oh, dear, what shall we do? I'm so worried."

"Rhodri's here; he'll see to her. Come with me."

Kate took Miss Chillingsworth into Rhodri's consulting room and put the cat basket on the examination table. "Take a seat. I'll get him."

Rhodri lifted the cat out of the basket and had to lay her on the table because she was too weak to stand. "Why, there's nothing left of her, just skin and bone." His hands gently moved over her body feeling her ribs, her stomach. He checked her gums, lifted a pinch of her skin, opened her eyelids, spoke to her and, getting no response, looked at Miss Chillingsworth and shook his head. "She's very ill, very dehydrated, starving too. I suspect she has been in labor for far too long and now everything has stopped. I'm pretty sure she has a kitten jammed and can't push it out. Would you leave me awhile, Miss Chillingsworth, and I'll see what can be done. Go and sit in reception if you wish."

Miss Chillingsworth looked searchingly into his face. "You're saying there's not much hope, aren't you?"

"I am."

"If the kittens survive and she doesn't, then I'm very good with tiny kittens. Ask Kate, she knows. I'd gladly help." She saw he was eager to do what he had to do to save what he could. "I'll wait." Before she left, she stroked the cat's head and momentarily her eyes opened and she looked at Miss Chillingsworth in mute agony. Miss Chillingsworth was choked with emotion, convinced the cat was thanking her for getting help.

She sat in the waiting room supposedly looking at magazines, but in reality she was in the consulting room with the cat, hoping things were going well for her. Half an hour went by and she could hear Kate apologizing about an emergency and yes, Mr. Hughes would soon be starting on his client list, but it was a cruelty case, you see.

Miss Chillingsworth imagined herself feeding the tiny kittens and saving their lives. She'd get poor Cherub's basket out again, the blankets were already washed. Her fingers twitched as though feeling the soft fur, the tiny ears. In her mind she was admiring the tiny, soft pink pads of their feet and could almost hear their mewing. Such joy!

This time she might even be brave enough to keep one for herself. Or should she have the mother instead? Maybe she needed a home more than healthy kittens did. Yes, she'd ask to keep the mother. That would be the kindest thing to do, the right thing to do. It was almost as if Cherub had been reincarnated, for the cat was white and black in very much the same pattern as she had been. Her dear Cherub. Then she remembered the kittens she'd reared playing king of the castle on the old apple box on the kitchen floor. Maybe she'd have a kitten instead and enjoy all the pleasure all over again. No, she'd have the mother and call her Cherub in memory.

Rhodri came out from the back. "Miss Chillingsworth, a word, please."

She followed him into the consulting room and he closed the door behind her.

"Take a seat."

"It's bad news, isn't it?"

"I'm afraid so. I was right; there was a kitten stuck, but it was already dead. I've managed to ease it out; there are more, possibly two or three, but the mother is far too ill for me to operate today."

"And . . . ?"

Rhodri paused and then said, "We've put her on a drip, given her medication and now all we can do is hope she'll last through the night and be able to withstand an operation to remove the remaining kittens. I must warn you she is very ill."

Miss Chillingsworth clasped her hands under her chin. "I know I can rely on you. If she's going to pull through, you'll do it. I desperately want her to live. You'll understand how strongly I feel because, being Welsh, you'll have a passionate soul, as I do. I'll take her home with me when she's ready and I'll adopt her. It's the least I can do. Can I see her?"

Rhodri hesitated. "I'd rather you didn't. It would upset you."

"I see. I'll wait."

"It could be a long wait before she turns the corner—if, in fact, she does."

"I could ring to ask."

"Of course."

"Thank you. I'm sorry I've held you up."

"I'm glad you found her."

"So am I. I'll ring tomorrow morning."

Miss Chillingsworth intended stopping to have a word at reception and report progress on the cat, but only Stephie was on the desk and Kate was nowhere to be seen, so she wandered bleakly out to face being alone, without a word of comfort from a twin soul, a whole day of worry and desperation.

In fact, Kate had departed to her accounts after telling Stephie exactly what she thought of her warning. She'd also remembered that Scott was taking a couple of days off, so she wouldn't be seeing him as she had expected, which did nothing to improve her temper. How could she be so happy one moment and so unhappy the next? Now she'd upset Stephie and as they had to work together, that was a stupid thing to have done. Her kind heart reasserted itself and Kate went to make coffee for Stephie and herself as a gesture of reconciliation.

Stephie accepted it gratefully. "Thanks. I need this. I was too late for breakfast this morning and when I do that, it always hits me about now. This is nice. Sorry I upset you; I meant it as a timely warning, etcetera, etcetera."

"I'm sorry too. But we don't know for certain it was his, do we?"

"No. But . . . I reckon it was, knowing Bunty and knowing Scott."

"But we don't *know*."

"You're saying that because you don't *want* to believe it.'"

Kate took on board what Stephie had said and quietly went away, disconcerted by how upset she was at how close to the truth Stephie had come.

Then she remembered how handsome Scott was, how attractive, how much she loved the touch of his hands, his sense of humor, the clowning he did, how dedicated he was to his work . . . and knew in her heart of hearts how transparently honest he was when he said he loved her. He'd always claimed he felt differently about her than any other girl he'd met, and those clear blue eyes of his couldn't lie, could they? Of course not. He meant every word. Cheered by her own well-reasoned argument, she switched on the computer and began work, knowing that before the day was out, Scott would ring to make arrangements for tonight.

But Scott didn't ring. Kate found all sorts of possible excuses for him, but pride forbade her to ring him and she spent an agonizing evening.

Chapter

· 14 ·

The following morning it was Joy who received the first intimation of what had happened. On her doormat when she went to get the mail was an envelope addressed to her. She didn't recognize the writing at first, but when she did, she frowned at the unexpectedness of it. A dreadful suspicion entered her mind. Surely not. Oh no. Surely not. But she bet her bottom dollar that she was right.

"Porridge or cereal?"

That was Duncan calling out to her, but she didn't answer because she was occupied reading the opening lines of Scott's letter: "I know you will be surprised."

Joy flopped down on the kitchen chair. This was just too much. Too much . . . "I have decided to return to Australia on the first available flight." She read on, seeing only the implications as far as staffing the practice was concerned and nothing more.

I know I should have given you notice of this holiday, but I had a phone call from my dad to say Ma was ill and

needing major surgery, so I had to make a decision quick
smart. Hopefully, I shall be back once Mother has recovered.
Sorry, Joy, for putting the staffing situation in jeopardy.
Will keep in touch.

Joy flung the letter down on the kitchen table and put her head in her hands. "I just don't believe what he's done."

"Who?"

"Scott. He's had it away on his toes. Done a runner. Hopped it. He can't help it. It's his mother, she's ill. But all the same."

"Didn't he say he was going?"

"Not a word. As far as I knew, he was off yesterday and today, then on call all weekend."

"He hasn't made his mother ill on purpose."

"I know, but I've a nasty feeling it will turn permanent, if you know what I mean. He won't come back; I feel it in my bones. There's been no sign up until now that he was getting itchy feet. I've sensed it before and been prepared—and taken steps—but none of them left quite as precipitately as this."

Duncan suggested it might be woman trouble and his mother's illness had given him a valid excuse.

"Surely he hasn't got someone else pregnant." She began spooning in cereal, not tasting it but eating out of habit. Then Joy choked and had to cough a lot to clear her throat. "Oh God! It can't be Kate, can it? With all her high hopes. It'll ruin things for her. The young devil! If it is, I'll fly out to Australia myself and have it out with him. Ruining her chances. I'll kill him!"

"Now, Joy, you don't know that."

"He was going to run out on Bunty if the baby had been his, but then she said it wasn't, so he didn't. I'm certain it was his, but she'd too much pride to admit it when he declared he wouldn't stand by her."

Tears began pouring down Joy's cheeks and Duncan got up to put an arm around her. "Now come on. This isn't like you. Go to work and see what the real picture is. Does he mention Kate at all?"

Joy pushed the letter toward him, shaking her head.

Duncan read the apologies, the thanks for all her help, about his enjoyment of working in the practice, and how he'd benefited from the experience and it would stand him in good stead, and how he hoped it wouldn't cause too much disruption, and how sorry he was for letting her down like this but he'd be back as soon as he could . . . "No, he doesn't. Maybe there's a letter at the practice for her. I suggest you ring Mungo right now and warn him. He should shoulder some of the responsibility for the practice. It can't all be laid at your door. Come on, Joy. Brace yourself."

Before she left, he said he would come to have lunch with her to cheer her up.

"That's kind. I don't suppose that during the course of your misspent youth you qualified as a vet?"

Sadly Duncan had to confess that no he hadn't, but if wishing . . .

"I'll see you about twelve, then."

At the practice, the Land Rover Scott had used was in the car park and on the doormat an envelope with the keys to it and the keys to the flat and a card saying in big letters SORRY.

Sorry indeed, thought Joy. *I'd give him sorry if I could lay my hands on him. Sorry! Huh!* At least Kate wasn't in until lunchtime today, so she had some time in which to pull her thoughts together on how to break the news.

Mungo came down from the flat with Miriam.

"So, Joy, how did all this come about?"

"Don't look at me; I'm just as surprised as you. No hint, not even an inkling that he was off. I was saying to Duncan before I left I've usually spotted when they've developed itchy feet and taken steps with the agency, but this . . ."

"But he hasn't said he's not coming back, so the big problem is his being on call this weekend."

"Exactly! He hasn't *said* he isn't coming back but reading between the lines, I'm sure as hell he won't. I'm declaring here and now that over my dead body do we employ another of our itinerant brothers or sisters from the Commonwealth. Never again."

Miriam interrupted with, "Oh! I don't know; they certainly add spice to life. He was definitely adding spice to Kate's life when they got back from that emergency calving at Lord Askew's. They were kissing very passionately in the Land Rover when I went out to walk Perkins."

Joy smiled grimly at her. "They were, were they? If he's done anything to harm Kate, I'll personally do for him."

"Look, if it's any help, I'll work on reception for you."

"Are you sure?"

"Of course I am. I've got to give a hand, haven't I? Can't let you sink. Would it help?"

"Of course it would; give me a chance to sort the staffing problem."

Mungo said he intended doing Scott's weekend on call, so that was covered.

"You two are angels. Thank you very much."

Miriam linked her arm with Joy's and said, "I'll pop out with Perkins first, then I'll be in. What I can't understand is why so suddenly, without speaking to anyone? Still, he says he will be back, so it's only for a short while. He always seemed happy enough."

"I don't know. I expect we shall never know." Unless Kate has the answer, thought Joy.

Miriam kissed Joy and dashed away to collect Perkins for his walk.

THE news of Scott's departure was the talk of the practice all morning and Joy had to confess to looking forward to having lunch with Duncan to get some respite from it. He appeared at ten minutes to twelve, wanting the keys to the car so he could leave his walking boots in there and change into the smart shoes he'd put in the trunk as Joy was leaving for work.

"Hello, Miriam, they've had to call in the support troops, then?"

"Duncan!" She went around the desk and gave him a big hug. "How nice to see you. All hands to the pumps this morning, but your dear wife is close to solving our problem. The agency is sending a temporary around for an interview this afternoon. They've faxed his details and he seems very suitable."

"Excellent."

"I don't know how we would manage without her."

"Is she ready for lunch?"

"Go and see for yourself."

"Joy! Ready?"

Joy slammed the filing cabinet drawer shut saying, "Get me out of here, quick."

"You'll need your coat. It's cold."

"Where are we going?"

"The sandwich bar down the road. We'll walk."

"I'll put up with that if you'll take me somewhere nice tonight. I shall need a bit of cosseting after the day I've had."

"Agreed. There wasn't a letter for Kate this morning, then?"

Joy shook her head. "I can't be long. I've still got to talk to her. What a shambles. I'm worried sick."

"Forget it for a while."

The brand-new, up-to-the-minute chromium and red-leather transformation of the sandwich bar took Joy's breath away. "This is definitely not how I remember it! It was so shabby before and the name's changed. Ned's Diner, no less. You knew, did you?"

"Yes. Thought we'd give the new management a chance."

"I do like it. Very 'New York,' I must say. Do they do anything as mundane as a bacon, lettuce and tomato sandwich with a caffe latte?"

"Let's see." Duncan picked up the menu. "They do. They do." Joy found a seat and Duncan went to order at the counter.

When he came to sit with her, he asked, "So, you haven't spoken to Kate yet?"

"No, and I must be back before one. Whether she knows or not, I can't leave her to all the tittle-tattle that's going on. The walls are bulging with speculation."

"Complete change of subject. I've discovered who my mystery walker is."

"You have?"

"Yes. He was waiting for me this morning. I knew something had happened because he wasn't wearing his business suit. He starts Monday in a new job. It's transformed him."

"Never mind about the transformation. Who is he? Someone we know?"

"You'll never guess." Duncan deliberately paused before he told her. "It's Adam Pentecost, Kate's old boyfriend."

Joy's face was alight with amazement. "No! Adam Pentecost! Of course. Of course. Why didn't I realize? Of course it was him. Well?"

"He's going to work near Weymouth for a company that all but fell on his neck with delight. He is the answer to their prayers, apparently. He's got an increase in salary and he's going to look for a flat or a room or something in Weymouth and leave home."

"Thank heaven for that. It'll do him a power of good."

"He hasn't told his mother he's moving out yet, though. She could be a big stumbling block."

"It's only what she deserves by the sound of it. I'm so pleased. I wonder if Kate knows. Fancy it being Adam! Kate will be pleased. At the very least it will have restored his self-confidence, which he was badly in need of, and it is a plus for her because it will get him off her back. Poor Kate. I feel so sorry for her about Scott's leaving. I just don't know how far she felt committed to him. She'd been fending him off for weeks, but I've an idea, well, in fact I know that . . ."

"Eat your BLT. Stop worrying about her; young ones have far more resilience than we credit them with. They get very badly hurt, but bounce back much more easily than older people do."

"Yes, but she's such a fine girl, I hate to think of her being hurt."

THE subject of Joy's concern was at that moment stuck in traffic on her way to work and also thinking about how hurt she felt. He'd never rung and he wasn't in today, and he was on call all weekend and she couldn't understand his silence. The phone at his flat was working, she knew, because she'd finally given in and rung him last night. But there'd been no reply to her calls and the answering machine was switched off, which was very odd indeed when he knew perfectly well she'd have gladly lost her all to him the night before last.

The line edged a little nearer to the road works.

After an offer like that how could he now ignore her? But he had. Unless he'd been involved in an accident? Maybe he was lying in a hospital bed somewhere, unconscious. Or worse still, dead. Her mind raced through all the possibilities.

The line moved forward another ten yards.

But he'd have to be around at the weekend because he was on call. That was it. He'd decided to go to visit a friend or something for a couple of days and he'd be back tonight to start his weekend on call. Of course! That was it.

She could see the temporary lights now, at red yet again.

Although he could have let her know. Maybe her offer to make love for the first time in her life had made this free-as-air Aussie feel the leg irons closing around his ankles and he was warning her off with his silence. That was it. She was going too fast for him. What a fool she'd been.

The temporary lights changed to green and she slid forward again.

Too fast for *him*! Whom was she kidding?

This time she got past the road works and was pulling into the car park, unfortunately ten minutes late. And there, parked for all to see, was his Land Rover. He was here! Thank heavens. Her heart leaped into her throat. Waves of vibrant joy surged through her veins. She punched the dashboard with her fist and shouted, "Yes!" Wherever he'd been, he was back. Thank God. The dear, darling man. Despite her overwhelming relief, she decided to be as cool as cool could be in front of him. Not to punish him, no, but to let him know that she, too, knew how to handle a relationship. Oh yes! The thought of him—of smelling his smell; of seeing his bright, approving eyes; hearing his footfall—pushed up her pulse rate and she walked to the back door desperately trying not to look too eager.

Kate deliberately went straight to her office, hung up her coat. Speaking to no one, she switched on the computer and began the end-of-month figures. She'd print them out too before she took one single step toward seeking him out. But she'd been working only about ten minutes when Joy put her head around the door.

"Oh! You're here." She closed the door behind her and sat down.

"Look! I'm sorry I was late, but there were road works and it took ages. I'll set off earlier tomorrow."

"That's all right; it happens to the best of us." Joy studied her face and could see none of the anguish she would have expected to see if Kate had already heard the news. "I had a letter this morning at home."

"You did?"

"Yes. From Scott."

Kate's heart lurched and she hoped Joy hadn't noticed. "From Scott?"

"Yes, I'm afraid so."

"What about?"

"Well . . ."

"He's here. Why should he need to write?"

"You haven't heard from him, have you?"

"No. Should I have?" This curiously stilted conversation felt as though it was turning into the overture to some bad news.

"I would have thought so." Out of her pocket she took Scott's letter and handed it to Kate. "Here, this is his letter. Read it."

"Should I?"

Joy nodded. "Yes, please. It explains something."

She'd make a good poker player, thought Joy. Her face had gone white, but apart from that there was nothing in Kate's demeanor to indicate that she'd received a mortal blow. She remained absolutely still, read it through twice, then slowly and neatly folded it and handed it back.

She didn't speak for almost a minute and then said in a voice not at all like her own, "You can feel underneath what he's written that he's not coming back, is he? He was supposed to be on call all weekend."

"Mungo's covering that. Like you I feel that he won't be back. With Zoe having wound down her involvement until after the baby, we are terribly shorthanded. At three I've got a temporary coming for an interview. Someone who's free to begin on Monday. So we've not been entirely annihilated by his departure. I can't begin to imagine what really made him go in such a tearing hurry. He doesn't say, you see, except about his mother. That seems genuine enough."

Kate didn't answer.

"I wondered if he'd said something to you about his mother?"

"No."

"It's come as a considerable shock."

Kate agreed. "Must get on, though. Going to print out the end-of-month figures."

"Oh, right. I've put the kettle on. Cup of tea?"

"No. Thanks all the same." *I wish she'd go! Just go and leave me alone.*

"I'll leave you to get on, then. We shan't need you on reception until Stephie goes at four. Miriam's been helping to free me to sort out a temporary. She'll cover when Mungo and I interview this one at three."

"Right. I'll press on, then." *Please go. Please. I can't hold on any longer.*

"I'll bring some tea in later."

"Thanks."

If he had to go, the only good thing that's come out of this is my eternal gratitude to Miriam for taking Perkins out for his walk when she did. No. Damn Miriam for coming out when she did. At least I would have known what it was to have been loved by him. Now I'll never have the joy of it. He would have been a tantalizingly passionate lover, she was sure. The tears were just beginning to come when the door burst open and in came Lynne.

"Have you heard? Bunty's flipped her lid. It's all that Scott's fault. Mungo's operating and Sarah One's having to take over assisting him and she's shaking like a leaf because he frightens her to death. Bunty's mother's going to come to take her home. Apparently it was Scott's baby after all and she's still carrying a torch for him. We all reckon he won't be back. Sorry about his mother and all that but . . . Good riddance, I'd say, wouldn't you? Catch me going to pieces over a man. I'd keep out of Mungo's way if I were you, by the way; he's furious at all the upset. Are you all right? You look quite flushed."

"I'm fine. Got to press on."

"Oh, all right, then. Just thought I'd keep you up to date with all the news. You should have been here this morning! Talk about rumors flying around, the air was thick. Aren't you glad you didn't get involved with him?"

"Oh yes. Not worth it, is it?"

"Mind you, he was a gorgeous hunk. Well, everyone thought so, but I saw through him. All right for a quick fling, but he's the type to run a mile if a girl began to get serious." Had Kate been looking at her, she would have seen a malicious grin on Lynne's face. "Must press on, as they say." She shut the door behind her with a cheerful slam, which Kate felt go straight through her, so fragile did she feel.

For fully ten minutes Kate sat quite still with her hands gripped tightly together to stop them shaking, her head bowed, trying to come to terms with Scott's departure. *Not a word from him to me. Not a word. How could he do that to one he said he loved? How could he?* His last words to her were, "Love you."

Where on earth had she gone wrong? To go without a word. If he couldn't face her, he could have written to her. But he hadn't, and she'd learned her first lesson about love. Never ever again would she allow herself to become so hopelessly involved. She had to get through the next few weeks somehow and she would. She wouldn't let a setback like this ruin things forever. No. She'd do as he had done and walk away without a backward glance. Some chance.

The afternoon dragged on. Too late she found she'd printed out the September figures in error and had to begin again. The printer paper got itself into a ruck and she had almost to dismantle the machine before it ran true. Altogether, an afternoon like today she never wanted again.

At five past four she was on the reception desk feeling like death because all the time in her mind's eye she could see Scott: his blue eyes more blue, his tan deeper than ever, his streaked hair more blond than she could have imagined, his tender mouth on the verge of a smile. He'd been so handsome. Such fun. Like no one she'd ever met before or would again. But Kate was brought back to earth by the hurly-burly of the afternoon clinic, so the pain and the heartbreak had to be put on hold for the time being.

SHE drove home a different way to avoid the road works and Mia was just beginning to worry when she heard Kate opening the front door. "Why, Kate! You are late! I was starting to worry."

"Hello. The clinic was so busy we overran and then we had to tidy up. Then I came home a different way to avoid the road works and all in all I'm tired out."

"You look it too. Sit down. I'll soon have your meal heated up. Gerry, get Kate a drink. She needs perking up."

"Hello, love. Long day? Gin and tonic?"

"Thanks, Dad; yes, I will."

Kate slumped down on her chair at the kitchen table and patiently waited to be ministered to.

"I think I'll join you. What about it, Mia?"

"Yes, please, after all it's Friday. Why not?" Mia could see that something was wrong with Kate but couldn't for the life of her put a finger on what it was. Maybe when she'd eaten she'd be able to tell them.

Kate drank down the gin in a trice but poked her food about without appetite and made a poor show of eating it.

"Kate! That's your favorite—my chicken and vegetable pie. Are you not well?"

"You remember Scott?"

"Well, of course we do, don't we, Gerry?"

Gerry nodded. "How could we forget? Such a nice chap. He really enjoyed working my train set. We'll have him around some time and he can have another turn."

"He's gone back to Australia."

Mia sat back, astounded. "Back to Australia! But you watched him deliver that calf only, what, two nights ago. How can he have gone?"

"Well, he has."

"Why? Did he say?"

"He sent a letter to Joy. He says his mother is seriously ill and he'll be back as soon as he can, but we all think he won't."

Anxious to ease Kate's obvious pain, Mia babbled, "But if his mother is ill, he had to go. He'll be back, surely, as soon as he can?" She saw she hadn't convinced Kate. "Perhaps he got fed up with the English weather; just needs a break from it. It's been diabolical recently. Perhaps all he wanted was some sun and warmth. Or maybe he wanted to see all those blessed sheep. Homesick—perhaps that was it. You can get it bad, homesickness, so bad you feel physically ill. Or perhaps he longed for all those wide-open spaces they have in Australia; here on this island in comparison we're so cramped." Mia stopped thinking up any more reasons to make sense of Scott's departure when she saw she wasn't lifting Kate's spirits. "Anyway, what's done's done."

Gerry, from behind his newspaper, said, "Not right that, leaving without giving notice. 'Spect it's left them in a hole."

"No. We've got a temporary starting Monday and Mungo's doing his weekend for him."

Gerry lowered his paper. "Surprising how the waters close over your head when you leave somewhere. You think you're indispensable, but in no time at all that phrase 'Oh, we shall miss you!' is as hollow as a drum. Never you mind about him, Kate, there's plenty more fish in the sea for someone like you."

Mia saw the heartache in her eyes when Kate looked at her briefly before answering her dad. "I expect there are, but it's not much comfort at the moment."

"Have your dessert, love. You'll feel better when you've eaten something, and you always like my treacle sponge." Mia was rewarded with a pale kind of smile. She whipped the treacle sponge into the microwave and had it in front of Kate, complete with custard, before she could change her mind. Kate plodded her way through it right to the last spoonful of custard, leaving the really treacly bit to the last as she always did.

"Thank you for that. I'll take my cup of tea upstairs with me and finish it in bed. I'm tired."

"Of course, love, you do that. And sleep late in the morning. You're not working tomorrow. Good night." Mia got up, gave her a kiss and sat down again, remembering how Kate had said she thought things were moving along with Scott. Obviously, this very day her whole world had been turned upside down.

When she'd gone, Gerry said, "It's not like her to go to bed this early; it's only half past eight. What's the matter with her?"

Mia sighed. "Oh, Gerry!"

NEXT morning there were letters for Kate and Mia, along with a parcel for Gerry. Mia tore hers open and to her surprise and delight found in it the confirmation for a commission: a miniature of a baby at the request of doting grandparents willing to pay a premium. She handed Gerry his parcel and paused for a moment to study Kate's letter. She didn't recognize the handwriting and couldn't read the postmark because it was too smudged.

She'd take it up along with Kate's breakfast. She had the tray already laid, so all she had to do was make a pot of tea for her.

"Morning, Kate. There's a letter and I've brought your breakfast up."

Kate's bedside table was cluttered with textbooks and papers, so Mia put the tray on the carpet while she opened the curtains a little to let the light flood in.

From under the duvet a cautious question came: "Who's the letter from?"

"I don't know, love. I can't recognize the handwriting."

But Kate could. She'd seen that writing on countless notes she'd typed into the computer at the practice. That was Scott's writing.

Mia noticed her reluctance to open the letter while she was there, so despite her curiosity she left Kate to herself.

Dearest Kate,

I'm at the airport awaiting takeoff. My mother is seriously ill with a heart problem. You will already know when you read this that I am going home to see her. I didn't intend writing to you, but at the last minute I can't help myself.

No one who saw your face when we delivered the calf that last night could fail to realize that the veterinary profession is for you. You were so alive that night. I knew if I stayed I would be tempted to want you to go home with me and that you would come, and in no time at all begin bitterly to regret not qualifying. I cannot stand in the way of your fulfilling your ambition.

I said you were different from any girl I'd kissed before and you are, so very special, to me. You will always be close to my heart. Take care, sweet one.

They're loading the plane. Must go.

All my love,
Scott

There was a splotch of a tear at the bottom of the letter and she didn't know if it was a tear of Scott's or one of hers. But it was still wet, so it must be hers. Though there was another splotch near the words *sweet one*, which had dried, or maybe that was a splash of lager. Whatever it was, Scott had written that letter and she knew he meant every word. There was no address at the top. So he really did mean it to be final, though in his letter to Joy he had said he'd be back in a couple of weeks. But like Joy, reading between the lines, she sensed he would not come. In any case, if she read her own letter a thousand times, it would still say she wouldn't see him again.

She lay back on the pillow, drained of emotion. Was she glad or was she not? Kate didn't really know. There seemed to be a great big hole somewhere in the middle of her, a hollowness that wouldn't go away. *Oh, Scott! Oh, Scott!*

He was right, though. If he'd asked her, she would have gone wherever he went and as he said would have been most likely, when it was too late, she would regret it all the rest of her life. She thought about how she felt when she saw the calf being born and tried hard to put it foremost in her mind, but Scott would keep creeping around the edges of her resolve and obliterating her determination not to think of him. *Oh, Scott! To sacrifice yourself for me. You surely belong to the great and the good.*

Maybe one day she would travel to Australia and look up his name in the Veterinary Register and seek him out. She wrapped her arms around her waist to stem the tide of pain. This was acute physical agony she felt, a very real gnawing in her innards. Whatever, she wasn't going to let anyone at the practice know just how much she missed him. She'd brace herself to speak of him without flinching and do all her grieving at home. She hid her head under the duvet and wept for him.

Oh, Scott! Oh, Scott!

THAT Saturday night Mungo rang Joy and asked if he and Miriam could come around for an hour. "Not for a meal, just for an emergency business meeting. If you're not going out, that is."

"We're not. Of course, come around; be glad to see you."

"That man from the agency—I wasn't keen."

"Oh, I see. Well, come around, then. If you don't mind Duncan being here."

"Course not. Colin's covering just for the evening, so I won't get called out."

"Right. See you then."

"About nine. Bye."

When they came, Miriam arrived with a gift, as she always did when she visited anyone. This time it was flowers.

Mungo kissed Joy, and Miriam kissed her and Duncan, and eventually Miriam and Joy went into the kitchen to put the flowers in water while Duncan poured drinks for them.

"Whiskey?"

Mungo nodded. "You're a man of leisure at the moment, then?"

"I am. Till the next project comes up."

"I can't understand how relaxed you are about it. I need to have daily work on a regular basis, on the go all the time. I wouldn't know what to do with leisure like you've got right now. Taking a holiday's a different matter altogether, but I find even that hard."

They could hear Joy and Miriam laughing together in the kitchen.

Duncan sat down. "They get on amazingly well, those two, don't they . . . considering?"

Mungo looked at him in surprise. "Considering? Considering what?"

There was a pause before Duncan replied, "Both loving the same man?"

"The same man?" Mungo went deathly still.

"You."

"Me?"

Duncan nodded. "You. Didn't you know?"

The shock of Duncan's revelation silenced Mungo. When he did eventually answer, his voice was harsh and belligerent. "Is this you having one of your plain-speaking moments—you know, when you vent your spleen for the hell of it?"

"No, it's the truth. I'm surprised you've never realized, all these years. She loved you when she married me and still does. It's not easy for a husband to live with."

"I've done nothing to . . ."

"I know you haven't."

"I'm stunned." Mungo's first thought was for Miriam. Slowly and deliberately, because he didn't want to know the answer but knew he must, he asked, "Does Miriam know?"

"Of course not."

"Joy speaks to you of it, then?"

"I've known for a long, long time, but we've never said it out loud to each other until a few nights ago."

"I'm very fond of her, always have been, we've known each other a lot of years, worked together, you know, right from the early days. God, man, I'd no idea. You must hurt."

Duncan agreed he did. "Like hell. I thought you should know."

"Why? I don't see what I can do about it."

"Neither do I. Just thought you ought to know." Duncan pointed a finger at Mungo. "If ever you do anything about it . . ."

"Don't be a bloody fool. There's too much at stake, in any case . . . If you're bandying threats about, you remember to keep your mouth shut tight and don't, whatever you do, tell Miriam. She is so very fond of Joy and it would ruin their relationship. I won't allow it."

"No."

The complex emotions that had surfaced between them hung in the air. They heard sounds of footsteps and both tried to appear amicable together.

Miriam was standing in the doorway looking at them. "What's the matter?" She looked from one to the other, awaiting their reply.

Duncan stood up. "Here's your drink. Come and sit down."

Mungo pulled an easy chair closer to the fire. "Sit here, look, next to me."

"Men's talk, then?" She squeezed Duncan's fingers as he handed her her gin. "Joy won't be a moment; Tiger's been paddling in her water bowl so she's mopping up. She's turning into a lovely cat, isn't she?"

Duncan nodded. "There's something you don't know."

Mungo half rose out of his chair believing that Duncan was still in his mood to shock.

Miriam asked Mungo, "What's the matter?"

"Nothing, nothing at all." He sat back down again but not before he'd shot a warning glare at Duncan.

Duncan continued speaking: "I never thought I would live to see the day when I loved an animal, but I have to confess I bloody love that cat."

Remembering his scathing attitude to Mungo over Perkins, Miriam laughed until she was almost helpless. "Wait till I tell Joy. Oh, dear! There's a crack appearing in your armor, then?"

"Indeed."

"Well, why not. It makes you more human."

Mungo, sitting morosely staring into his whiskey, looked up and said snappily, "Where's Joy? Is she coming?"

Joy answered his question by appearing in the sitting room. "I'm here at your service. Where's my drink?"

They talked business, deciding that the temporary could stay till they found someone else, but there was no question of his being permanent.

Mungo expressed his feelings in no uncertain terms. "I didn't take to the chap, not one bit. He's too businesslike. It's a job, not a vocation, to him and I don't like that. With Valentine and Cohn and Rhodri and Graham and Zoe, and for that matter Scott, they all *like* animals and put their welfare first. This chap seemed to talk too much about making money."

"Excuse me, but we do need to make money. We've got wages to pay," Joy said.

Mungo nodded. "Of course, but there's a limit. We'll put up with him until we find the person we want. Right?"

Joy added, "Colin *is* your partner. Do we know what he thinks? Shouldn't he have a say?"

"Oh, Colin! He'll go along with our decision. You know what he's like: anything for an easy life. And Zoe's too preoccupied with the imminent arrival of the baby to be bothered."

Finally they talked of this and that, of Scott leaving, of Kate and her hopes, and it was midnight before Miriam and Mungo were saying their good-byes.

"Good night! Good night!"

"Thank you."

"Thanks for coming."

Miriam called out from the car, "The pleasure's all ours. Did you know that Duncan's confessed to loving Tiger? Isn't it a laugh? I'll speak to you Monday about lunch next week. There's something about my future I need to discuss. OK?"

Joy waited to wave to them as they turned into the road because Miriam always gave a big wave out of the window just before they disappeared and Joy didn't want to disappoint her. She followed Duncan in, locked the front door and went to find him in the kitchen washing glasses.

"I'm so lucky to have Miriam for a friend. I don't deserve her."

Duncan didn't answer.

"She's so kind to me, isn't she? She must never know what we talked about the other evening. I couldn't look her in the eye if she did. You won't ever tell her, will you?"

"Never."

Chapter

· 15 ·

B ack at work on Monday, Kate hoped she was getting away with her pretense of finding Scott's sudden disappearance no problem at all. As she'd promised herself, she was keeping her grieving for home. At work she intended to be as she always was—pleasant, efficient and happy. Meeting the clients was no problem, but working with Stephie and Lynne needed more willpower than she had ever imagined. All weekend the pain of Scott's leaving kept surfacing and real life became a nightmare. She longed to put back the clock and pretend that she'd never let on to Scott how she felt about him, that he was still here and she could look forward to his coming into the practice for his list, or halfway through the day with an armful of samples for the lab, or ringing up and saying he'd be another half hour before he'd finished and should they go out somewhere? But he wouldn't, not ever.

This was the day Miss Chillingsworth was going to be able to take new Cherub home. It had been a fight to keep new Cherub alive, but with intensive nursing and Rhodri's brilliant piece of surgery, she had survived. None of the kittens had been alive when Rhodri operated and Cherub had been close to death too, but the two Sarahs and Bunty had given her forty-eight hours of round-the-clock nursing and she was now fit to go home. Kate had fully expected Miss Chillingsworth to be there before the morning clinic opened, but it was almost lunchtime when she came in, beaming from ear to ear, carrying her old cat basket.

"Kate, dear. Is she ready?"

"She is. Give me your basket and I'll get her for you. There's tablets for her to take too. Don't go without them."

Miss Chillingsworth leaned her elbows on the reception desk, wondering if she should divulge the reason for being so late collecting her dear new Cherub. She decided not. They would only think her a foolish old lady, which perhaps she was, and they wouldn't be interested. She wouldn't tell them how she'd spent the morning crying. How it had struck her that bringing her new Cherub home to her big house, with its echoing, shabby rooms, had filled her with dread. Of how she had wept for the lost companionship of old Cherub, for her teenage boyfriend drowned at Dunkirk, for the years spent in shackles nursing her tyrannical father, for the paintings she'd had to sell to keep going, and that she'd wondered what use she had ever been to anyone at all, and where was it all going to end?

Weeping was a new experience for her, for despite all the vicissitudes of her life, she'd never before weakened and found relief in crying. But the tears she'd shed today had swept away the debris of that past life and when finally she could cry no more, she'd dried her eyes and decided that old memories didn't keep you warm, or put food on the table, or enrich your life, or provide companionship. Old memories were old memories and nothing more, and at this moment she'd had enough of them.

She'd recollected that an estate agent had pushed a leaflet through her door weeks before, saying that properties like hers were in great demand and why not take advantage of the boom in property prices in the area? Why not? Why shouldn't she have a slice of the good life? Sell, buy a garden flat and provide a *real* home for new Cherub. For she deserved something better than this old, cold, comfortless house. She *would*. And for once in her life, she'd have spare money to spend on luxuries for herself and for new Cherub.

But she'd have to get rid of lots of things. There wouldn't be room in a flat for all this big furniture, or for all the things she'd kept in case they might be useful some time. She could begin today and collecting Cherub would be the start of her new life. Consequently, she'd been delayed by making arrangements at the estate agent's. But now she was here and she couldn't wait to tell Cherub all about her plans.

Kate came through from the back with Cherub safely stowed in the old basket. Miss Chillingsworth poked a finger through the wire door. "Hello, Cherub dear. We're going home. I've got some lovely chicken ready for your dinner tonight. Now, Kate, what do I owe?"

"We haven't finished doing the bill yet. We'll mail it."

"I'll give you a hundred pounds on account, shall I? I have it with me."

Memories of the last one hundred pounds she'd left in her care made Kate blush. "No, thank you. You hang on to it until you get the bill, Miss Chillingsworth." Kate diverted her from talking about money by remembering the tablets. "Now you see, we almost forgot the tablets. One each day. There's sufficient until Sunday and she should be fine by then. Bring her back a week from today for her checkup. What she needs now is some loving care."

"She'll get that; don't worry. Come along, then, Cherub, off we go home. Bye-bye, dear. See you next week, Kate. Take care, dear. Send me the bill as soon as you can."

Kate watched her trot away, glad that her new cat had put

the spring back in her step. Poor Miss Chillingsworth with nothing to look forward to but enjoying her new cat. She thought about growing old and having achieved nothing at all. That was definitely not going to happen to Kate Howard. Definitely not. Had Miss Chillingsworth known that the sight of her had strengthened Kate's resolve to qualify and make a challenging life for herself, she would have been very gratified to have been proved to be of some use after all.

Kate went to fill the fire bucket because it was the first Monday of the month and Adolf was due. Though she hated dogs to fight, she had to confess to enjoying the thrill of Perkins and Adolf squaring up to each other. They truly meant nothing by it; it was simply something they both felt a need to do.

She placed the heavy bucket under the reception desk and checked through the small-animal appointments for the afternoon clinic at four. It was so quiet today for a Monday morning. Coffee. She'd make coffee for Lynne and Joy.

Joy liked it not too hot, two sugars and plenty of milk. Lynne liked it hot, no sugar with hot milk. As she waited for the milk to heat up in the microwave, she thought of Scott and how he'd grown to love her making his coffee for him. Black with two sugars. She remembered how he cupped his hands around the mug, not using the handle when he drank. She indulged herself by thinking about those long, strong fingers, the brown hair streaked with blond, the broad shoulders, the clean smell of him, and then she saw in her mind's eye how he'd looked the day he'd fallen into Phil Parsons's slurry pit and she laughed.

"What are you laughing at?"

It was Lynne.

"Life, I suppose."

"Mm. Glad you find it a joke. I don't."

Kate turned to look at her. "Why?"

"Sick of everything. Time I moved on. Did something different."

"Why don't you, then?"

Lynne shrugged her shoulders. "Such as?"

"I don't know. Whatever takes your fancy, I suppose."

"You're lucky."

"I am?"

"Yes, you've got an aim in life. What will you do if you don't get your chemistry, though?"

Kate groaned. "Don't mention it. I honestly don't know."

"You will, you wait and see. You'll make a good vet. It must be hard doing a day's work and then studying."

"It is, but I enjoy it."

"Worth it?"

"Of course."

"I might give it a go. Not veterinary but something else."

"You should."

"I might do that very thing. Why not?" Lynne went to sit outside on the bench by the back door and think about her options. Kate went back to the reception desk.

To stop herself from thinking about Scott, Kate worked all afternoon instead of taking her three hours off.

Joy put her head around the door halfway through the afternoon. "You really shouldn't, you know, you should go out or go home or something."

"I know." She pondered whether or not to tell Joy her reasons. "Better keeping busy at the moment."

"I see. He shouldn't have done what he did."

"He explained."

"You've heard, then?"

"A letter from the airport."

"I see. All part of life's rich tapestry, if that's any comfort."

"It is. I suppose. A little." Kate gave her a rueful smile.

"Brave heart, that's what's needed."

Kate nodded.

I⊤ must have been just after six when an enormous bouquet of flowers appeared to be making its own way into the reception area. Lynne said, "What on earth . . . ?"

Finally it emerged through the glass door with a pair of very long legs below it and made its way to the desk.

To Kate there was something very familiar about those legs.

It couldn't be.

But it was.

All the fear she'd felt when he'd threatened her that time and when he'd stalked her came rushing into her heart and she instinctively stepped back from the desk, unable to stop herself from trembling. She sensed beads of sweat between her shoulder blades and her scalp prickling.

The flowers were laid down in front of her and there was Adam.

"Kate!"

"Adam."

They both stood staring down at the bouquet, not speaking.

Stephie, embarrassed by the silence between them, tried hard to fill it. "Aren't they lovely! You are lucky! I love the roses."

"Thank you." Kate made herself look at Adam. Disappointed, she saw he was still the same Adam: his cheeks were as thin as always, his Adam's apple as large, his skin as sallow, his hair as nondescript, his hands as large and bony as ever. What had she seen in him? Poor Adam.

Adam saw the lovely girl he'd loved. And lost. "I started my new job today; it's just up my street. I've come straight from work to bring you these. To say . . ." He glanced at Stephie and disliked her avid interest. Leaning toward Kate, he whispered,

"Is there anywhere we could talk, you know, all these clients listening."

"I can't ask you in the back; it's not allowed. We'll go outside. Won't be a minute, Stephie." She led the way out, hating herself for the fib she'd just told, but knowing she couldn't bear to be shut in a small room with him. The beads of sweat turned cold and made her shudder.

"I've brought the flowers to say sorry."

"Right."

"I am, really sorry. I should never have done what I did. I was so desperate, you see. I didn't mean to harm you. It was losing my job like I did. I couldn't tell Mother. How could I? She's always been so ambitious for me, driving me, you know. It was that Scott as well. He always got the better of me. Whatever I did, no matter how hard I tried."

She opened her mouth to tell him Scott no longer posed a threat, but instinct told her not to and she closed it.

"I'm going home to tell Mother that I've got the chance to share a flat with two chaps from work."

"Good."

"I don't know how she'll take it, but I'm determined."

"Good. I hope it works out OK."

His Adam's apple bobbed up and down. "If I gave you a ring some time . . . bowling one Tuesday, perhaps . . . oh, no, not bowling, cinema, perhaps?"

"No. Best not."

"I hoped . . ."

She got a sudden image of Adam as he hopped about clutching his bruised hand after he'd missed punching Scott the night they'd had the fight. "No, Adam, I'd rather not."

Adam's sloping shoulders slumped. "Good luck, then. We had some good times."

"Good luck to you. Glad the job's turning out well. Stand tall with your mother. Thank you very much for the flowers; they're beautiful."

As Kate closed the door behind her, a terrible sadness came over her and she wished she could like him. But she couldn't. Not after Scott.

"I'll put these in the fire bucket under here. Mr. F. mustn't be coming."

"No, don't. Mr. Featherstonehough is coming. His camper thingy broke down this morning and he's been waiting to get it mended, and he rang to say he'll be in before we shut."

But the waiting clients weren't going to let her get away with it so easily and one of them called out, "My word, he must be keen!"

Another said, "I've gone wrong somewhere. No one's ever come out of the gloaming and presented me with a bunch that size."

"Nor me," offered a client, hanging on for dear life to a particularly spiteful cat.

Stephie called out, "Nor me. Some people have all the luck without even trying." She gave Kate a nudge and grinned, and Kate mouthed her thanks.

On impulse Kate said, "Dad and Mia are both out tonight, so I'm supposed to be getting my own meal when I get back. I don't suppose you'd like the idea of window-shopping in the mall and a meal?"

Stephie nodded. "Thanks, I would. Bit short this month, though, so I can't go anywhere smart."

"So am I. We'll go to the fish restaurant. You can get some quite cheap meals there and their chips are fantastic."

"Right, you're on. Let's hope we don't run late tonight, then."

There was a kerfuffle at the door and in came Adolf, dragging Mr. Featherstonehough.

"Good evening, Mr. F." Kate leaned over the desk to welcome Adolf. "Good evening, Adolf. Take a seat. Graham won't be long; a client's just gone in and then it's your turn. You've got the car mended, then, at last."

"I have. Three hundred and fifty-two pounds it's cost me. It's not worth it. If I sold it, I'd only get about five hundred for it. Good money after bad, but I can't manage without it, so what's the alternative?"

"Buy a new one."

Mr. Featherstonehough's bushy eyebrows shot up his forehead. "And pigs might fly. I've had that Dormobile twelve years. I can't bear to part with it. I know all its little idiosyncrasies; take the clutch, for instance . . ." He leaned his elbow on the desk. "You just have to let it up until . . ." He let go of Adolf's lead, dropping it on the floor and anchoring it with his foot while he demonstrated with his hands the delicate maneuver needed to let in his clutch.

Unbeknownst to him, though, Perkins had achieved his freedom and was silently racing down the stairs from the apartment to get at Adolf. Mungo was calling him, but Perkins had cast his normal obedience to the winds as he charged through to meet the challenge. Adolf seized his freedom with all four feet and met Perkins halfway down the corridor. There ensued a bitter, fearful fight, the worst they had ever had. The sight of their swirling bodies and the flashing of their fangs was terrible to see. It was impossible for Mungo, trapped on the far side of them, to interfere for fear of being bitten, so it was Kate who separated them with the well-aimed fire bucket full to the brim with water. Mungo, unprepared for this remedy, leaped back far too late and that, combined with the limited space in the corridor, meant that he as well as the dogs got drenched.

After the two of them broke apart, Adolf strutted up the

corridor into reception and shook himself all over Mr. Feather-stonehough, and Perkins did the same to Mungo, then grinned at him and wagged his tail.

Mungo, dressed ready for an evening out, was steaming with temper. "Bert!" he roared. "Bert!"

Mr. Featherstonehough peered cautiously around the door into the back.

"If it weren't for the fact that you've been a faithful client of ours for years, I'd tell you to take that bloody Adolf home and never come back. He's a menace. An absolute menace. If it hadn't been for Kate having that bucket ready, heaven alone knows what damage would have been done to Perkins. Have a care in future."

Mr. Featherstonehough began to smile. Mungo, pausing in his attempt to brush some of the water from his suit, glanced at him and saw the smile. "If I'm about when they have a return match, and there'll definitely be one because Perkins has a long memory, I'll . . . I'll . . ."

"Do what? They're both as much to blame. Just happens this time Adolf got in there first. That's Graham calling my name; I'll go and keep my appointment if you'll excuse me, for which, I might remind you, I pay you good money." With great dignity Mr. Featherstonehough took hold of Adolf's lead and marched to Graham's consulting room.

Mungo caught Kate's eye and when he saw her trying hard not to laugh, he succumbed to amusement himself and gave her a broad grin. "Where did you learn that trick, then?"

"The first morning I was here."

"Well, aim more carefully next time." Mungo took hold of Perkins's collar, gave her another grin and disappeared up the stairs. The clients still waiting gave her a round of applause and a mild cheer, so Kate bowed to them all and disappeared into the back to fetch the mop, with a beaming smile on her face.